Praise for *Nosy Neighbours*

'Touching, entertaining, and deeply compassionate, *Nosy Neighbours* is a tribute to the power of unexpected community and a portrait of two women who take the risk of healing.'   —Shelf Awareness

'Freya Sampson is a master at creating complicated, nuanced characters you care deeply about, and *Nosy Neighbours* is no exception! While a mystery is the central engine of the book, the true story lies in the mundane lives of the residents of Shelley House and the pain each person carries within them. A fun and beautiful book about the devastating power secrets can have on our lives and the many ways community can help you heal.'

—Mia P. Manansala, author of the Agatha, Anthony, and Macavity Award–winning *Arsenic and Adobo*

'Sampson delivers a lovely cosy crime mystery! A pair of mismatched sleuths cleverly unites their mistrustful London apartment building community in a story of found family that brims over with warmth and charm.'   —*USA Today* bestselling author Sherry Thomas

'*Nosy Neighbours* is addictive reading. Freya Sampson has a wonderful talent for creating characters that feel vividly true to life, and it really shines here. This warm and moving novel is layered with mystery, emotion, and heart as it explores its powerful themes of guilt and community. I just know readers are going to love it as much as I do.'

—India Holton, international bestselling author of *The Geographer's Map to Romance*

'A fun, heartwarming community caper, this book reminds us that while we can't choose our neighbours, we often end up with exactly the ones we need – even if they infuriate us at first.'

—Mikki Brammer, author of *The Collected Regrets of Clover*

'A sweet, uplifting story that explores how a group of strangers can ultimately become a community – and perhaps solve a mystery or two along the way!'

—Nikki Erlick, *New York Times* bestselling author of *The Measure*

'*Nosy Neighbours* is an utterly adorable novel filled with heart and mystery. Freya Sampson gets better and better.'

—Clare Pooley, *New York Times* bestselling author of *Iona Iverson's Rules for Commuting*

'Freya Sampson never fails to make me cry in the best possible way, and *Nosy Neighbours* is no exception. While the characters try to solve a mystery in their quest to save their beloved home, it becomes apparent that the real mystery is how they ended up in that situation in the first place – a mystery Sampson slowly unravels with the utmost care for their humanity and abundant charm. It's impossible not to root for Dorothy, Kat, and even Shelley House itself.'

—Tori Anne Martin, *USA Today* bestselling author of *This Spells Disaster*

'*Nosy Neighbours* is a real hug of a book, full of dynamic characters, intrigue, courage, and kindness. I loved it!'

– Hazel Prior, bestselling author of *How the Penguins Saved Veronica*

'Touching and thrilling all at once. I loved this clever mystery about friendship, loss, and the power of community. Highly recommended!'

—Tess Amy, author of *The Confidence Games*

'The ultimate cosy mystery. . . . If you love *Only Murders in the Building*, you'll love this.'

—theSkimm

'A story that will make you laugh, make you try to guess whodunit, and also feels like a warm hug!'

—Chick Lit Central

'Sampson once again presents a charming story about intergenerational friendship leading to healing. . . . This heartwarming tale is full of subtle humour and rich characters.' —*Booklist*

'The tenants are as crafty and charming as the house in this all's-well-that-ends-well tale.' —*Kirkus Reviews*

Praise for *The Girl on the 88 Bus*

'It's as sweet as it sounds – a literary cup of cocoa. Sampson reminds us that there's value in the "failures" in life – missed connections, broken relationships, unattained college degrees. They may, inadvertently, set us on the right path. Same for small daily interactions like a conversation on public transport. . . . If you're looking for a little hope, or a reminder of how chance encounters can change life for the better, this is the ticket.' —*USA Today*

'A heartfelt story about chance, loss, and aging, populated by messy characters you will root for in this delightful ride.'

—*Montecito Journal*

'Freya Sampson's writing is like a feel-good magical potion made of everything that's beautiful in life: a hug, a cup of tea, a warm blanket, a puppy. *The Girl on the 88 Bus* is the perfect sophomore novel: the descriptions of London are whimsical and immersive; the characters are relatable and lovable; the story is uplifting and romantic, full of emotions and heart, celebrating the importance of making human connections and embracing our dreams. This book is my happy place! Whatever Freya writes next, I'm on board.'

—Ali Hazelwood, #1 *New York Times* bestselling author of *Deep End*

'It's hard to think of another book quite as delightful as this one. *The Girl on the 88 Bus* is basically the best hug in the world in book form. It's a story about love and second chances and the best kind of unlikely friendships. Pick up this book if you're yearning for some joy in your life!'

—Jesse Q. Sutanto, *USA Today* bestselling author of
Vera Wong's Guide to Snooping (on a Dead Man)

'*The Girl on the 88 Bus* is one of the loveliest novels I've read. Gorgeously written, it's brimming over with hope, inspiration, and endearing humour. I completely adored this wonderful, warm hug of a book.'

—India Holton, international bestselling author of
The Geographer's Map to Romance

'Freya Sampson's *The Girl on the 88 Bus* is an unputdownable masterpiece of heart, hope, and humanity. I cheered, swooned, and gasped with each turn of the plot, staying up well past my bedtime because I needed to know what would happen next. Sampson's lovable cast of characters will steal your heart, lift your spirit, and make you wish you were a passenger on the 88 bus. Do yourself a favour and buy this book; you won't regret coming along for the ride.'

—Sarah Grunder Ruiz, author of *Last Call at the Local*

'A gorgeous story that's equal parts heartbreaking and heartwarming. A reminder that love is unwavering and ageless and will always carry us through. Freya Sampson is a brilliant writer.'

—Lia Louis, author of *Better Left Unsent*

'In these chaotic times, this is a much-needed story about kindness, the importance of friendship, and the wonder of hope. *The Girl on the 88 Bus* is a delight, a beautiful example of how the ripples from one chance encounter can change many lives for the better. I loved it. Everyone should read this book!'

—Jenny Bayliss, author of *Kiss Me at Christmas*

'Sampson's true gift is bringing to life an improvised family of three-dimensional characters with real struggles and real humanity. In a way, *The Girl on the 88 Bus* is the ultimate literary British Invasion, uniting the Beatles' "With a Little Help from My Friends" with the Rolling Stones' "You Can't Always Get What You Want".' —*BookPage*

'Sampson has done a masterful job of misdirection, offering tidbits of information that seem to lead one way but then are shown to have been leading somewhere else altogether. This is an engaging read that touches on aging and the physical incapacities it brings, lost and misplaced love, the power of accepting people as they truly are, finding the reliance to build a life on one's own, and the family that can be forged in friendships. A warming story of love and happiness found despite hardships, difficulties, and the passage of time.'

—*Kirkus Reviews*

Praise for *The Last Library*

'A wonderfully warm and uplifting story of kindness, community, and love that made me laugh, cry, and cheer.'

– Clare Pooley, *New York Times* bestselling author of
Iona Iverson's Rules for Commuting

'*The Last Library* is a heart-squeezing and charming story about grief, love, and the power of community. An absolute delight.'

—Colleen Oakley, *USA Today* bestselling author of
Jane and Dan at the End of the World

'*The Last Library* is absolutely irresistible! Curl up and indulge in Freya Sampson's charming novel about a shy librarian in a small town with a great cause. You'll have such a good time, and you'll love the unexpected twist at the end!'

—Nancy Thayer, *New York Times* bestselling author of
Summer Light on Nantucket

TITLES BY FREYA SAMPSON

The Last Library
The Girl on the 88 Bus
Nosy Neighbours
The Busybody Book Club

The Busybody Book Club

FREYA SAMPSON

RENEGADE BOOKS

First published in the United States by Berkley
An imprint of Penguin Random House LLC
First published in Great Britain in 2025 by Renegade Books
An imprint of John Murray Press

1

A CIP catalogue record for this book is available from the British Library.

Paperback ISBN 978-1-408-74973-9

Book design by Nancy Resnick
Printed and bound in Great Britain by Clays Ltd, Elcograf S.p.A

John Murray policy is to use papers that are natural, renewable and recyclable products and
made from wood grown in sustainable forests. The logging and manufacturing processes are
expected to conform to the environmental regulations of the country of origin.

Carmelite House
50 Victoria Embankment
London EC4Y 0DZ

The authorised representative
in the EEA is
Hachette Ireland
8 Castlecourt Centre
Dublin 15, D15 XTP3, Ireland
(email: info@hbgi.ie)

www.dialoguebooks.co.uk

John Murray Press, part of Hodder & Stoughton Limited
An Hachette UK company

For Hayley Steed: dream maker, cheerleader and agent extraordinaire.
Thank you for everything.

Prologue

Nova

'I call this emergency meeting of the St Tredock Community Book Club to order,' Phyllis said, rapping her knuckle on the desk.

'Hang on a sec, who put her in charge?' Arthur grumbled.

'Technically, Nova's our chair, so she should start the meeting,' Ash said.

'Can you all stop arguing, please!'

Nova looked at the ragtag group in front of her. Phyllis had clearly come straight from bed, as she was wearing an old-fashioned nightie under her coat and her hair was held in place by rollers. Arthur's weathered face was still red and puffy from all the crying he'd done during his confession earlier, and Ash was tapping away on his phone, his teenage brow furrowed in concentration. When Nova had set up this book club, it never occurred to her that one day she'd be holding a late-night meeting with this motley crew. But then again, it never occurred to her that one day they'd be investigating a murder either.

'Are you sure your theory's right?' Ash asked, looking up from his phone. 'It just seems so unlikely.'

'I know it does, but how else do you explain all this?' Nova signalled to the evidence laid out on the desk in front of them.

'It's all very well knowing who did it, but how are we going to prove it?' Arthur said. 'This lot doesn't mean anything unless we can get a confession, and that's hardly likely to happen.'

Nova glanced at Phyllis, who had gone quiet. *Too quiet.* 'You've got a plan, haven't you?'

'Of course I have,' the older woman said indignantly.

'Let me guess; is it inspired by an Agatha Christie novel?' Ash asked.

'Haven't I said all along that she'd have the answer?' Phyllis said. 'Now, Nova, how would you feel about having a couple of extra guests at your wedding?'

Nova swallowed; in all the drama of the past hour, she'd barely thought about the fact she was getting married in little more than twelve hours' time. Assuming the wedding went ahead and she wasn't arrested before then, of course.

'Craig's parents have invited most of the village to the church, so I suppose a few more guests won't make any difference.'

'Excellent!' Phyllis turned to Arthur and Ash. 'I hope you've both got clean suits, because tomorrow we're going to catch a criminal: Miss Marple style.'

Chapter One

Nova

Nova Davies closed her eyes and thrust her arm into the murky depths. She could feel the chill of the water through her rubber gloves as she groped around, reaching for the body.

'Any luck?' her colleague, Lauren, asked behind her.

'There's something here, but I can't get a proper grip on it.'

'Try and grasp a leg, that might give you something to pull on. Or else the hair.'

Nova delved further, trying not to think too hard about what else might be down there. Finally, she managed to close her fingers round a foot, and she yanked her arm back hard, freeing the victim with a loud splash.

'Got her!'

She stood up from the toilet and turned round triumphantly, a soggy plastic doll in her hand.

Lauren shook her head as she opened the black bin bag she was holding. 'I bet it was that Daryll Robins. I saw him lurking round the toilets earlier with an evil smirk on his face, plotting our downfall.'

'The boy's only six! Here, take Toilet Barbie while I wash my hands.' Nova dropped the offending doll in the bag, along with her rubber gloves, and crossed to the sink.

'Man, we do *not* get paid enough to deal with this nonsense,' Lauren said with a dry laugh.

'Good thing we love what we do, hey? And thanks for staying to help.'

'No problem. You know St Tredock Community Centre rule number 17: never leave a comrade to face a blocked toilet alone!'

They headed down the corridor together, and Nova stopped outside the small meeting room, sighing when she saw the circle of empty chairs inside.

'No one's coming tonight, are they?' she said.

'Of course they will; you still have a few minutes.'

'I'm not so sure. There were only four people last month, one of whom looked like he'd gotten lost on the way to the pub. Honestly, this book club is a disaster.'

'Don't be so defeatist. I once ran an over-sixties yoga class here for more than a year and it only ever had one member, and I don't think he even mastered a downward facing dog. Now, *that* was a disaster.'

Nova smiled. 'Thanks, that makes me feel a bit better.'

'Just give it time. I've told you, this lot are deeply suspicious of anything – and anyone – new, but they'll come round to you eventually.'

'This lot' was how Lauren referred to the residents of St Tredock, the small, picturesque Cornish village where the two women worked. Nova had moved to the area five months ago, but Lauren had lived here her whole life and took great pleasure in affectionately mocking her fellow natives.

'I'm sorry I can't stay and give you moral support, but Sam will never forgive me if I miss tonight's pub quiz. I've got a parting gift for you though.' Lauren reached into her rucksack and pulled out a packet of digestive biscuits. 'I know what Phyllis is like, and your evening will be considerably easier if you have snacks.'

'Oh, thank you. I meant to buy some earlier but forgot.'

'No worries. Also, I've never been to a book club before, but don't you need a copy of the book?' Lauren's eyes scanned the empty chairs, and Nova grimaced.

'Ah, yes. Ideally you do, but I can't find mine anywhere. I must have left it at home.'

'It's *Where the Crawdads Sing*, right? I'm sure I saw it on your desk this morning, under a pile of papers.'

'Really? You're a lifesaver!'

'Right, I'd better get to the Anchor,' Lauren said. 'Will you join us later?'

'I'll see how it goes here. If I don't make it, tell Craig I'll see him at home.'

'Will do. Good luck with your crawdads!'

Lauren headed towards the front door, and Nova glanced at her watch; 6:59 and there was still no one here. She walked down the corridor, her footsteps echoing through the empty community centre. Nova hated being here alone, and she hummed as she unlocked the door and flicked on the light. The office was really a glorified cupboard, with barely space for the desks of her, Lauren and their boss, Sandy. Nova's was nearest to the door, its surface invisible under assorted junk modeling from the after-school art club, some wilting potted plants she was trying to resurrect and several dirty coffee mugs. No wonder she kept losing things; she really must keep it tidier. Nova located her copy of *Where the Crawdads Sing*, which as

Lauren had said was under a teetering pile of papers, then put on a slick of red lipstick and grabbed a plate for the biscuits.

She flicked off the office light and stepped back out into the corridor. As she was locking the door, Nova heard a sudden bang to her right. Her heart leaped and she swung round, adrenaline coursing through her veins as she prepared to defend herself.

'That wind! There's a storm coming tonight, Craddock, you wait and see.'

Phyllis Hudson was stepping into the entrance foyer, untying a plastic rain-hood from under her chin. The septuagenarian was a familiar sight at the community centre. Nova saw her squat figure and distinctive blue-rinsed perm at the knit and natter group on a Monday, at the Silver Swans senior ballet class on a Thursday and at the food bank on a Friday. In fact, she was such a regular that Nova had been told to turn a blind eye to Craddock, the elderly, arthritic English bulldog that accompanied Phyllis at all times, in blatant contravention of the centre's no-animals policy. The dog was lumbering in through the door now, wheezing like a sixty-a-day smoker.

'Evening, Phyllis,' Nova said, fixing a smile on her face.

'What's wrong with you? You look like you've witnessed a murder.'

'Nothing, I'm fine. Come on in, I'm just setting up.'

Nova hurried to the meeting room and began laying out the biscuits. As she did, she took a deep breath, trying to slow her racing heart. *It was just the door banging in the wind.*

'Digestives?' Phyllis wrinkled her nose as she fed a biscuit to Craddock. 'If you want people to come to your book club then you need to do better than this.'

'Sorry, I'm afraid these are all I've got today.'

'They're not even McVitie's ones. Beryl used to get us shortbread from M&S.'

Beryl had been Nova's predecessor at the centre, a St Tredock local who'd been in the job for thirty years until Sandy caught her drinking whisky out of a coffee mug during the Under-Fives Stay and Play. Although Nova hadn't even been living in Cornwall at the time, she was pretty sure there were some who blamed her for Beryl getting sacked, Phyllis included.

'Next time you want to get some proper biscuits, like a Hobnob,' the older woman continued. 'But not the chocolate ones, mind, as Craddock can't eat those.'

'Noted, I promise,' Nova said.

Phyllis sat down in a chair and Craddock lay heavily at her feet, farting with the exertion. Nova glanced at the clock and saw it was almost 7:05. *Please, please let someone else come so it wasn't just her and Phyllis for the next hour.* They sat in silence for several minutes, the only sounds Phyllis munching biscuits and the snuffling snores coming from the dog's direction.

'Right, well it looks like it's just us tonight, Phyllis. Shall we—'

'Evening all, sorry I'm late!'

The door flew open and in strode Arthur Robinson, a giant of a man dressed in a thick woollen jumper and a pair of green corduroy trousers, his white beard in stark contrast to his ruddy, weather-beaten face. He was followed by Ash, a gangly teenager who was clearly still adjusting to his new height as he bumped into both the doorframe and a chair while crossing the room. He sat down at the far side of the circle and gave Nova an embarrassed nod of greeting before hiding behind his long, dark fringe.

'Good evening both of you,' Nova said, trying not to smile at

Arthur. Although she knew she shouldn't have favourites, she was always delighted to see the pensioner. He'd stumbled into her first book club meeting by accident, when there was a room mix-up with the Carers Support Group summer social, and the eighty-one-year-old retired dairy farmer was now Nova's most enthusiastic participant. Or rather, her only enthusiastic participant.

'You look lovely tonight, Nova,' Arthur said, nodding at her 1950s gingham swing dress. 'You always bring a touch of glamour to the community centre. Oh, digestives, my favourite.' He helped himself to a biscuit and sat down. 'I've been looking forward to tonight all week. A hell of a book pick, I have to say.'

'You enjoyed it, then?' Nova said.

'Absolutely! What a cracker, a real page-turner. Esi and I stayed up well past our bedtime to find out what happened.'

'What did she think of it?'

'She loved it, especially the bits with Tate. You know how my wife enjoys a proper love story.'

Nova had never met Esi Robinson, but Arthur had told her all about the woman. They'd been married for almost sixty years and lived on a farm a couple of miles inland from St Tredock. Esi was now housebound and Arthur was her carer. The woman apparently loved romance novels but was no longer able to read them herself, so Arthur read aloud to her every day. Part of the reason Nova had picked Delia Owens's book was because she hoped Esi would enjoy the romance plot.

'I didn't think much of it at all,' Phyllis said with a sniff. 'Far too slow.'

'I thought you might appreciate the whodunit part?'

'I would if the story had focused on that, but instead there was all that nonsense about insects and birds. Honestly, reading it was like getting stuck behind Jimmy Wallis in the post office queue, waffling on about his twitching holidays.'

'Esi and I loved all the nature bits,' Arthur said. 'Although I've never been to America, I felt like I was there among the herons and fireflies of the North Carolina marshes.'

'What about you, Ash? Did you enjoy the book?' Nova smiled encouragingly at the teenager, who looked panicked at being ad-dressed directly.

'Erm . . . eh . . . yeah? I mean, I've not really read anything like it before, so, I don't know . . .'

'You're right, lad, it was different, wasn't it?' Arthur said, and Nova saw relief flash across the boy's face before he retreated behind his hair. 'Esi and I thought the same, that we weren't sure we'd read anything quite like it.'

'It wasn't even a proper murder mystery,' Phyllis grumbled. 'I worked out who did it by chapter three. And where were the red herrings? The misdirection and twists? And don't get me started on that terrible ending. When he—'

'Before we discuss the ending, why don't we chat about some of the themes in the book?' Nova said. 'I thought we could start by talking about Kya's abandonment, which is a running theme starting from—'

She was interrupted by a loud creak as the door swung open. Nova glanced up to see the miserable-looking man who'd come for the first time last month, and who she'd been sure wouldn't come back. His expression was even unhappier this evening, exhaustion etched around his eyes, and there was a large splatter of ketchup on the front of his shirt. He had a bulging bag slung over his shoulder and was clutching a copy of *Where the Crawdads Sing*.

'Oh, hi . . .' Nova faltered, trying to remember his name.

'Michael,' the man said quietly.

'Of course, lovely to see you again. Come on in, we've only just started.'

He hovered in the doorway for a moment, his eyes flicking around the occupants of the room. There were two free seats between Arthur and Phyllis, and he took the one next to the older man.

'I see you've got the book with you,' Nova said. 'Did you enjoy it?'

Michael looked at the book in his hands as if only just realising it was there. 'I only read a bit.'

She waited to see if he'd elaborate but he just stared at the cover.

'Right, well we were about to discuss Kya's abandonment by her family,' Nova said. 'I was interested to know what impact you all thought this had on the young girl, and how it shaped the woman she became?'

She looked round the circle, but the only person willing to catch her eye was Arthur. She gave him a small nod.

'I thought it was heartbreaking. Especially her being left by her own mother aged just six. It made Kya think she was unlovable, and she carried that her whole life.'

'It wasn't the mother's fault,' Phyllis said, squinting at Arthur through narrow eyes. 'That husband of hers was a violent thug who drove her away and threatened her kids if she ever came back.'

'That's true,' Nova said. 'Clearly Kya's mother was terrified of her husband and—'

'That's no excuse,' Michael interrupted.

They all turned to look at him; at the last meeting he'd not uttered a single word.

'How do you mean?' Nova asked.

'Given she knew how awful life would be for Kya when she left, why didn't she take her daughter with her? What kind of a monster abandons her own child like that?'

'Hang on a second,' Phyllis said, crossing her arms. 'The book tells us the woman had a nervous breakdown, and yet somehow you're blaming the poor bird for everything. That's typical bloody men!'

'Here we go again,' Arthur muttered to Nova. Last meeting, Phyllis had taken umbrage when Arthur had made a critical comment about Agatha Christie's *The Murder at the Vicarage*, and she'd spent fifteen minutes berating the man.

Nova cleared her throat to cut Phyllis off before she could launch into another rant. 'I thought it was interesting how Kya uses examples from the animal world to try and understand the behaviour of humans. Did anyone else pick up on this?'

'Like that mother fox who abandoned her babies for her own survival,' Michael said with a grunt. 'Kya's mother did the same, leaving her kids in danger to protect herself like a—'

He stopped as his phone pinged. Michael pulled it from his pocket and looked at the screen, the colour draining from his face as he read the message. He thrust it away again and closed his eyes. Nova was about to ask if he was okay when Ash spoke up.

'I don't think it was the mum's fault,' he said, his voice so quiet Nova had to strain to hear him. 'I think even Kya comes to understand her mum's actions.'

'Kya could empathise but *these* two clearly can't,' Phyllis snapped, nodding towards Michael and Arthur.

'Okay, shall we move on?' Nova said quickly. 'The residents of Barkley Cove treat Kya as an outsider, and I wondered—'

But she didn't get to finish her sentence, as at that moment Michael jumped up so abruptly that his chair fell over with a crash, grabbed his bag and ran out of the room.

Chapter Two

Nova

For a moment no one said anything as they all stared at the open door. Arthur was the first to speak.

'What do you suppose is up with him?'

'I don't know, but something fishy is going on there, you mark my words,' Phyllis said.

'I'm sure he'll be back any minute,' Nova said. 'Shall we carry on?'

They continued discussing the book, but after Michael's sudden departure, all the energy seemed to have disappeared from the room. Ash had retreated into silence and Phyllis only piped up to disagree with Arthur. Nova tried to get the conversation going again, but her efforts fell flat, and after twenty minutes of stilted chat, she decided to admit defeat and wrap the meeting up early.

'Before we head off, shall we pick our book for next month?'

No one answered, and Nova's heart sank. This was the moment they were about to tell her they weren't coming back again, and she could hardly blame them.

'I'm happy to make a suggestion if no one else wants to,' Arthur said.

'If you're sure, that would be great.' Nova gave him a grateful smile. 'You're a fan of biographies, aren't you? I don't read much non-fiction so it would be great to try something new.'

'Actually, I was going to suggest some fiction . . .' He paused, and Nova saw his cheeks were even redder than normal. 'As you know, my Esi loves a good historical romance. And while they're not my cup of tea, I thought maybe we could read one of them for her?'

'Oh, for goodness' sake, not another soppy love story,' Phyllis said, rolling her eyes. 'In Beryl's day we used to have a proper rota for who chose the books.'

'I think that's a lovely idea, Arthur,' Nova said, ignoring Phyllis. 'Do you think your wife might be able to join us at the next meeting?'

'Oh no, I don't think so. She finds it difficult to leave the farm these days, her eyesight's gone and she's not so steady on her feet. But I always read our book choice to her, and she loves hearing what everyone has to say about them.'

'And is there a particular book Esi would like us to read?'

He gave an embarrassed cough. 'Well, she loves those Bridgerton books. They're all codswallop to me, but she likes all the corsets and balls and the like. So, I thought maybe we could read *The Viscount Who Loved Me*, which is her favourite.'

'That sounds great, thanks Arthur,' Nova said, over Phyllis's exaggerated groan. 'Thanks for coming tonight, everyone. Our next meeting is on twentieth November, so I'll see you then.'

There was the sound of scraping chairs as they all rose. Arthur and Ash said good-bye while Phyllis muttered under her breath and Craddock waddled behind them out the room. Once they were gone, Nova began tidying. As she straightened up the fallen chair, she found Michael's copy of *Where the Crawdads Sing* abandoned under it. In his haste to get away, he must have forgotten it. She opened the book and flicked through the pages, but there was only an

ancient-looking leather bookmark with faded lettering saying something about lizards. Nova shut the book and put it in her bag to leave
in the lost property drawer tomorrow. Not that she imagined Michael would ever come back to get it.

The community centre was eerily quiet as Nova switched off the
lights, and she hurried to lock the front door and run across the rain-
lashed car park. It wasn't yet eight, so she still had time to join Craig
at the pub quiz, yet as she climbed into her rusty old Fiat, all Nova
wanted to do was drive back to the house, put on her pyjamas and
curl up with her current Kiley Reid novel.

It wasn't that Craig's friends and family wouldn't make her feel
welcome at the Anchor. Everyone had been friendly to Nova since
she moved down here, especially Lauren and her boyfriend, who
had been best friends with Craig since primary school. Yet despite
their efforts, Nova still felt like the odd one out when she was with
his friends: the city girl who wore colourful vintage clothes, liked
old-fashioned music, and couldn't join in any of the in-jokes or old
stories that bandied around. She knew it would get better with time:
that at some point she'd stop being seen as 'Craig's quirky girlfriend
from London' and just be 'Nova'. But right now, after a ten-hour shift
at the community centre, all she wanted was a few hours alone with
a good book.

Thankfully, no one was standing outside the Anchor in tonight's
storm and Nova was able to drive past unnoticed. In fact, she didn't
spot a soul as she wound her way through the steep, narrow cobbled
streets down to the harbour. When she'd first moved to St Tredock,
back in May, the place had been bursting with life: the pavements
crowded from morning to night with hordes of holidaymakers visiting the fishing village's pretty beach and old-fashioned, picture-
postcard streets. But now it was mid-October and the tourists had all

gone home, many of the shops and restaurants had closed up for the winter, and the village felt like a ghost town.

It was only a three-mile drive along the coastal road back to Craig's parents' house, but Nova took it slowly as the rain and wind lashed her ancient car. The lights were all off when she pulled into Craig's parents' driveway; the Wednesday night pub quiz was a sacrosanct Pritchard family tradition and they'd all be there until closing. Nova let herself in and walked through the silent rooms, each decorated in muted shades of cream and beige, to the huge modern kitchen that ran along the back of the house, overlooking the sea. She always felt nervous cooking in here, as she was a notoriously messy chef and Pamela Pritchard liked her kitchen pristine, so Nova made herself a simple cheese sandwich, put her favourite Billie Holiday album to play on her phone, and sat down at the glistening marble island to eat.

She was a few mouthfuls in when her phone rang, interrupting the music. She assumed it was Craig, who liked to check in with her when she was alone, but when she lifted up her mobile, she saw it was her mum. Nova pressed answer and her screen was filled with her mum's tanned, grinning face.

'*Buenas noches*, Nono!' Maddy had to shout to be heard above the background noise.

'Hey, Mum! Where are you? It sounds like you're at a rave!'

'Sorry, hang on, let me go outside.' There was a blur on the screen as she moved, and Nova caught flashes of what looked like a beach bar, with a sandy floor, bamboo walls and colourful flags lining the ceiling. Then there was a sudden brightness as her mum stepped outside, and the background noise died away.

'Sorry about that, darling, that was louder than I thought.' Maddy's face was back on the screen and Nova drank it in. Her mum's hair had gone lighter in the South American sunshine, and she had a new silver ring in her nose. As she sat down, Nova heard the familiar jangle of bangles that her mum wore clustered on both wrists.

'How are you, Mum? Adopted any more stray cats lately?'

'I'm good, thanks, and I have! She's a little tabby who reminds me of that kitten we found in Goa when you were seven or eight; the one you wanted to smuggle back to London in your rucksack. Do you remember?'

Nova tried to place the incident, but her childhood memories were a blur of sandy beaches, vast blue skies and friendly stray cats. Her parents were lifelong travellers, and so while Nova's friends had spent their holidays in places like Wales or Spain, her childhood getaways had always involved backpacking on a budget in far-flung places. They had been some of the happiest times of her life.

'How are you feeling about leaving next week?' Nova asked.

'Oh, a bundle of emotions. It's gone so fast, and there's still so much I want to do here. But I can't wait to see you, eat Marmite on toast and drink Yorkshire Tea again!'

Maddie's face radiated happiness as she spoke, and Nova felt a surge of love for her mum. It had been almost seven months since they'd last seen each other in person, when Nova had dropped Maddy at Heathrow airport to send her off on her work secondment for an NGO in Colombia. They video-called every week, and Nova had watched as her mum had slowly transformed from a gaunt, grief-stricken widow to the glowing woman she was now.

'How are you, Nono? How are things at the community centre?'

'It's good. I think I'm really starting to fit in now and forming some good relationships with the visitors.' Nova took a sip of water; she hated lying to her mum, but she also didn't want to worry her by admitting just how hard she was finding it to settle in here.

'That's fantastic! I knew they'd all fall in love with you quickly, everyone always does. And how's Craig?'

'He's great. He's out at the pub quiz tonight; I'm just on my way to join him. And Pamela and David send their love.'

'Ah, give them my love, too, and tell them I'm looking forward to seeing them. I can't believe it's just ten days now, it's so exciting!'

'I can't wait either,' Nova said, a sudden lightness in her chest at the thought of being able to hug her mum again. 'I've got so many fun things planned for when you get here. I want to do some big coastal walks and maybe take a boat out and see if we can spot any seals. Craig told me there's a colony just down the coast, but we've not had a chance to go and look yet.'

'That all sounds perfect. Although there's something else pretty exciting we have to do first . . .' Maddy grinned and Nova laughed.

'Yes Mum, don't worry; it's not like I can forget about my own wedding.'

'How's all the last-minute planning going?'

'Yeah, all good. Pamela has everything under control so it's really not that much work for me. I just have to turn up and say *I do*!'

'I'm so glad she's been able to help you with everything.' Maddy paused and Nova saw something cloud her face. 'You don't mind that I haven't been able to help more, do you? I know it's not been great timing with me being the other side of the world right before your wedding.'

'Of course I don't mind, I'm delighted you're travelling again, and this job was an amazing opportunity. Besides, no offence, but you'd be shit at organising a wedding. If it was up to you, I'd be getting married in a field wearing a bikini and no shoes.'

'There's nothing wrong with getting married barefoot, your dad and I did it in Thailand!' Maddy laughed, but then she grew serious again. 'I just worry that maybe I should've waited until you were more settled. Maybe I left too soon after—'

'Mum, stop it,' Nova interrupted. 'We've been over this before and you didn't go away too soon. I'm absolutely fine.'

'I know you say you are, but I still worry I abandoned you when you needed me most. After losing your dad followed by everything that happened with Declan, then moving to Cornwall and planning a wedding – these are huge things and I've not been there for you.'

'You've been on the end of the phone whenever I need you,' Nova said. 'And I have Craig now too. He's been the most amazing support, so it's not like you left me on my own.'

'He has been amazing,' Maddy said, smiling again. 'I know I had my reservations about you getting married so young, but I can see now that I was wrong. The life Craig is offering you in Cornwall – that stability and love – is a wonderful thing. And I know your dad would be delighted you're so happy.'

'He'd be delighted that you're travelling again too. Remember he said he wanted you drinking ice cold beers on a beach the day after his funeral!'

As she said the words, Nova pictured her dad sitting in the tiny, cluttered kitchen of their old London flat, a glass of wine in his trembling hand and Duke Ellington playing in the background. *I don't want you two moping around once I'm gone*, he'd said. *You've wasted too much time already. The second I'm in the ground, I want you both out there, living your life in full colour, having adventures and causing trouble.* Nova glanced around her at the large, spotless white kitchen she was sitting in now and felt a pang of longing for her dad so sharp she almost moaned.

'I miss him so much,' Maddy said, as if reading Nova's thoughts. She paused before she spoke again. 'I was thinking the other day, one of the worst things about his illness was that it didn't just steal his life, it took both of ours too. For years we became side characters in the story of his disease. And so, while I miss your dad with all my heart, I can't deny it feels good to finally be living my own life again; to have the sand under my toes and fresh air in my lungs. Does that sound awful?'

'Of course it doesn't,' Nova said, swallowing the lump that had formed in her throat.

'It's all your dad ever wanted: for us to be the main characters in our own wonderful, messy stories. And in ten days' time, I'm going to walk you down the aisle as you start this next amazing chapter of yours. I'm so proud of you, darling, and he would be too.'

Tears pooled in Nova's eyes, and she wiped them away.

'Right, enough of this moping!' Maddy said, her face brightening. 'I'm going to have a cold beer and dance on the beach, and you've got a pub quiz to go and win. But I'll see you very, very soon. I love you.'

'Love you, too, Mum.'

The screen went dark, and Nova was plunged into silence.

Chapter Three

Nova

The storm was still raging the following morning, and so after eating breakfast with Craig and his parents, Nova left the house and headed into work early. Wet days inevitably meant the community centre would be extra busy. As soon as the doors opened at ten, young families would start to arrive for the under-fives drop-in session, the Tai Chi class would no doubt turn into an extended coffee morning, and the after-school club would be full of restless kids who'd rather be playing outside. Plus, there would inevitably be leaks to deal with; the centre's ancient roof was in desperate need of repair and let water in whenever it rained heavily. Work to fix it was due to start the week after next, but until then, Nova knew that she and Lauren would have to spend the day emptying buckets around the building.

Sandy and Lauren were on the early shift and their cars were already parked up when Nova arrived at the community centre, as was a police patrol car. She ran inside, shaking the rain out of her curly hair as she walked down the corridor towards the office. As she approached, she heard the raised voice of her boss. This in itself wasn't unusual; Sandy was a woman who'd been known to have emotional outbursts over everything from too many e-mails in her inbox to not enough sugar in her coffee.

'I know it's horrible to even suggest it, but Nova was the last one here.'

Nova ground to a halt a few metres from the open door. Why was Sandy talking about her?

'Are you sure you didn't take it home by accident?' Lauren said. 'Maybe you put it in your handbag without thinking and—'

'Of course I didn't! I put it in the tin before we locked up the office together. You saw me do it, remember?'

'Did anyone else know it was here?' This was an unfamiliar male voice.

'Not a soul,' Sandy replied. 'I only collected it yesterday afternoon, and it was just me, Lauren and Nova who knew it was on-site.'

Nova's heart rate started to climb. She straightened her dress and stepped into the office. Sandy was sitting behind her computer, her face flushed and her curly grey hair even more chaotic than usual. Lauren was on her hands and knees on the floor, going through a drawer, and a young male police officer was leaning against Nova's desk. They all turned to look as she walked in.

'Morning. What's going on?'

'The roof money's been stolen.' Lauren's eyes were wide, and Nova felt her stomach drop.

'How? Did someone break in?'

The police officer shook his head. 'There's no sign of a break-in, the windows and doors are all secure. I'm PC Yusaf Khan, by the way. You're Craig's fiancée, aren't you?'

Nova nodded. 'Yes, hi. How did the thief get in?'

'We don't know, but the office door was unlocked when I arrived this morning.' Sandy made no attempt to hide the accusation in her voice.

'It was definitely locked when I left last night.' As she said this, Nova ran over the evening in her mind. She'd gone to get her copy of *Where the Crawdads Sing* from the office before the book club meeting, but she'd locked it afterward – she clearly remembered the key in her hand – and then she'd not gone back to the office again. 'Someone must have come in after I went home.'

'We've already checked the CCTV footage from the front door,' Yusaf said. 'Sandy left at 6:50 and Lauren at 6:59, after which the only people to enter the building were the four members of your book club.' He consulted his notepad. 'One of them, a guy none of us recognised, ran out at 7:24. Then Phyllis Hudson, Arthur Robinson and Ash Chalabi all left together at 7:46 and you left six minutes later. After that, there's no one else on the CCTV camera until Sandy arrived at 8:35 this morning.'

'Which means that the money must have been taken by someone during the book club meeting,' Sandy cut in, staring at Nova with beady eyes. 'Did you go back into the office last night?'

'I did, but I promise I locked it again,' Nova said, more emphatically this time. 'How much was taken?'

She saw Sandy blink before she answered. 'Ten thousand pounds. The first instalment for the roof repairs, to be paid to the builders up front today.'

'Oh shit!'

The community had spent more than a year trying to fund-raise for a new roof, and they still hadn't hit the full target. Nova knew that first ten thousand pounds had been vital so that emergency work could be done to stop the roof literally collapsing on them before the whole thing could be replaced. And now that money was gone. She looked at Sandy, who had slumped over her desk and was letting out a low moaning sound.

'Nova, can you talk me through what happened during your book club?' Yusaf said. 'Where did it take place?'

'In Tintagel, the small meeting room.'

'And apart from when people arrived and left, did anyone go out of the meeting room during the book club, say to the toilet?'

'No, we all stayed in the room.'

Yusaf studied his notepad. 'Right, well Phyllis arrived first and on her own so potentially she could have broken into the office and taken the money then.'

'No, I met her in the hallway,' Nova said. 'I was just locking the office when she came in and she and I walked to the room together.'

'Okay, that's helpful.' He scribbled something down. 'Arthur Robinson and the teenager, Ash, arrived together and they both left with Phyllis, which means that if any one of them stole the money, there would have been a witness.'

'I'm sure it wouldn't have been one of them,' Lauren said. 'Arthur and Phyllis use this place all the time, they'd never do anything to harm it. And I've known Ash since he was a baby; he's a good kid too.'

'Who was that other man?' Sandy asked Nova. 'I've never seen him here before.'

'His name's Michael. This was his second time at the book club.'

'He arrived on his own and then left after ten minutes,' Yusaf said. 'So theoretically, he could have stolen the money on his way in or out.'

'But how did he unlock the office?' Lauren said.

'He might have picked the lock, I guess. Although he did a bloody good job, as I already checked, and it doesn't look like it was tampered with.'

'So maybe it wasn't locked in the first place,' Sandy said, looking at Nova again.

'Sandy, I swear—'

Nova stopped as a thought occurred to her. She remembered stepping out of the office and putting her key in the lock, but then the front door had banged open when Phyllis came in and scared the life out of her. She felt her insides curl.

'What is it?' Yusaf asked.

'I don't know, but it's possible I might not have locked the door properly. I got distracted when Phyllis arrived and—'

'Bloody hell, Nova!' Sandy exploded. 'You know you have to keep the office door locked when we're not in here.'

'I know, and I was definitely in the process of locking it when Phyllis came in,' Nova said quickly. 'She just made me jump so there's a chance I didn't turn the key.'

'Do you realise what this means? If you did leave the office unlocked, then the money won't be covered by our insurance. We're screwed!'

'Hang on a second, Sandy,' Lauren said. 'Even if Nova did forget to lock the door – which we don't know for certain – she can't be blamed for the money going missing, can she? I mean, she didn't steal it herself.'

Nova felt a rush of gratitude for her friend, but Sandy ignored her.

'It must've been that Michael man,' she said, looking at Yusaf. 'You can see him running out on the CCTV footage: he clearly took a chance on the door, saw the petty cash tin and swiped it on his way out.'

'He does seem like our most obvious suspect,' the police officer said. 'Do you have any contact details for him?'

Nova nodded, relieved she'd at least remembered to get the names and addresses of each member when they started at the book club. 'I've got it written down, hang on.'

She crossed to her desk and began searching through the piles of paper with shaking hands, aware the others were all watching her as she sent pages flying. Finally, she located the records from the book club.

'His name is Michael Watkins,' she said, and Yusaf scribbled it down. 'His address is 8 Mountfort Close, Port Gowan.'

'I have to get to the station now, but I'll pay this Michael Watkins a visit later,' Yusaf said. 'And I'll chat to the other book club members as well, just to be safe. Have you told the council yet?'

Sandy shook her head, and Nova saw her shoulders sink. 'They're going to have a field day with this.'

'What do you think they'll do?' Lauren asked.

Sandy didn't reply, but her eyes flicked to Nova, and she felt a wave of nausea. Of course; someone would need to take the rap for the missing money, and as the person who forgot to lock the door, it was going to be her.

'Let's just hope it was all an innocent mistake and this Michael hands the money back,' Yusaf said as he walked to the door, but it was such an unlikely idea that no one bothered to answer.

Chapter Four

Phyllis

The door swung open, and Phyllis jumped back as PC Khan came striding out. She waited for him to accuse her of eavesdropping, but he strode off without even glancing at her. Not that this was a huge surprise; people rarely noticed her these days, unless she was complaining about something.

Phyllis turned back to the room and made a quick mental note of the tableau inside. Sandy was sitting behind a desk, her face the same colour as her bright red hand-knitted sweater. Nova, who was dressed like an extra from the film *Grease*, had her eyes closed as if she was about to cry, and Lauren was staring at Nova with an expression of concern in her eyes. Phyllis looked down at Craddock as the door slammed shut.

'I told you that Michael was up to something fishy, didn't I?'

Phyllis prided herself on being an excellent judge of character. Like her heroine, Miss Jane Marple, she'd made a hobby of studying human nature, and as a result she almost always got it right: like the too-chatty postman who turned out to be stealing ladies underwear from washing lines, or the girl in the newsagents who refused to let Craddock in the shop and was caught with her hand in the till.

Phyllis had known they were both bad eggs the first time she met them, just as she'd watched Michael Watkins at the book club, with his shifty behaviour and refusal to meet her eye, and known he was dodgy too.

'How do you fancy a little trip to Port Gowan?' she asked Craddock, and the dog let out a slow wheeze in response, like air escaping from a balloon.

They had to catch a bus to get there but Phyllis didn't mind; bus journeys gave her an excellent opportunity to ponder the key questions of the case. Questions such as why would a man from Port Gowan come to a book club in St Tredock? There must be book clubs in his hometown, which was five miles along the coast and much bigger than St Tredock. Besides, it wasn't like theirs was a particularly good one. A few years ago they'd had a decent turnout, but numbers had dwindled as Beryl's behaviour got more erratic, and the book club had stopped altogether after the unfortunate incident involving Eric Forsythe and the women's toilets. It had been restarted by Nova, the out-of-towner who'd taken over Beryl's job, wore funny old-fashioned clothes, and looked like she was going to scream every time anyone made a sudden movement. Then there was the teenager, Ash, who barely spoke and gave off an air of indifference, although Phyllis saw that he always paid attention to every word that was said during the meeting. Finally, there was Arthur Robinson, whose over-friendly exterior and forced joviality were obviously covering up some dark secret. In fact, if Michael turned out to be innocent then Arthur was definitely the next suspect for Phyllis to investigate.

She smiled to herself as the bus pulled into Port Gowan. This case might be rather tame compared to those of Miss Marple, a woman who had single-handedly solved dozens of murders and outwitted countless master criminals and chiefs of police. Yet Phyllis still felt a thrill at the thought of catching the person who'd stolen ten thousand pounds before the police. For a brief moment, she allowed herself to imagine the look of admiration in everyone's eyes when they found out that she was the one who'd apprehended a thief and helped the community centre in the process. Not that she would gloat, of course, but it would be nice to get a little recognition for once.

It had stopped raining by the time she disembarked from the bus, and Phyllis consulted her street map and then set off towards Michael's address. Her pace was slow, thanks to Craddock's short legs and incontinent bladder, but she studied her surroundings as they went. Port Gowan was modern and considerably less charming than St Tredock, its high street filled with clothes 'boutiques' – not shops – and silly fancy restaurants where fish and chips cost more than £20. As they got nearer to Mountfort Close, the houses became bigger and more spaced out. This Michael had obviously done well for himself, not that you'd be able to tell by the state of the man. In his first book club meeting, Phyllis had noted the dandruff on his shoulders and the fact his shirt was buttoned up incorrectly, as if done in a hurry, and last night he'd had what looked like red paint splattered on his shirt. Still, Phyllis had long observed that the richer the person, the more shabbily they dressed. Her own mother, who had been as poor as a church mouse, never left the house without a hat and gloves, and Phyllis remembered once being made to stand in the back garden for three hours in the driving rain, because her mother had caught sight of her walking home from the library with her skirt rolled up above her knees. And yet many of the 'Tarquins' and 'Amelias' who invaded St Tredock every summer dressed as if they were vagrants.

'Here we are,' Phyllis said as they rounded a corner and entered Mountfort Close.

It was a cul-de-sac containing twenty or so semi-detached houses, each set back from the road by a wide driveway. There were few cars around at this time of day, and Phyllis imagined the residents commuting to well-paid jobs in Plymouth or Exeter. There were, however, three vehicles parked in Michael Watkins's driveway: a red MINI Cooper, a black Ford van and a police car.

'Damn it, Craddock; it looks like PC Khan got here first.'

So much for catching the thief before the cops. Still, Phyllis had come all this way so she might as well stay to watch the criminal being arrested; if nothing else, it would make a good story to tell everyone back at the community centre. Reaching into her handbag, she retrieved a woollen bobble hat and a pair of sunglasses. It wasn't a very sophisticated disguise, but she was confident that if PC Khan glanced over, he wouldn't recognise her. This was one of the few occasions when it was useful that older people like her were invisible to the rest of the world.

Phyllis adopted a hunched posture and began to shuffle across the road towards number eight, but as she reached the far pavement, the door to the house swung open. Phyllis froze. There was a large black wheelie bin to her right, and she just had time to pull Craddock behind it before someone appeared in the doorway.

They had their back to Phyllis, but she could see it was a man dressed in protective overalls. Was this Michael? No, he looked too young, and his posture was different, taller and more confident. He said something to a person out of view and began to move backwards away from the door. How strange, why was he reversing like that? And then Phyllis saw something that made her gasp.

Behind the man was a contraption on wheels, one Phyllis recognised from the countless murder mysteries she'd watched on TV. It was a wheeled stretcher, covered with a long, human-shaped object cloaked in a white sheet.

A dead body.

Phyllis's heart was hammering so hard she could hear it in her ears, but she kept her eyes trained on the house. A woman was pushing the stretcher from the other end, and the two of them loaded it into the back of the unmarked van. Once the rear doors were shut, the man walked back to the front door and said something to a figure inside the house who Phyllis couldn't see. She strained round the side of the bin to get a better look and was rewarded with a quick glimpse of a dark-haired woman in her mid to late fifties, her face pinched as she closed the front door. The van engine burst into life, and a moment later the man had climbed in and they were pulling past the police car and out of the driveway. Phyllis ducked low in case one of them spotted her, but the vehicle turned right and drove out of the cul-de-sac before disappearing from view.

Phyllis's mind was racing as fast as her heart. Who had died and how? Why were the police involved? Was the woman in the doorway Michael's wife, and if so, where was he? And, most importantly, how was this dead body connected to the community centre money?

She inhaled deeply, trying to calm herself; after all, Miss Marple never allowed her emotions to get the better of her. And now, *finally*, Phyllis had a chance to put all these years of Agatha Christie reading to good use. With a quick glance back at the house, she straightened up and strode across the road, Craddock trotting to keep up with her.

Chapter Five

Nova

The storm had passed by the time Nova finished work that evening, leaving behind a dramatic pink-and-orange sky that cast St Tredock in a gorgeous, sleepy glow. Beautiful sunsets always reminded Nova of her dad, who'd loved watching them wherever they were in the world, and so usually she'd stop to appreciate the sunset too. Yet tonight, Nova paid it little attention as she drove home, her attention fixed on the missing money and what it meant for her future. When she reached Craig's parents' house, she turned off the engine but sat in her car for a few moments longer, psyching herself up before she went inside.

'Nova, sweetie, you're home!' Pamela Pritchard's voice assailed Nova as she opened the front door. 'How was your day? Everything good at the centre?'

'Fine, thanks.' At least the news about the stolen money hadn't reached Craig's parents yet.

'We're through in the kitchen. I've made roast chicken, Craig's favourite.'

'Great,' Nova said, although in truth, all she wanted was to hide upstairs with Craig and a bottle of wine. Unfortunately, Pamela and

David liked to eat dinner at 6:30 p.m. sharp, and always meat and two veg, despite the fact Nova was a lifelong vegetarian. She'd volunteered many times to cook some veggie meals for the family, but her future mother-in-law insisted that Craig and his dad needed meat every day.

'Hey, gorgeous!' Craig's handsome face lit up when he saw Nova walk into the kitchen, and she slid into the seat next to him and gratefully took the glass he handed her. 'Good day?'

'Mm-hmm.' She took a long swig of wine so she didn't have to outright lie; she'd save the bad news until she was alone with Craig later. 'How was yours?'

'Busy. Dad's been working me to the bone, as per usual.'

David Pritchard let out a deep laugh. 'Just training you up properly, son. If you're going to be taking over the garage one day, then I want to know it's in good hands.'

'Of course it'll be in good hands with Craigy,' Pamela tutted, as she carried over a towering plate of Yorkshire puddings.

'Wow, these look amazing,' Nova said.

'My secret recipe. I'll have to teach it to you before you move out.'

'Speaking of which, how's the house hunting going?' David asked.

'There's nothing out there at the moment,' Craig said. 'I think it's just the wrong time of year.'

'Did you manage to speak to the estate agent about that cottage in Mawham I sent you?' Nova asked Craig.

'I called him this morning, and it sounds like it's a no-go, I'm afraid. The guy said it's a 'fixer-upper', which is estate agent code for an absolute dump.'

'I don't mind a bit of a renovation project. It could be fun to make a place our own.'

'Oh no, you don't want to be taking on a big project; those things are a money pit,' Pamela said, putting two dry-looking vegetarian sausages on Nova's plate. 'Besides, there's no hurry. David and I love having you both here, so you can stay with us as long as you need to.'

'Thanks, Mum,' Craig said, helping himself to three roast potatoes.

'We could go and take a look on Saturday, just in case we love it?' Nova said to Craig.

'Sure, if you—' Craig started, but Pamela interrupted.

'Not this Saturday, young lady. We've got the final fitting of your wedding dress, remember?'

Craig laughed and winked at Nova. 'Ditsy Davies strikes again! You must be the only bride who's ever forgotten about her own wedding dress fitting.'

'Sorry, silly me,' Nova said, forcing a smile. Her forgetfulness was the last thing she wanted to laugh about right now.

'I thought we could stop by my shop first so I can show you what I've got planned for the altar flowers,' Pamela said to Nova. 'I know you'd said dahlias, but the chrysanthemums are looking lovely at the moment and—'

'Oh dear,' David interrupted, and when Nova looked over, he was staring at his phone, a roast chicken–laden fork suspended in front of his mouth.

'What is it?' Pamela asked.

'I've just seen a message in the country club WhatsApp group. Apparently, there was a break-in at the community centre last night and someone stole thirty thousand pounds.'

'What?' Pamela shrieked. 'Nova, is that true?'

Everyone turned to look at Nova and she took another sip of wine before she answered. 'It was ten thousand, not thirty. But yes, money was stolen from the centre.'

'What the hell was £10k doing lying around the place?' David said. 'Sandy Reynolds is always going on about how cash-strapped that place is.'

'She'd taken it out of the bank to pay the builders for the emergency roof work.'

'Shit, Nova,' Craig said, reaching over and taking her hand.

'Yeah, it's been a rough day.'

'How did the bastards break in?' David asked.

For a moment, Nova wondered if she could lie and claim not to know, but she knew the truth would get out soon enough. 'It wasn't a break-in, as such. They think that the money was stolen during the book club meeting last night.'

'*Your* little book club?' Pamela said. 'Well, at least that'll make it easy to find the thief, given you hardly have any members.'

'Do they have any idea who it might have been?' Craig asked gently.

'It seems the most likely suspect is a guy called Michael, who left the meeting early.'

'I still don't understand how he managed to steal the money,' David said. 'Surely it was locked in a safe?'

Nova had been dreading this: the moment she'd have to tell them it was her fault. She took a deep breath.

'The safe has been broken for months so the money was in the petty cash tin. And then it looks like I forgot to lock the office door, so we think he must have gone in and taken the tin.'

There was a moment of stunned silence round the table.

'Oh, babe,' Craig said eventually, and she felt him squeeze her hand.

'Yeah, Ditsy Davies strikes again.' She gave a faint laugh, which fell flat.

'I hope Sandy's not trying to blame this on you?' David said.

'My God, you're not going to get sacked before the wedding, are you?' Pamela's hand flew to her pearl necklace.

'I don't know. Sandy has an emergency meeting with the council this evening and then she wants to see me first thing tomorrow, so I guess I'll find out then.'

'If they try and sack you, we'll get our solicitor involved and sue the council for unfair dismissal.' David skewered another roast potato and Pamela nodded in agreement.

'Absolutely! And on the upside, if you do get sacked then you can always come and work for me at the florists.'

Nova's face must have gone pale because Craig raised his hands. 'Mum, Dad, stop it! You're freaking Nova out.'

'Sorry, let's talk about something cheerier,' Pamela said. 'I wanted to chat to you both about the wedding favours, and whether you wanted the sugared almonds in boxes or . . .'

Four hours later, Nova lay curled up in Craig's arms in bed. Downstairs, she could hear the TV playing, although not loudly enough to cover David and Pamela's muttered conversation about her.

'Don't listen to them, Mum loves a drama,' Craig whispered into the back of her head.

'I'm so sorry I've brought this on us,' Nova said. 'Moving down here was supposed to be a fresh start, and I've ruined it already.'

'Stop it, this isn't your fault. That money should never have been left in the petty cash tin in the first place.'

'But what if we don't manage to get it back?' Nova turned to face him, her eyes wide in the dark. 'I can't lose my job again, not after everything that happened with—'

'Shh, don't upset yourself,' Craig said, reaching out and stroking her hair.

'If they sack me for gross negligence then I'll never get another job,' Nova said, fighting back a sob.

'Of course you will.' Craig brushed a tear from her cheek. 'And if for any reason you can't, it wouldn't be a total disaster. I'm earning a decent salary at the garage, so if the worst comes to the worst, I could support us both for a bit.'

'But I love being a youth worker; it's all I've ever wanted to do.'

'I know, but all I'm saying is that I don't want you to panic if you do end up losing your job. We'd be okay, I promise. I'll look after you.'

Craig pulled her into his chest and Nova closed her eyes, inhaling his comforting soapy scent. This was one of the many things she loved about Craig: his ability to make her feel safe. Back in the darkest days after her dad died, days when Nova thought she might never be able to get out of bed again, Craig had spent hours holding her like this while she cried. He'd been the one who'd brought her endless cups of sugary tea and made sure she ate, even when the thought of food made her sick; the one to gently wash her hair and pick out her clothes when even the simplest decision overwhelmed her. So, although the thought of what was to come at work was terrifying, at least she knew she'd always have Craig by her side.

The following morning, Nova spent ages choosing what to wear. One of the things she loved about clothes, and vintage ones in particular, was how they could shape her mood for the day: how she could go from feeling fun to serious to sexy by simply putting on a certain dress or the perfect pair of boots. With this in mind, she'd initially dressed in a pair of wide-legged, houndstooth trousers and a chic 1930s cropped jacket she'd found in a flea market in London. The outfit made her feel smart and self-possessed, but then she'd asked

Craig his opinion and he'd gently suggested that she might want to wear something a bit more 'normal' for her big meeting with Sandy – that maybe today wasn't the day for 'fashion statements' – and so Nova had changed into a pair of jeans and a simple blouse. She also toned down her make-up, although she did put on her favourite red, faux-fur coat, which she and her dad had found years ago in Camden Market.

It was usually just her and Sandy on the early shift on a Friday, but as Nova pulled into the community centre car park, she saw Lauren waiting for her by the front door, holding two takeaway cups.

'I thought you could do with a bit of moral support,' she said, handing Nova one of the cups as she got out of the car. 'How are you feeling?'

'Pretty nauseous. I've been up since five a.m., panicking.'

'How did the Pritchards take the news?'

'Pamela and David freaked out, but thankfully Craig was super supportive.'

'As he should be, otherwise I'd have kicked that boy's arse! Now, shall we go inside and find out what's going on?'

Nova took a deep breath and nodded, and together the two women headed into the centre. The office door was open and the light on inside, and as they walked in, they found Sandy behind her computer. From the toast crumbs and empty mugs on her desk, it looked as if she'd been there for a while.

'Morning, Sandy,' Lauren said.

'Morning.' She was scribbling on a piece of paper and didn't look up as they walked in. 'You two had better sit down.'

Nova glanced at Lauren and grimaced. They both sat in their chairs and waited for her to finish what she was doing.

'So, I met with Tina and the team at the council last night,' Sandy said, and when she looked up, Nova saw that her eyes were red-rimmed behind her glasses. 'As you can imagine, it wasn't a particularly pleasant meeting. They're furious about the missing money and—'

'They're going to sack me, aren't they?' Nova interrupted.

'I'm afraid it's more complicated than that,' Sandy said, thrusting a pen into her thick curls. 'I knew it was trouble the moment I walked into the room. The head of finance was there, awful man, and he gave a long, waffling speech about reduced central government funding and budgetary constraints. And then he told me the community centre was a poor return on the council's investment and they'd been considering "alternative arrangements that might help alleviate the council's current funding deficit."'

'Which means?' Lauren said.

'Which means they want to end our lease on this place and sell the building off. And this stolen money has given them the perfect excuse to do it.'

'What?' Lauren spat. 'Those bastards!'

'They can't do that, can they?' Nova's voice was high-pitched, and she cleared her throat. 'Where would everyone go if it closed down? The centre is always so busy.'

'You don't have to tell *me* that, I've worked here for twenty-four years!' Sandy breathed in through her nose before exhaling loudly. 'I know how much the community needs this place. But the council is short of money, and we're sitting on a piece of prime Cornish property.'

'Surely they must realise how unpopular it would be to close us down?' Lauren said. 'If nothing else, it would piss off a load of voters.'

'They know that, which is why they're being so conniving about the whole thing. Rather than simply saying they're going to end our lease, they've given me ten days to show how I can recoup the stolen money from our existing budget.'

'But that's impossible. We can barely afford toilet roll; how the hell are you meant to find ten thousand pounds?'

'Of course it's impossible, that's the point. And when I say I can't do it, that'll mean the roof repair work can't be done, and they'll have the perfect excuse to close us down on health and safety grounds.'

'I take it the insurers won't pay out?' Nova said.

'No. As I feared, the unlocked door invalidates our policy.' Sandy's eyes flicked to her as she said this, and Nova felt her cheeks burn.

'What if we tried to find the money another way? Could we delay the roof repairs and fund-raise again?'

'That's not an option. The inspector made it very clear that this roof won't last another winter, and we're already in mid-October. Besides, it's taken us more than a year to raise this money, and we're still well short of the full amount we need.'

'This is absolutely ridiculous,' Lauren said. 'How are you supposed to magic ten thousand pounds out of thin air in ten days?'

'I have no idea,' Sandy said. ' I'm going through the budget with a fine-tooth comb, but there's no reserves in here, thanks to the bloody Tories and fourteen years of their cuts.'

'Have the police had any luck tracing Michael?' Nova asked.

Sandy shrugged. 'I've not heard back from Yusaf yet, but that's the kind of miracle we need.'

The room fell into silence, and Nova felt her stomach twist. She'd been worrying about losing her job, but this was *so* much worse. Where on earth would everyone go if the centre closed? The parents who relied on the play group, the young people who used the centre as a safe space, the older people who came for somewhere warm to socialise, not to mention the dozens of different community groups from all around the area who hired their rooms each week. All that could be lost, and it would be her fault.

'What are we going to do?'

Sandy let out a long, exhausted sigh. 'Give me a couple of days to keep working on this budget, just in case there's a way of recouping the money somehow.'

'Is there anything I can do to help?'

'Find the missing money?' Sandy gave a humourless laugh. 'In all seriousness, just keep your head down and try not to cause any more trouble. The council are going to be watching us like hawks, and I don't want to give them any more ammunition.'

Nova nodded, the word *trouble* ringing in her ears.

Chapter Six

Nova

Nova stumbled out of the meeting to find the community centre in its usual Friday morning chaos. Every week, a volunteer-run food bank was held in the main hall, and from nine thirty until one o'clock, there was a constant flow of people coming through the centre doors to stock up on food for their families, as well as have a cup of tea and a friendly chat. As Nova walked past the front door, she saw a queue had already formed outside, even though they didn't open for another fifteen minutes. Her stomach lurched again at the thought of what all these people would do if the centre closed and the food bank could no longer happen.

'Morning, Nova.' Arthur Robinson, who volunteered every week making tea, was standing in the main hall, trying to coax the ancient urn into life. 'Any chance you know the magic spell for this thing?'

'Let me have a look.' Nova joined him behind the table and began to fiddle with the temperamental cable.

'I had young PC Khan on the phone this morning,' Arthur said, lowering his voice. 'He told me about the theft during book club.'

'I'm sorry about that,' she whispered back. 'I did try to tell him it wouldn't have been you.'

'Oh, never mind that. I just can't believe anyone would steal from this place.'

'It looks like it might have been Michael.'

Arthur's white eyebrows shot up. 'The man who ran out? He didn't look the thieving type.'

'I don't know who else it could have been. No one apart from us came in or out of the building on Wednesday night.'

'It's always the quiet ones, isn't it? And how are *you* doing, lass?'

Nova opened her mouth to say she was fine, but something caught in her throat and for a horrible moment she thought she was going to burst into tears.

'It's not been great,' she managed to mumble. 'We just have to really, really hope that we get the money back, otherwise . . .' She trailed off, not wanting to finish the sentence.

'Well, I'm happy to donate money again if needs be. Esi and I don't have much, but we'd happily give what we can to help this place.' Arthur paused, his eyes scanning the room. 'The community centre means a lot to us, you know. We got married in Esi's home-town in Ghana, but we had our British wedding celebration in this very room, back in 1966.'

'How amazing! Has it changed much since then?'

Arthur didn't reply, and Nova could tell he was back there on his wedding day, dancing with his bride. A small smile passed over his lips, but his eyes were misty.

There was a shout over by the main door, and Nova looked up to see one of the food bank volunteers trying to remonstrate with a figure in the lobby. She couldn't see who it was behind the man, but she had a good idea. Sure enough, a second later she heard a familiar voice.

'You can't stop me going in here; this is a free service for the whole community.'

'You're welcome to come in when we open, but the dog has to stay outside. It's a health and safety rule.'

'This is discrimination! Would you stop a blind person bringing in a guide dog?'

'No, but that's different; guide dogs are assistance animals.'

'Well, Craddock *is* my assistant.'

'I said assistance not . . . Ow!'

The man bent over to nurse his shin as Phyllis barged past him, Craddock at her side. She scanned the room until she spotted Nova.

'Oh Lordy,' Arthur muttered, as Phyllis bowled towards them.

'I assume you've heard?' The woman's voice reached them before she did. 'I told you there was something strange going on with that man, and I was right!'

'Phyllis, shhh!' The last thing Nova needed was her announcing the theft to the whole centre. 'Let's go and talk somewhere quieter.'

She took Phyllis's arm and steered her out the hall, past the volunteer who glared at the older woman.

'We can go into Tintagel, it should be free.'

Nova opened the door and ushered Phyllis inside, Craddock and Arthur hot on their heels. As soon as the door closed, Phyllis let rip.

'The second I saw him, I knew something was up. But never in my wildest dreams did I imagine something like this would happen.'

'We still don't know for sure it was Michael,' Nova said.

'Oh, it was him all right. I've considered all other explanations and that's the only one that fits with the evidence.'

'Well, PC Khan was hoping to speak to him yesterday afternoon so we should know whether he confesses to the crime soon enough.'

Phyllis let out a snort. 'He's not going to have much luck interviewing Michael now. Not unless they have a spirit medium over at Port Gowan police station.'

'What do you mean?' Arthur asked.

Phyllis's head snapped to look at him, and then a satisfied smile spread across her face. 'Are you telling me you don't know yet?'

'Know what?'

The older woman pulled her shoulders back and took a deep, dramatic breath before she spoke again.

'Michael's dead!'

Nova felt her stomach drop. 'What?'

'I saw his body being taken away from his house under a sheet yesterday.' Phyllis was practically hopping from foot to foot in her excitement.

'My God, the poor man,' Arthur said.

'Poor man, my arse! He stole ten thousand pounds from this place, remember?'

'But still, he didn't deserve to die!'

'How do you know it was Michael if the body was under a sheet?' Nova said.

'By a process of elimination. Aside from the police car and the coroner's van, there was only one car in his driveway, suggesting there were only one or two driving-age adults in the house. The body being carried out was heavy – the two people pushing it looked like they were exerting themselves – and Michael must have weighed at least fifteen stone. Plus, I saw a woman around his age standing in the doorway with smudged mascara, who I assume was the grieving wife. Ergo, it must have been Michael.'

'Imagine stealing ten thousand pounds and then dropping dead a few hours later,' Arthur said, shaking his head. 'All that effort for nothing.'

'Assuming he did just "drop dead",' Phyllis said.

Nova looked at her in surprise. 'What are you suggesting?'

Phyllis smiled, as if she'd been hoping for this question. 'Let's look at the facts, shall we? Michael Watkins, a man who lives five miles away in Port Gowan, chose to come to a neighbouring book club rather than one closer to home. Odd, no?' She turned from them and began to pace across the room. 'He behaved suspiciously the whole time he was here; clearly the man's no bibliophile. On his second visit, he arrived late and seemed distracted but showed no obvious signs of ill health. Then, having received a text message that alarmed him, he ran abruptly from the meeting halfway through. These are peculiar things, wouldn't you agree?'

Nova opened her mouth to answer, but it had clearly been a rhetorical question as Phyllis continued.

'Yesterday morning, ten thousand pounds was discovered missing from the community centre, and yet there was no sign of a break-in, and CCTV footage showed that no one else entered or left the building, suggesting Michael was the thief. And then, most peculiar of all, a few hours after the missing money was discovered, our main suspect is dead, and the police are at his property investigating.'

'You're not seriously suggesting you think Michael was murdered?' Nova said.

'The great Miss Marple always said that if all the facts fit a theory, it must be the right theory. And all the facts point to Michael's death being suspicious.'

'But isn't there another explanation?' Arthur said. 'What if Michael came to our book club because he actually liked books, then got some bad news in the text, and on his way out he saw the unlocked office and stole the petty cash tin on a whim? And then, completely unrelated, later that night he had a heart attack or died from some other unfortunate natural cause. It could be a complete coincidence that the two things happened so close together.'

Phyllis let out a grunt of impatience. 'Another of the many things I've learned from reading Agatha Christie's novels is there's no such thing as coincidence. Miss Marple knew this and always paid attention to the small, peculiar things, as she knew they were likely relevant. Like when Elvira Blake just happened to turn up at the same hotel as her long-lost mother in *At Bertram's Hotel*, or Anne Protheroe accidentally not carrying her handbag in *The Murder at the Vicarage*. Others dismissed these as irrelevant coincidences and yet Miss Marple knew they weren't. Just as I know that a man attending a faraway book club on the same night money goes missing and then his dead body turning up the following day are not mere coincidences. The man was murdered, and I propose that his death was linked to our stolen money.'

Phyllis stopped and looked at them as if expecting a standing ovation, but Nova's mind was racing. The older woman was well known for having an overactive imagination: Lauren had told Nova about the time Phyllis had accused Sandy of running an international drug smuggling ring, all because she'd caught the woman with several boxes of donated talcum powder for the Christmas fete and been convinced they were cocaine. But however carried away Phyllis might sometimes get, Nova had to admit that everything that had happened in the past thirty-six hours did seem a bit, well, suspicious.

'How did you get Michael's address in the first place?' she asked Phyllis. 'In fact, how did you even know about the stolen money yesterday? Nobody knew outside of the staff here and the police?'

'I might just be a little old lady, but I know more than you think.'

'Have you told your theory to the police?'

Phyllis let out a guffaw of mirth. 'Of course not! They'll dismiss me as a dotty old lady, just like they always did with Miss Marple.'

'I still can't believe Michael's dead,' Arthur said softly. 'Do you think we should go and pay our respects to his wife?'

Nova was about to say no, but then she remembered how grateful she'd been for all the people who'd come to offer their condolences after her dad died, even the ones she'd never met before.

'That's an excellent idea!' Phyllis said. 'And while we're there, we can ask a few gentle questions about the missing money.'

'No!' Nova said. 'You can't ask anything about the missing money, or the circumstances around Michael's death. All we'll do is say how sorry we are and then leave, okay?'

'Whatever you say, boss,' Phyllis said, not even attempting to hide the excitement in her voice.

Chapter Seven

Nova

Nova spent the drive to Port Gowan kicking herself for agreeing to this. Sandy had told her to keep her head down and stay out of trouble, and yet here she was, visiting the wife of a recently deceased (possible) thief, with a wannabe Miss Marple in tow. And what would Craig say when he found out? After everything that had happened in her old job, he'd freak out when Nova told him she'd driven to the home of a (possible) murder victim. Maybe she shouldn't mention this outing to him? Although how she'd explain the strong smell of dog in the car, Nova wasn't sure. She wrinkled her nose and wound down her window.

'I think this is a bad idea,' she said as they reached the end of Michael's cul-de-sac. 'If Michael really was murdered, the last thing his widow's going to want is random strangers turning up on her doorstep so soon after. Let's come back in a few days' time.'

'We're not strangers, we were in a book club together,' Arthur said. 'And if the tables were turned and I was the one who'd died, I'd like to think you'd all visit Esi to pay your respects.'

Nova sighed but she could hardly argue with that. She turned the car into Mountfort Close and pulled up by the pavement.

'That's his house, over there on the left,' Phyllis said. 'That red car is the one I saw yesterday. It belongs to his wife.'

'How do you know that?' Nova asked, turning to look at Phyllis in the back seat. 'Please tell me you haven't been searching car records?'

'Of course not, but it's obvious. For one, no man in his sixties drives a red MINI Cooper. And secondly, at the book club meeting last month, Michael was wearing a golfing tie, and you'd never fit golf clubs in the boot of that car.'

Nova hated to admit it, but that logic did make sense.

'I wonder if it was his wife who killed him?' Arthur said absent-mindedly as he stared at the house. 'It happens all the time in Esi's romance novels; a lovers' tiff that turns nasty. A crime of passion, they call it.'

'Not you as well with the fictional theories,' Nova said with a sigh, and Arthur chuckled. 'Right, let's get this over and done with, shall we?'

They climbed out of the car and headed up the driveway. When they reached the front door, Phyllis pressed the doorbell.

'Remember, we're just giving our sympathies and then leaving,' Nova whispered as they waited.

'Yes, yes, yes,' Phyllis snapped.

'I mean it, Phyllis. No interrogations about money or murder or—'

At that moment, the front door swung open to reveal a woman with salt and pepper hair pulled back from her make-up-free face. She was dressed in a black sweater and slim trousers, and had a look of confusion on her pale face as she took in the strange trio and wheezing dog standing on her doorstep.

'Can I help you?'

Nova opened her mouth to speak but Phyllis got there first.

'Hello, deary.' An unfamiliar soft, quivering voice emerged from the woman's mouth. 'I'm so sorry to trouble you when I'm sure you're busy, but we just wanted to pay our respects.'

What on earth was Phyllis doing? She may be many things, but a sweet, timid old lady she certainly wasn't.

'Sorry, who are you?' the woman asked.

'We're friends of your husband's. We were in a book club with him over at St Tredock community centre and—'

'Did you say a book club?' The woman's eyebrows shot up. 'I'm sorry, but I think you must have made a mistake. My husband isn't the book club sort; not unless all you read are golfing manuals.'

'Oh, have I got the wrong address?' Phyllis's face fell. 'Sorry, I'm getting ever so forgetful in my old age, maybe I remembered it incorrectly. Is this not Michael Watkins's home?'

The woman frowned. 'A book club, you say?'

'That's right. You're welcome to join yourself, when you feel up to it. The book choices need improving and the biscuit selection is poor, but we do have a good debate, and it'll get you out of the house. We meet on the third Wednesday of every month.'

The woman shook her head, as if not believing what she was hearing. 'The third Wednesday; as in the day before yesterday?'

'Mm-hmm, that's right. This month's pick was *Where the Crawdads Sing*, although I don't think poor Michael thought much of it. How sad to think the last book he read was such a bad one. If only we'd gone with my—'

'Bloody hell, that man!'

They all startled at the rage in the woman's voice. Nova knew better than anyone that grief brought a roller coaster of emotions with it, but she'd never heard someone swear quite so angrily at their recently deceased spouse.

'What's that, deary?' Phyllis said, leaning forwards. 'Sorry, my hearing's not what it was, you're going to have to speak up.'

'It's nothing, I'm fine,' the woman said quickly, although the two red dots on her cheeks suggested otherwise.

'We should leave you in peace,' Nova said. 'We just wanted to come and say how sorry we are for your loss, but we'll be going now.'

She grabbed Phyllis's arm and began to pull her back before she could say anything else. Nova expected Arthur to turn around and join them, but instead he bowed his head.

'I'm very sorry, too, Mrs Watkins. I didn't know your husband well, but he seemed like a good'un.'

His voice was low and respectful, and Nova saw the woman's expression change.

'I beg your pardon?'

'My wife, Esi, always says that anyone who loves books can't be a bad person, so I'm sure your husband was a fine man. I'm only sorry I didn't get to know him better before he passed.'

The woman stared at Arthur for a moment, and then she threw back her head and let out a loud bark of laughter.

'My God, you think *Michael's* dead?'

'Isn't he?'

'No, he's very much alive. Although if he turns up at your book club, you can tell him that Cynthia says if I ever see him again, I'll kill him myself!'

Nova was too shocked to speak and even Phyllis seemed to have been stunned into silence. Only Arthur managed to find his voice.

'I'm so sorry, ma'am. Someone saw a body being taken away from here yesterday and we thought it was Michael's.'

'No, that was his mother, God rest her soul. I was the one who found her when I came back from staying at my sister's yesterday morning.' The woman, Cynthia, visibly shivered as she said the words.

'Oh dear, how awful for you,' Phyllis said, regaining her strange, quivering voice. 'That must have been a terrible shock for you and for Michael. Would you be able to give us his phone number, by the way? Only we think he might have taken something when he left the book club on Wednesday, and we're very keen to get it back.'

'I can give you his number, but it won't do you any good. If the police's theory is correct then Michael, and whatever it is you want back, will be long gone by now.'

'What do you mean the police's theory?' Nova asked.

For a moment Cynthia didn't speak, and Nova could see her weighing something up. Then she sighed and lowered her voice. 'I might as well tell you, seeing as word's bound to get out sooner or later. The police think Michael's mum was murdered. I found her body at the bottom of the stairs, and from the way she was lying, they think she was pushed.'

'Oh, dear God, how awful!' Arthur said.

'Do they have any idea who killed her?' Phyllis asked.

Cynthia leaned closer to them, dropping her voice even further. 'They think it was Michael.'

'What!' Arthur said with a gasp. 'But that's rubbish, surely? He didn't strike me as the murdering sort.'

'That's what I told the police. But he was overheard arguing with Eve before she died, and he has been behaving strangely recently. I'm sorry but could you please control your dog?'

Nova looked down to see Craddock humping a garden gnome.

'So Michael's run away?' Phyllis said, pulling back on the lead.

'He was seen driving away from the house around the time the police think Eve was killed, and he's not been seen since. Although by the sounds of things, he came to your book club before he disappeared.' Cynthia stopped as a thought occurred to her. 'Is *she* in your book club? Is that why he came?'

'Who?'

'That *woman*.' Cynthia's voice was thick with vitriol. 'He thinks I don't know, but of course I do: the hushed phone calls, the money gone from our bank account, all those evenings he came home late with no decent explanation of where he'd been.' Her eyes flicked to Nova. 'It's not you, is it?'

'Of course not!'

'I suppose you're not really his type. I wondered if it might be Wendy, the barmaid from the golf club. She's in her fifties, big breasts, very stupid. Is she in your book club?'

'I'm afraid not,' Phyllis said. 'Do you know where this Wendy lives? Maybe that's where Michael is now.'

'I've got no idea, and quite frankly, I don't care,' Cynthia said, although behind the angry words, Nova could hear a wobble in her voice. 'Do you have any idea the mess he's left me to deal with? I came home to find Eve's body, and then there's been police and forensics buzzing all over the place. And now I have a funeral to organise on top of all the legal business around this house and sorting Eve's stuff. And he hasn't even bothered to send me a text!'

'It sounds like you've got a lot on, so we should get out of your hair,' Nova said. 'Thanks for your time, and I'm sorry again about your mother-in-law.'

'Yes, if there's anything we can do to help, please just ask,' Arthur said. 'You can find us at the St Tredock Community Centre.'

'And you're absolutely sure you don't know where Michael is?' Phyllis added, but Cynthia had already shut the door.

Chapter Eight

Phyllis

Phyllis climbed into the back seat of the car, heaving Craddock in beside her. She heard Nova and Arthur get into the front seats but paid them little attention as her mind spun with everything she'd just learned. So, Michael wasn't dead, but he *was* now a murder suspect, which explained so many things. For one, the red stain on his shirt that Phyllis had thought was paint had clearly been his mother's blood. And the way he'd ranted about Kya's mum in the Crawdads book, even calling her a monster, now made sense too. God knows what Eve Watkins had done to make her son hate her so much, but the man clearly had major mummy issues. And now they had the explanation for why he'd stolen the community centre money too: to fund his escape. But for every answer, there were still many questions hanging in the air, and lots of new avenues to explore. Phyllis couldn't help but smile at the thought of the days ahead.

'Bloomin' heck, I wasn't expecting any of that,' Arthur said as he closed the front passenger door. 'And to think he was sitting with us at book club, chatting about *Where the Crawdads Sing*, while his own mother lay murdered at home.'

'It would explain why he was so jumpy in the meeting,' Nova said.

'Imagine killing your own mother in cold daylight and then eloping with your mistress?' Arthur said. 'It reminds me of this book Esi loves, *A Rogue and a—*'

'For goodness' sake, tell me you two didn't fall for that nonsense?'

Nova and Arthur both turned to look at her, and Phyllis felt a thrill of satisfaction. Finally, people were paying attention when she spoke.

'What do you mean?' Nova said.

'I mean, not a word of that was true. The woman was lying from the moment she opened the door.'

'So, you don't think Michael killed his mother?' Arthur asked.

'No, I think that bit was true. But she definitely wasn't giving us the whole picture.'

'She seemed genuine enough to me,' Nova said.

'The problem with you two is you're far too trusting,' Phyllis said, leaning back in the car seat. 'Miss Marple knew—'

'Not Miss bloody Marple again,' Arthur muttered.

'*Miss Marple* knew never to give anyone the benefit of the doubt,' Phyllis continued. 'She always believed the worst in people, and she was always proven right.'

'Phyllis, she was a fictional character,' Nova said. 'Whereas Cynthia Watkins is a real woman, dealing with a murdered mother-in-law and a runaway husband.'

'Didn't you see the way her hands fidgeted while she spoke? And the way she couldn't look us in the eye? No, that whole thing was a story, as fictional as anything Agatha Christie wrote, only considerably less well-constructed.'

'So, what do *you* think happened, then?'

'Well, that's interesting indeed.' Phyllis rubbed her chin and then stopped in case it was too much. 'Let's take a step back for a moment and ask ourselves what Michael's motive was for killing his mother. In murder mysteries, there are usually five main motives for committing murder: jealousy, revenge, anger, fear, and the most common, greed.'

'Perhaps Michael's mum found out about his affair and threatened to tell Cynthia about it?' Arthur said. 'So, Michael killed her out of fear, to keep her quiet.'

'That theory might work *if* there was another woman involved, which there isn't. That's another of Cynthia's lies: a cover story to distract us from the truth.'

'What truth, Phyllis?' Nova wasn't even bothering to hide the scepticism in her voice, but Phyllis didn't care. She was used to people dismissing what she said; after all, even her own mother had never listened to her.

'Cynthia wants us – and the police – to believe that Michael's motive was anger; that he killed his mother after an argument and then fled with his lover, while Cynthia was safely tucked away at her sister's, oblivious to what was going on. But did you see the way her eyes shifted to the right when she told us she'd been staying at her sister's? That was a lie, a fake alibi, just like Michael came to our book club so that he could have an alibi for the time of the murder as well.'

'So, you think Cynthia was involved in the murder too?' Arthur said.

'Without a doubt. All that supposed anger at Michael, her shock when we told her he'd been at our book club; it was all an act. She may not have committed the murder herself, but she definitely knew what Michael was up to. And my bet is that Cynthia knows exactly where he is now, and she intends to join him as soon as the police are looking the other way.'

'Perhaps she was involved in the theft too?' Arthur said. 'Maybe they're serial thieves who target community centres up and down the country? And then Michael's mother discovered what they were up to and threatened to tell the police, so he killed her to keep her quiet!'

'I suppose that's one possible explanation,' Phyllis said, trying not to sound impressed. Perhaps the old farmer wasn't as stupid as he looked?

'Oh my God, listen to you both!' Nova said from the front seat. 'Cynthia isn't some master criminal, she's a woman whose life has fallen apart in the past forty-eight hours. As will mine if I don't get back to the community centre before my lunch break ends in fifteen minutes.'

'The next question is: What are Cynthia and Michael going to do now?' Phyllis said, ignoring Nova. 'My guess is they'll try and leave the country with their ill-gotten gains. So, I propose we take turns to stake out this house, so we can follow Cynthia when she goes to join Michael.'

'Phyllis, are you joking?' Nova exploded. 'If Michael's mother really was murdered, then you have to stay out of this and leave it to the police.'

Phyllis let out an exaggerated sigh. 'Have you never read a murder mystery? The British police never manage to solve a crime without the help of an amateur detective.'

'Yes, but this is the real world, not St Mary Mead. The police will be using all their resources to find Michael, so please just leave this to the experts.'

'Then what about the missing money?' Phyllis demanded. 'Now there's a murder to solve, do you think the police are going to care about a few thousand stolen pounds? And what does that mean for the community centre? I know the place is in financial trouble, Beryl was always complaining about it, so shouldn't you be doing everything you can to help the community centre?'

Phyllis could see her words had hit home as Nova went quiet, clearly mulling it over. Then she blinked and shook her head.

'This isn't some murder mystery game, Phyllis. This is a real police investigation, and we have to stay the hell out of it. Now let's get back.'

She started the engine, and the car pulled forwards. As it did, Phyllis glanced back at number eight. Was it her imagination or did she see the downstairs curtain twitch? She pictured Cynthia inside on the phone to Michael, telling him about her visit from the members of the St Tredock Community Book Club. *That damn old woman is onto us*, Cynthia would tell him, and Michael would curse. *I thought she was just a doddery old bird, but clearly I underestimated her.*

Phyllis smiled to herself and stroked Craddock's wrinkled head. *Just you wait, Michael and Cynthia Watkins. Miss Hudson has only just begun.*

Chapter Nine

Nova

It was gone two by the time Nova got back to the community centre, and she was late for her afternoon shift. But as she ran in through the front door, she crashed into a tall, broad-shouldered figure clutching an oversized potted plant.

'No running in the community centre!' shouted a deep, booming voice. 'Oh, it's *you*.'

Nova's heart sank as she saw her predecessor, Beryl, blocking the corridor. Although she'd been fired five months ago, the woman still found excuses to visit several times a week. On Wednesday, she'd come to retrieve a large box of tea bags and had proceeded to spend an hour sitting at Nova's desk, counting the tea bags individually to make sure none had been used in her absence.

'Hi, Beryl.' Nova tried to dodge past the woman, but she stood with her legs astride.

'I came to rescue Stephen.' Beryl indicated the yucca plant in her arms.

'Ah, is that yours? I've been trying to revive it.'

'Kill him, more like,' Beryl muttered. 'Sandy told me about the stolen money.'

'Yeah, it's been a nightmare but—'

'Do you have any idea how long it took us to raise that? It's not like London down here; we don't just get *handed* money on a plate.'

From further along the corridor, Nova heard a raised voice coming from the office. For once, it didn't sound like Sandy.

'I'd better get down there, it sounds like something's going on.'

Beryl didn't move. 'The whole of St Tredock pulled together to raise that money, and we won't forget whose fault its theft was.'

'Beryl, I need to get past, *please*.'

For a moment, the woman stayed where she was, glaring down at Nova. Then she slowly and deliberately stepped aside. Nova squeezed past her and hurried along the corridor. As she got nearer to the office, the voices inside grew louder.

'I have this afternoon slot on a permanent booking and have done for years.' Nova recognised the rich baritone of Serge, the yoga instructor who ran a session from the centre every Friday.

'I was told the hall was free when I made the booking,' said an irate female voice. 'And I've got thirty four-year-olds and Cornwall's premier Elsa impersonator about to turn up for a party.'

As Nova stepped into the office, she saw Sandy standing between Serge and a woman dressed as Olaf from *Frozen*, complete with carrot nose.

'All right, please let's stay calm,' Sandy said, fiddling with the worry beads round her wrist. 'I'm sure there's a simple explanation.'

'If the community centre is going to cancel my slot without warning, then I'll take my business elsewhere,' Serge said.

'I paid my deposit for the room, look!' The woman thrust her phone in Sandy's face, almost knocking her glasses off. Sandy spotted Nova and scowled.

'Ah, there you are. Please can you check the bookings diary? There appears to be a mix-up.'

'Of course.' Nova opened the calendar on her computer and cringed when she saw that the regular yoga class had been taken out and a birthday party booked in for a two-hour slot.

Sandy spent the next ten minutes grovelling to the group of middle-aged ladies who'd turned up for their yoga, and had to give them each a full refund and offer Serge a month of free room hire to stop him complaining to the council.

'How the hell did that happen?' Sandy demanded once they'd all left. 'Serge is always in the diary, who put the party in instead?'

Nova swallowed as she saw her own name next to the woman's details. 'I'm sorry, I must have accidentally deleted Serge's booking.'

Sandy didn't say anything as she stalked back to her desk, and Nova felt her chest tighten. *Try not to cause any more trouble*, Sandy had said this morning, and just five hours later, Nova had already door-stepped a grieving woman and messed up an important booking.

Nova kept out of her boss's way for the rest of the afternoon, dealing with the sugar-hyped four-year-olds from the party running wild round the community centre while their parents ignored them and drank wine. Once the party had finished, the main hall looked like a bomb had hit it – the mother hadn't cleaned up, despite Nova's pleas – and so she fetched some black bin bags and began to sweep up the mountains of confetti, glitter and crushed Pom-Bears.

'Need a hand?' Lauren appeared in the doorway, brandishing a dustpan and brush.

'Thanks,' Nova said. 'How are you? Today's been so hectic, I've barely seen you.'

'Fine, thanks, although Sandy's in another stinking mood: I offered her a cup of tea earlier and she bit my head off. I know she's stressed about the budget, but she doesn't have to be such a cow about it.'

'I think her mood is partly my fault.'

Lauren looked over at her. 'Nova, you have to stop beating yourself up. I know leaving the office unlocked was an unfortunate mistake, but not everything that's gone wrong since then is your fault.'

'No, this really was. I double-booked the main hall and Sandy had to deal with the fallout.'

'Oh, shit,' Lauren said. 'That will explain all the shouting I heard earlier.'

'I just don't know what's wrong with me.' Nova slumped down in a chair. 'I used to be really efficient, but at the moment I'm all over the place. I've caused nothing but trouble since I started here.'

'That's not true. And look: you've moved to a new town hundreds of miles from home, you've got a new job *and* you're getting married a week from tomorrow. Your life is a whirlwind, so it's no wonder if you've let a few things slip.'

'Craig keeps calling me Ditsy Davies,' Nova said. 'And his mum thinks I'm completely useless. I swear, she must have texted me about ten times to remind me I need to confirm the timings with our wedding photographer.' She held up her phone to show Lauren the stream of messages, many of them in caps lock.

Lauren gave a soft chuckle. 'Don't take that personally, Pamela is a complete control freak. Sam and I always joke that it's remarkable she's letting this wedding go ahead at all. In all the years we've known Craig, his mum has never thought anyone was good enough for her precious son.'

'Yeah, well I think she's quickly changing her mind about me.' Nova sighed and shook her head. 'Sorry, I shouldn't moan to you; you've got your own problems to deal with, all thanks to me.'

'Don't be silly, you can moan all you want.'

'Thanks. Honestly, if it weren't for you and Craig, I think I'd have already run back to London with my tail between my legs.'

'I don't think anyone would blame you if you did. I can't imagine leaving my friends and family to move two hundred miles away, let alone living with Pamela Pritchard!'

'I didn't mind moving; to be honest, after my dad died, I was glad of the change of scene.'

'Yeah, but give yourself credit too. The way you've uprooted your life for Craig is impressive.'

'And now this place might close and I won't even have a job. Neither of us will.' Nova's stomach lurched at the thought. 'Do you think the council will really shut us down?'

'God knows. They've been slashing our budget for years, so I guess it's not a complete surprise. Although the way they're trying to pin this on the missing money, rather than just being honest and saying they want to sell the building, makes my blood boil.'

'Everyone's going to blame me for this, aren't they?' Nova said, remembering Beryl's words earlier. 'If this place closes, I'll forever be known as the girl who got the community centre shut down.'

'People's memories are short, they'll soon forget about this once a new piece of gossip comes along. And if they don't, you can always—'

Lauren was interrupted by the bang of the front door opening.

'Sorry, we're closed,' she called out, but a moment later they saw PC Khan put his head round the door.

'Afternoon,' he said, nodding to them both. 'I've just popped in to give Sandy an update on our investigation. Is she still here?'

'She's in the office,' Lauren said. 'Okay if we come too?'

Nova and Lauren followed him down the corridor. Sandy was sitting behind her computer, but her head jerked up as soon as she saw the police officer walk in.

'Yusaf, please tell me you're here with good news?'

He waited until Nova had closed the office door. 'I'm afraid not. In fact, things are a lot more complicated than we originally thought. As well as being the main suspect for the theft of your money, Michael Watkins is also now the prime suspect in a murder investigation.'

'What?' Sandy said, at the same moment Lauren muttered 'Bloody hell!' Nova did her best to feign shock, given she didn't want any of them knowing she'd been to visit Michael's wife and already knew this.

'On Wednesday, Michael's mother was killed in the home she shares with Michael and his wife. I can't go into too much detail at this point, but it appears Michael packed a bag and fled the house soon after, and he hasn't been seen since. In fact, as far as we can ascertain, it seems likely that Nova here was the last person to see him at her book club.'

'So that means our money has disappeared too,' Sandy said, slumping back into her chair. 'Shit!'

'Do you have any leads on where he might be?' Lauren asked. 'A man doesn't just disappear, for God's sake.'

'I'm afraid it seems he has,' Yusaf said. 'This morning, his car was traced to a deserted lane in the middle of Bodmin Moor, but there was no sign of Michael. It seems likely that he drove there after your book club and then abandoned his car and carried on by foot or transferred to another vehicle.'

'Can't you track him via his mobile phone signal?' Nova asked.

'We've tried but he must have switched it off, or else it's run out of charge.'

'He must have an accomplice,' Lauren said. 'You can't just disappear off the face of the earth without help.'

'His wife has mentioned a possible other woman in Michael's life, and this is another line of investigation.'

'So, what's the plan now?' Sandy asked. 'How are you going to find him?'

'We have teams out searching for him around the Bodmin area, in case he's gone into hiding there, and obviously we've alerted our colleagues nationwide as well as Border Control. Assuming he's still in the UK, then at some point in the coming weeks he'll have to emerge from hiding, and we'll be ready to catch him when he does.'

'But we don't have weeks!' Sandy said, her voice sounding horribly desperate. 'We need to find our money now or the council will shut us down.'

Yusaf shrugged. 'I'm afraid that without Michael, there's not much we can do about that. I interviewed the other members of the book club and, as you know, they all have alibis for arriving and leaving the centre. So, it seems the only person who could have taken the money was Michael or . . .' He trailed off and there was an awkward silence.

'It wasn't me, if that's what you're suggesting,' Nova said, feeling her face flush. 'Why would I steal from my own place of work and risk losing a job I love?'

'Aren't you and Craig getting married next weekend?' Yusaf's tone was soft, but Nova knew what he was insinuating.

'Craig's parents are paying for the wedding. But even if they weren't, I'd never do anything to hurt the community centre. Sandy, you believe me, right?'

She looked at her boss, but Sandy was staring at the squeezy stress ball in her hand and wouldn't catch Nova's eye.

Chapter Ten

Arthur

Every Saturday morning, Arthur Robinson visited St Tredock library to collect new books for Esi.

Before she lost her sight, his wife used to go herself, spending hours choosing a stack of historical romances, which she'd bring home and devour in bed at night, her reading glasses balanced on the end of her nose and a mug of home-grown herbal tea in her hands. Even when her eyesight started to fail, Esi would still make her weekly pilgrimage, although as time passed, she became more and more reliant on Arthur to not just help her choose the books, but also to read them to her as well. Eventually, her eyesight became so bad that Esi found it too overwhelming to leave the farm, and she asked Arthur to go to the library for her.

To begin with he hated it, embarrassed in case someone saw him browsing the romance shelves, and he used to go to the library as soon as it opened and hide her books under his own biographies. But over time, Arthur had become less self-conscious and began chatting to the librarians, getting recommendations for books that Esi might enjoy. Now they all knew him by name, and they'd often set aside new historical romances for him to collect on his Saturday visits.

Today, Arthur greeted the librarian and headed straight to the familiar shelf. As he approached, he saw a gangly figure hunched over it.

'Ash! How are you, lad?'

The boy visibly jolted at being addressed and took a hurried step back from the shelf.

'Eh, hi . . .' he mumbled, flicking his long fringe over his face.

Arthur smiled in recognition; not so long ago, he'd been as embarrassed as Ash.

'Don't worry,' he said, lowering his voice. 'You're near enough to the horror shelf that you can always pretend you're looking at those if anyone spots you.'

Ash gave a shy smile. 'I was just trying to find *The Viscount Who Loved Me* for book club.'

'Reading that already, are you? Well, it'll be here if they have it.' Arthur bent down to the small row of Julia Quinn books on the lowest shelf. 'You're in luck.' He pulled out a well-worn copy of the paperback and handed it to Ash.

'Thanks,' the boy mumbled and turned to leave.

'Did you hear about the theft at the community centre?'

Ash looked back. 'A police officer came to my house yesterday. He said he thought it might've been someone from the book club.'

'It sounds like it was that Michael man, the one who ran out.'

'Have they arrested him?'

'Not yet. The police think he might've also murdered his mother and done a runner, although I'm still not convinced that man had a murdering temperament.'

'And he's disappeared?' Ash's eyes were wide. 'If he didn't kill his mum then maybe he's been kidnapped? Or abducted?'

'Abducted?' Arthur couldn't help but chuckle. 'You sound like Phyllis!'

The teenager gave an embarrassed smile. 'Sorry. I've just been reading this science fiction book where a character gets abducted by aliens, so I guess that's on my brain.'

'Oh, that sounds like a good story. You like science fiction, do you?'

The boy nodded. Arthur waited for him to say something, but he'd clearly lost his confidence again.

'I have to confess, I've not read much myself, although I have watched a few science fiction films in my time. I used to like those Star Wars ones.'

'I love *Star Wars*!' Ash's face was suddenly alight. He pulled back his jacket to reveal a well-worn *Return of the Jedi* T-shirt.

Arthur smiled. 'I've only seen the original ones. My Esi was always fond of that Han Solo.'

'Maybe your wife would enjoy the *Solo* film, which is all about his backstory?'

'Thanks, I'll tell her about it. Although between you and me, I think it's the young Harrison Ford she likes more than the character,' Arthur said with a wink, and Ash gave a shy laugh when he realised what Arthur was referring to. 'Maybe one month we could read some science fiction in book club. How about that one you just mentioned, about the alien abduction?'

'Oh no, I don't think that's a good idea. I'm not sure the others would enjoy it very much.'

'You'd be surprised. And even if they don't, that won't matter. I'm no expert, but I think the whole point of a book club is to read things you wouldn't normally.'

'I've enjoyed all the books we've read so far,' Ash said, then frowned. 'Not that you'd know.'

'What do you mean?'

'I mean, I can never think of anything to say about them in the meeting. Everyone else has clever ideas but my mind goes blank.'

'Oh, I never say anything clever,' Arthur said. 'I just spout any old waffle and hope someone interrupts me.'

'That's not true. You always have excellent ideas.'

'Well, any I do have I'll have nicked off Esi. She's the smart one in our relationship; any good idea I've ever had has been hers first.'

Ash smiled but didn't say anything, and Arthur kicked himself for blabbing on about his wife to the teenager.

'Well, I've talked your ear off enough. I look forward to seeing you at the next book club and hearing what you think of this one.' Arthur nodded at the book in Ash's hand and turned to leave. But he'd not got more than a few paces when he heard a new voice behind him.

'Ash, hey!'

Arthur glanced back to see a tall, strapping lad with blond hair walking across the library towards Ash. The boys must be about the same age, yet while Ash looked like he wanted the earth to open up and swallow him, this boy oozed confidence. He was dressed in a muddy football kit, a rucksack slung over one shoulder and a pile of books in his hands. Arthur remembered boys like this from his days in school: the ones who always got picked first for sports and got the attention of all the prettiest girls.

'Oh ... eh ... hi, Dan.' Ash's cheeks had gone bright scarlet, and

Arthur could see him trying to hide *The Viscount Who Loved Me* behind his back.

'You getting books for English?' Dan said. 'I started reading *Much Ado About Nothing* the other night but fell asleep a few pages in.'

'Erm . . .'

'What's that you're holding; anything good?'

Arthur saw Ash's eyes go wide in panic. He tried to step back, but that only resulted in him knocking into the romance shelf and sending books scattering to the floor. With a groan of embarrassment, Ash bent down to pick them up, flashing the cover of *The Viscount Who Loved Me* in the process. Arthur saw Dan's eyebrows shoot up in surprise.

'Is that—'

'Ash, there you are, lad!' Before he knew what he was doing, Arthur was striding towards the two boys. 'Have you got that book for me yet?'

Ash looked up at Arthur, his mouth hanging open like a cow. Arthur held out his hand for the book, but Ash stared at it blankly.

'Thanks for finding it for me,' Arthur said, speaking slowly to try and communicate to the teenager what he was doing.

Ash finally seemed to cotton on and thrust the book towards him. Arthur gave him a quick nod and stepped away. But as he started to leave, he heard the other boy speak again.

'Hi, I'm Dan.'

Arthur turned back round to see the teenager looking at him with curiosity.

'I'm in English class with Ash.' Dan paused, clearly waiting for Arthur to explain his connection.

'Hello. I'm, eh . . .' Heck, what should he say? Something told him

Ash wouldn't want his friend knowing he went to a book club with a load of old fogies. 'I'm Arthur, Ash's grandfather.'

He saw Ash blink in surprise, but what else was he meant to say?

'Ah, lovely to meet you, Arthur.' Dan's face split into a warm smile.

'Ash was just helping me find this book for his grandma. My wife loves these soppy romances, doesn't she, Ash?'

The teenager nodded, clearly struck mute with the horror of it all.

'Yeah, my mum loves the Bridgerton books too,' Dan said, and then he lowered his voice to a stage whisper. 'Between us, I've watched all the series on Netflix with her.'

He laughed and Arthur laughed, too, although Ash still looked like he wanted to die of shame.

'Well, I'd better go. I've got to pick my car up from the garage,' Dan said. 'It was nice to meet you, Arthur. And Ash, see you around.'

He gave them both a farewell wave and then strode towards the door. Arthur glanced at Ash and saw him staring after Dan, an expression on his face that Arthur recognised from the hundreds of romance novels he'd read Esi: a mixture of terror and longing that could only mean one thing. The poor boy was hopelessly in love.

Ash blinked and turned back to Arthur. 'Thanks for helping me out.'

'No worries. I guessed you might not want your friend to know you were reading it.'

'Oh . . . he's not my friend,' Ash stuttered. 'I mean, we're in the same class, but I don't know him very well. I didn't even realise he knew my name . . .' He trailed off, his cheeks flushed as he stared at his feet.

'He seems like a nice young man,' Arthur said gently.

Ash's head snapped up, his eyes wide again. 'Oh no, it's not—'

'It's all right, Ash.' Arthur smiled to try and reassure the boy he understood.

There was a moment of awkward silence and then Ash's shoulders sunk as he let out a long, forlorn sigh. 'Was I that obvious?'

Arthur couldn't help but chuckle. 'No, of course not.'

'I just freeze every time I see him. It's so embarrassing, it's like I forget how to speak. And Dan is so confident. You should hear him in English class, he always has such smart things to say about every book.'

Suddenly, Arthur understood something that had been bothering him. 'That's why you come to book club, isn't it?'

Ash stared at his feet again. 'I just wanted to learn how to talk about books so maybe I wouldn't look like such a dick in front of Dan. But it's no use, I'm just as useless there as I am in class.'

'I can help if you want?'

Ash's head jolted up. 'You?'

'I know I might look and sound like an old farmer – well, to be fair, I am one – but I've spent decades listening to my Esi talk about books. So I think a little bit of her knowledge must have rubbed off on me over the years.'

Ash chewed his fingernail, visibly weighing the offer up.

'It can be our secret, if you're worried about anyone knowing,' Arthur added.

'Are you sure you wouldn't mind?'

''Course not or I wouldn't have offered. What are you reading in class at the moment?'

'We're doing *Much Ado About Nothing* next,' Ash said, with all the enthusiasm of a criminal about to face the gallows.

'That's by Shakespeare, isn't it? I'll be honest, I've not read much of his, but I'll take a look and see what I can come up with. How about we meet at the community centre on Tuesday?'

'Next week is half term so that would be great, thank you!' The boy grinned and Arthur felt a small, unexpected swell of pride.

'Grand. And don't worry, I promise I won't tell a soul.'

Chapter Eleven

Nova

There were many ways Nova would have liked to spend her Saturday morning: lying in bed reading, going house-hunting with Craig, or for a coastal walk and a pub lunch with Lauren and Sam. And yet instead, here she was, standing in Blushing Brides dress shop in Port Gowan, being poked, prodded and squeezed by two bickering women.

'It's too loose here. We need to tighten the corset,' Pamela said, pinching a piece of fabric and causing Nova to gasp as the remaining air was squeezed out of her lungs.

'If we go any tighter then Nova might be too uncomfortable on her big day,' said the dress fitter.

'It's not about being comfortable, it's about looking beautiful,' Pamela snapped. 'We want the corset to really show off Nova's lovely curvy figure.'

'If we take in any more fabric then it might disrupt the shape of the bodice. Plus, I don't have time to resew all the crystals before next Saturday. What if . . .'

Nova allowed the conversation to wash over her. It wasn't that she didn't care what she looked like on her wedding day. It was just that, despite her love of clothes, she wasn't someone who'd grown up dreaming about her wedding dress. To be honest, she'd always been ambivalent about the whole marriage thing, and had only said yes to Craig's proposal because she knew it was important to him. Her initial plan had been to buy something colourful and fabulous from a vintage shop, but Pamela had been adamant that Nova would regret that decision. *Your wedding is the one day in your life when you get to look like a fairy-tale princess*, her future mother-in-law had insisted. *Trust me, you don't want to be wearing some old secondhand thing on your wedding day; you want to look and feel a million dollars.* After many attempts to argue her case, Nova had decided it wasn't a battle worth fighting, although she'd drawn the line at wearing a veil.

She and Craig similarly had to relinquish their idea of a small, intimate ceremony in a registry office followed by a knees-up in the Anchor for family and close friends. *I won't have my only child celebrating his wedding in a pub*, Pamela had complained when Craig had tried to convince her. *You're only getting married once and you should do it properly.* It had all ended up getting quite heated, with Pamela threatening not to attend the wedding if they did it at a registry office, and David saying he'd only pay for it if they had the reception at his country club. Privately, Nova had told Craig they should elope and have a tiny wedding, just the two of them on a beach somewhere far away. But Craig couldn't bear the idea of upsetting his parents, and so it was that next Saturday, Nova was going to walk down the aisle of St Piran's church watched by most of St Tredock, and then have a party for 200 at the Tennis and Country Club, complete with a champagne reception, three-course sit-down meal and disco.

'Ouch!' She winced as a pin jabbed into her side.

'Sorry, love,' mumbled the shop assistant.

'There, that's much better,' said Pamela with satisfaction. 'Don't you think that's better, Nova? Although I still think it's such a shame you won't wear a veil.'

Nova looked in the mirror but barely recognised the woman in the sparkly white dress staring back at her. Once she'd changed back into her own clothes, she had to sit down with a glass of water because she felt so dizzy.

'It'll be all the stress with everything that's happening at the community centre,' Pamela said. 'I think it's outrageous the way they're treating you. Trying to blame the whole thing on you when the money should never have been left lying around.'

'They're not blaming it all on me.'

'Oh, but they are,' Pamela said. 'I was at the hairdressers the other day, and Danny, my colourist, was telling me that he'd heard from Jenny Brazier that apparently Tina Farleigh and her mafia at the council wanted Sandy to sack you on the spot as soon as they heard about the theft. According to Jenny, Sandy refused, and she and Tina had a stand-up row about you.'

Sandy had defended her to the council? That seemed remarkable, given how annoyed the woman had been at Nova, and she felt a glow of gratitude towards her boss.

'Frankly, if I were you, I'd just quit now and walk away while you still can,' Pamela said, crossing to a row of hats and picking one up to inspect. 'It sounds like the centre is going to end up closing anyway, so why not get out now with your head held high?'

'The centre might not have to close. Sandy's still trying to find a way of recouping the missing money from the budget.'

'But even if she does, that place is doomed. Besides, I see how tired you are when you get home, your job is exhausting. How are you going to cope when you and Craig live alone and you have a house to run as well?'

'Craig will share all the domestic chores with me,' Nova said pointedly.

'Of course he will, I raised my Craigy to be a modern man. But still, you want to enjoy the early years of married life, not be knackered all the time. My offer of having you work at the florists still stands,' Pamela said, picking up another hat. 'I know you worry you have no experience, but you're a smart girl and I'm an excellent teacher.'

'Thanks, but I've worked hard for my career, and I don't want to give it up.'

'There are advantages of working for me too,' Pamela continued. 'The hours are decent, and I pay my girls a proper wage, plus it's a family-friendly job. It's something Craig and I have discussed.'

For a moment, Nova didn't know what to say. Pamela had never made a secret of the fact she was keen to have grandchildren, but she'd never been quite so overt about it before. And had Craig really talked about this with her?

'We're a way-off thinking about that yet.'

Pamela must have heard the edge in Nova's voice as she gave a placatory wave of her hand. 'Of course. All I'm saying is that the offer is there if you want it.'

'I think I feel better now. Shall we get going?' Nova stood up and headed towards the door before her future mother-in-law could say anything else.

'Right, I've got the cake lady coming over at one to show us the decorations she's made for the top tier,' Pamela said as they stepped outside.

'Actually, I'm going to stay here for a bit and do some shopping,'
Nova said. 'I can catch the bus back later.'

Pamela looked like she wanted to argue with her, but then gave a
tight smile. 'Fine, I'll see you at home.'

Nova said good-bye and headed in the opposite direction. She
had no real desire to go shopping and the bus would take ages, but it
was still better than being trapped in the car with Pamela banging on
about babies. The idea that she and Craig had discussed it behind her
back still nagged at Nova; she'd have to talk to him about that later.

Up ahead, Nova could see a Cancer Research charity shop, and
she walked in and exhaled slowly. Charity shops had always made
her feel calm, perhaps because she'd spent so many wonderful hours
exploring them with her parents. God, how she wished they were
both here today. They'd have found a wedding dress in a charity
shop, no doubt; something original and full of character.

Nova spent a happy twenty minutes browsing the shop; twenty
minutes in which she didn't think once about the missing money, the
community centre or her perilous career situation. She had great fun
trying on clothes, in particular a bright yellow eighties boiler suit
that would have given Pamela a heart attack if she went home wearing it. Nova didn't buy it, but she did get a cool old teapot shaped like
a pineapple, which for some reason reminded her of her mum, and a
small, framed painting of a coastal scene. Both of these would look
great in her and Craig's home, once they finally managed to find one.

Nova paid for the items, and when she stepped out onto the pavement, her mood was considerably lighter than it had been half an
hour ago. But as she turned towards the bus stop, she spotted two
familiar figures walking down the pavement towards her. One was
short and dressed in a woollen hat and a men's overcoat three sizes

too big for her, with a pair of ancient-looking binoculars swinging round her neck. The other was squat and carrying what looked like a rotting fish in his mouth.

'What have you been up to, Phyllis?' Nova asked the approaching woman, dreading her reply would have something to do with Michael and Cynthia.

'I've been bird-watching.'

That definitely wasn't the answer Nova had been expecting. 'Oh. That sounds . . . fun.'

'It's a trick from *They Do It with Mirrors*. Miss Marple pretends to be bird-watching, but really she's spying on suspicious activity.'

Nova groaned. 'Please tell me you haven't been bird-watching near Mountfort Close?'

The older woman ignored her as she looked into the box Nova was holding, studying its contents with a critical eye. 'I hope you didn't pay much for that horrible painting.'

'Phyllis, you can't keep stalking their house; if Cynthia sees you there again, she'll probably call the police. Besides, it's not as if Michael's just going to turn up with the stolen money in his hand.'

'What's that?' Phyllis asked, jabbing a finger at the newspaper-wrapped teapot.

'It's just something I got for . . . Oi, what are you doing?'

Phyllis had pulled the parcel out of the box and was ripping off the newspaper around it.

'Be careful, that's fragile!' Nova said, as Phyllis threw the teapot back into the box, her eyes fixed on the newspaper sheet in her hand. 'What on earth's the matter with you?'

The woman didn't answer, her eyes scanning the page she was holding. Then a smile spread across her face. 'That's it!'

'What's it?'

She looked up at Nova, her eyes shining. 'Agatha Christie was a genius!'

'What *are* you talking about?' Nova said, but the woman just gave her an infuriating grin and sauntered off, the newspaper clutched in her hand.

Chapter Twelve

Phyllis

Phyllis had never confessed this to anyone, but she hated Hercule Poirot. She'd read all the novels, of course; she'd read every book Agatha ever wrote and wouldn't hear a word said against them. But secretly, she found the Belgian detective deeply irritating. That silly little moustache, the annoying way of talking, not to mention his constant self-aggrandisement. Unlike Miss Marple, who knew that the key to being a good detective was to be inconspicuous, Poirot liked to put himself at the centre of everything, preening and posturing like a peacock. Phyllis had therefore been somewhat disappointed when she'd seen the notice for Eve Watkins's funeral in the newspaper and realised that the answer to catching the murderer and thief Michael Watkins lay not, as she'd hoped, in a Miss Marple novel, but in a Poirot one instead.

And so it was that on Tuesday morning, Phyllis found herself standing outside the gates of St Piran's church, wearing a black coat, sunglasses and a head scarf to disguise her blue-rinsed hair. She'd had to leave Craddock at home, much to his annoyance, but he was far too conspicuous. Now though, as she stared up at the tall, imposing face of the church, Phyllis wished she had her companion with her.

When her mother was alive, Phyllis had come to St Piran's twice a week. There had been other churches nearer to their home, but Eliza Hudson had been a devoutly Christian woman and had preferred the monotone, joyless sermons of Reverend Platt to the more modern, upbeat style at their local church. And so, every Wednesday and Sunday, come rain or shine, Phyllis and her mother had silently trudged three miles along the rocky clifftop path from their home to the church, which stood on a small, exposed headland between St Tredock and Port Gowan. The last time Phyllis had been here was the day of her mother's funeral, eleven years ago. She hadn't realised at the time that it would be her last visit. But the following Sunday, Phyllis had found herself sitting at the kitchen table at ten o'clock, drinking a cup of tea, without the slightest inclination to leave the house. She had not entered this – or any – church since.

An icy gust of wind blew in off the sea and Phyllis pulled her coat around her. Perhaps this was a bad idea? Just because this was how Poirot solved the mystery in *After the Funeral* didn't mean she'd have the same luck today. Besides, Craddock didn't like being left alone and—

Phyllis stopped and took a deep breath, asking herself the same question she always asked when something was unclear. What would Miss Marple do? Adjusting her head scarf, she set off up the front path towards the church.

As soon as she stepped inside, Phyllis's senses were assaulted. That distinctive smell, a mixture of sea salt, wood polish and piety so strong that it used to stick to her Sunday coat. The damp chill in the air; somehow the church always felt five degrees cooler than outside. The almost deafening silence of the vaulted space. It was all so familiar that for a moment Phyllis expected to see her mother sitting rigid-backed in one of the front pews, her head bowed in prayer.

But your iniquities have separated you from your God;
And your sins have hidden His face from you,
So that He will not hear.

'Hello! I'm afraid you're a little early.'

Phyllis jolted at a posh voice. A tall, silver-haired man was smiling down at her.

'Come on in, it's freezing out there. Would you like an order of service?'

Phyllis took one and hurried towards the back of the nave. She slipped into one of the rear pews, removed her sunglasses, and studied the order of service while she waited for the mourners to arrive. *Eve Louise Watkins*, it said on the front, along with the dates *1933–2024*. So, the old bird was ninety-one? Not a bad innings, although rather irritating to be murdered; by that age, you'd be expecting pneumonia or a urine infection to see you off.

Under the writing was a photo, an old black-and-white image of Eve in her thirties or forties. She was a striking woman, although not in a good way, with a square chin, pointed nose and thick black eyebrows. The idiom 'the kind of face only a mother could love' popped into Phyllis's head and she snorted softly. That expression had never meant anything to her, given her own mother hadn't been able to stand the sight of Phyllis's face.

Behind her, she heard the church door creak open, and she put the order of service down and turned to pay attention to the people coming in. As was to be expected for the funeral of a ninety-one-year-old, the majority of the mourners were elderly, too, and a slow procession of wheelchairs, walking sticks and Zimmer frames made their way into the church. Phyllis kept her eyes trained on each new face as they arrived, paying particular attention to the male mourners.

In *After the Funeral*, Agatha Christie had the murderer attend a funeral in disguise, pretending to be a relative of the deceased. While Phyllis had not particularly enjoyed the book when she first read it – Poirot was at his most insufferable when he made his big reveal – she was now grateful for the story. Because even though Michael had murdered Eve, stolen money and was now on the run from the police, surely he might still attend his own mother's funeral?

Phyllis continued her vigil over the growing congregation. Was that elderly man in the wheelchair actually Michael, with his head shaved to make himself appear bald? What about the man wearing a blue anorak and tracksuit bottoms, who seemed to be taking a suspiciously long time to find his seat? Or even the elderly lady with the large, feathered hat who was limping in now?

Phyllis glanced at her watch. It was past midday so the funeral would be starting at any moment. It was a large congregation for such an elderly person. When Phyllis's mother died, aged ninety-eight, there had only been three people at the funeral: Phyllis, the vicar and the organ player. Not that Phyllis had expected it to be busy. Her mother hadn't been an easy woman to love: pious, sharp-tongued and judgemental. But still, Phyllis had hoped that at least some of the regular members of the congregation might attend, if for no other reason than to support her.

'Mind if I sit here?'

She looked up to see the silver-haired man who'd been handing out the order of service looming over her. Phyllis was about to say no, but then the organ burst into life, filling the air with a loud, slightly out-of-tune chord, and before she knew it, the man had slid into the pew next to her. Phyllis shuffled to the other end of the bench as the church doors swung open and the coffin appeared.

The congregation rose to their feet – at least those who were mobile enough did – and Eve Watkins began her final journey through the nave. The coffin was carried by four pallbearers, but a quick scan of their faces told Phyllis that none of them were Michael. There were three figures walking behind: one was Cynthia Watkins, wearing a silly hat and an expensive-looking coat, and the other two were women in their thirties who must be Cynthia and Michael's daughters. The trio followed the coffin to the top of the aisle and then slipped into the front pew on the right. As they took their places, Cynthia leaned over and whispered something into the ear of the man standing next to her.

Phyllis's heart began to pound. Was this Michael, brazenly standing in the front row of St Piran's church while the Cornish police scoured Bodmin Moor for him? If so, it was an audacious move, although criminals had been known to do worse: just look at *Murder Is Easy*.

'Good turnout, isn't it?'

The silver-haired gentleman was leaning towards Phyllis and speaking in a low voice. She ignored him, her eyes trained on the back of the suspect's head, willing him to turn around and reveal his face. He and Cynthia had exchanged a few more words, their heads bowed towards each other conspiratorially.

'I had no idea Eve had so many friends,' the man continued. 'Mind you, Cynthia's promise of a cream tea at the wake might have incentivised a few. People will do anything for a good scone.'

Phyllis sighed loudly, hoping that might discourage the man from talking. Her mother could never stand people making noise in church and had once hit a man over the back of the head with her prayer book after he'd yawned too loudly.

'Of course, I imagine all the gossip has helped attract a crowd too.'

At the word *gossip*, Phyllis's ears pricked up. She had no time for tittle-tattle herself, but like Miss Marple, she knew it was often a useful way to get information.

'What gossip?' she asked, then winced as if her mother might reach out from beyond the grave to give her a clip round the ear.

'Dearly beloved . . .' The vicar's voice rang out at the front of the church as he welcomed the congregation.

The silver-haired man slid closer to Phyllis, his voice dropping to a whisper. 'They think Eve's son killed her! His fingerprints were all over her and he hasn't been seen since.'

Phyllis sighed; she'd been hoping for something new that might help her investigation.

'The police came and interviewed me about it on Friday,' her companion said, and she could hear a tinge of pride in his voice.

'Why did they interview you?'

'I live next door to Eve and was the one who saw Michael run out of the house. I didn't think anything of it at the time; I'd heard him and Eve arguing shortly before, so I assumed he was just going out to clear his head. Little did I know what had really happened.'

Oh, now *this* was interesting. Phyllis turned to face the man properly. He must be about the same age as her and was cleanly shaven, wearing a smart suit and black tie. His eyes were the brightest blue she'd ever seen and fixed on her face.

'Did you say you heard Michael and his mother arguing?'

A few rows in front, one of the congregants let out a pointed cough. The man leaned closer to Phyllis, his breath brushing her ear as he lowered his voice further.

'I wasn't eavesdropping, of course. But I'd just got back from walking my dog, Bella, and Eve must have had a window open, as their voices drifted out.'

'What were they arguing about?'

'I could only hear the odd bit, but from what I picked up, Eve was furious at Michael. She kept shouting about a letter and some debts, and how he should never have kept it a secret from her. But then Bella started barking for food, so I took her inside, and the next thing I knew, I heard a door slam and saw Michael's car speeding out of the drive.'

Phyllis found she was holding her breath. Michael was in debt! That must have been why he stole the community centre money. And – Phyllis felt her chest tighten as another penny dropped – maybe he killed his mother to get his hands on his inheritance? At last, now she knew the motive: *greed*.

'Do you know—'

'Shh!'

The pointed cougher turned to glare at them both. The silver-haired man gave an apologetic nod, and when the woman turned back to the front he glanced at Phyllis with a mischievous twinkle in his eye. Despite herself, Phyllis felt her cheeks flush, and she turned back to the altar. As she did, her heart dropped.

The man from the front row had disappeared.

Chapter Thirteen

Arthur

Arthur had arranged to meet Ash at four o'clock at the community centre, and so over the weekend he spent every spare minute reading *Much Ado About Nothing*. It wasn't easygoing, filled with strange old words and long, nonsensical rambles, and several times he almost gave up. This was why he'd hated school so much; teachers forcing them to read these old stories that were impossible to follow. It had damn near put him off reading altogether, and when he left school at sixteen, he'd sworn he was never going to read a book again.

Of course, all that changed when he met Esi. Arthur could still remember the first time he'd seen her as if it were yesterday. It had been the Port Gowan fair, back in the summer of 1964. She'd been sitting on a hay bale, engrossed in whatever book she was reading, absentmindedly twirling a braid round her finger while the fair raged on around her. She was the most beautiful woman he'd ever seen, like a radiant rose in a field of wheat. Of course, Arthur hadn't dared speak to her that day. Later, he told her it was because he didn't want to bother her while she was reading, but the truth was he'd been terrified he'd open his mouth and say something stupid, just like poor Ash worried about with Dan. But he'd sworn that next year he would pluck up the courage, and the very next day, Arthur had headed to the library and borrowed a book. It hadn't made much more sense to him than the Shakespeare they'd read at school, but he persevered, reading a few pages every evening when he got back from the cow sheds. It had taken him almost a month to finish that first book, and then he'd swapped it for a new one, and on it went. A year later, he'd returned to the county fair, and when he saw the beautiful woman with the book, he'd strolled straight up and said hello.

'Arthur Robinson, stop daydreaming or you'll never finish it.'

Esi's softly scolding voice interrupted his memories. Arthur chuckled; she could always tell when he was drifting off.

'Sorry, love.' He turned his attention back to the text in front of him. 'So, let me get this straight. Claudio wants to marry Hero, but he's tricked into thinking she's having it off with Borachio, and so instead of marrying her, Claudio humiliates her at the altar.'

'That's right. I never understood what Hero sees in Claudio. The man is a dolt.'

'And in the meantime, Benedick and Beatrice don't like each other and bicker all the time.'

'Benedick doesn't believe in love and has sworn he's never going to get married, which we all know means he's going to end the story loved up and happily married.' Even without looking up from the page, Arthur could hear the smile in his wife's voice.

'And Benedick and Beatrice's friends play a trick on them so they both realise that actually, rather than hating each other, they love each other,' Arthur continued. 'And then Hero pretends to be dead, and that makes Claudio see what a fool he's been, and then Hero's dad says you can marry my other daughter, who isn't dead. And that turns out to be Hero all along.'

'Yep, that's about it.'

Arthur exhaled. 'Bloomin' heck, this Shakespeare chap doesn't half make it complicated.'

Esi laughed, a sound that still made his heart sing even after all these years. 'It's not that complicated! Now read me the scene where Benedick and Beatrice finally realise their feelings for each other. I always loved that bit.'

Arthur flicked to the page. When the problems with Esi's eyesight had started, he'd felt like a right lemon reading to her. He was no actor, after all, and he could never do all the voices. But Esi told him to stop being so soft, and now, after ten years of reading to her, he didn't think twice. And so, he took a sip of tea, cleared his throat, and began to read aloud.

At three-thirty, Arthur left home and walked the two miles from his farmhouse into the village. He must have done this walk thousands of times over his eighty-one years, but he didn't think he'd ever tire of the view as he crossed the fields and came over the brow of the hill to see St Tredock nestled far below at the bottom of the cliff. When he was a boy, the village had been little more than a small, steep high street leading up from the harbour and a huddle of whitewashed stone fishermen's cottages. Much about St Tredock had changed since then, the village expanding as new houses were built up the hill like vines growing on a wall. The fishermen were long gone, too, their cottages now converted into overpriced holiday lets. Not that Arthur minded: unlike many of his generation, he'd always embraced change, and he loved seeing the village come to life every summer, with barefoot children playing on the beach and crabbing off the harbour walls, their parents drinking pints of cider outside the Anchor and eating steaming hot pasties from the bakery. And whilst so much about the village had changed, some things remained the same: the high street with its traditional butcher and greengrocer, the old library, and of course, the community centre.

Arthur had called Sandy this morning and asked if there was a free space he could use – he'd not gone into detail why – and been told he could borrow the room they usually held book club in. When he arrived at the centre, he found Ash waiting for him by the entrance door, scuffing his trainers on the gravel.

'Afternoon, lad!'

'Hi, Arthur.'

They headed into Tintagel, closing the door behind them.

'So, how did you get on with *Much Ado About Nothing*?' Arthur asked as they sat down.

'Not good,' the boy said with a sigh. 'It's all gobbledygook to me.'

'I'll be honest, I felt the same for much of it. All that fancy language is intimidating, isn't it?'

'I don't know why they make us read all this dead white guy stuff in the first place, it's completely irrelevant.'

'I used to think that too. But do you know what? Reading Shakespeare again after sixty-odd years, I realised it's not so different to modern books after all.'

Ash raised a disbelieving eyebrow.

'Look, it might be written strangely, but when you boil the whole thing down, it's basically just your common or garden enemies-to-lovers rom-com.'

Arthur had been quite pleased with that summary, but Ash was squinting at him as if he was speaking in Shakespearean English himself.

'Enemies-to-lovers? What's that?'

'It's a common trope in romance novels and one of Esi's favourites. Two people hate each other, or at least they think they do, and there's always lots of back-and-forth between them. And then eventually they come to realise that they're actually in love.'

'You mean a bit like Anthony and Kate in *The Viscount Who Loved Me*?'

Arthur looked at Ash in surprise. 'Yes, exactly like that! Have you read that one already?'

The boy gave a guilty shrug. 'I found the Shakespeare so confusing that I gave up on it halfway through and read the book club one instead.'

'And what did you think of it?'

'It was okay. Much better than Shakespeare.'

'Well, you're right, Anthony Bridgerton and Kate Sheffield are a brilliant example of enemies-to-lovers. They drive each other mad, and it takes them forever to work out that's because they fancy each other. They're one of Esi's favourite romance couples, because she says you can feel the chemistry between them sizzling off the page when they're arguing.'

'It reminded me a bit of . . .' The boy faltered and Arthur gave him an encouraging nod.

'Yes?'

'You'll think I'm stupid; it's not the same at all.'

'Go on, lad, give it a go. It's just you and me here.'

He watched Ash take a deep breath.

'Well . . . Anthony and Kate just reminded me a bit of . . . of Rey and Kylo Ren in the Star Wars films.' He rushed the last words out, as if embarrassed to be saying them out loud.

'Oh, is that so? I'm afraid I've not seen any of the new Star Wars films so you're going to have to fill me in.'

'Well, Kylo Ren is the Supreme Leader of the First Order – those are the baddies. And Rey, she's a Jedi, so these guys are sworn enemies: they literally spend two and a half movies trying to kill each other.' The boy pushed the fringe out of his face, his eyes shining with enthusiasm now that he was talking about something he clearly loved. 'But they also have this really strong connection with each other, in fact they're a dyad, which is a bit complicated to explain but basically means they're connected to each other through the Force and can see into each other's minds.'

'I see,' Arthur said, although he didn't see at all.

'Anyway, they have this whole mortal-enemies-chasing-one-another-round-the-universe-trying-to-kill-one-another thing going on. But then they have this big fight, and Rey impales Kylo Ren with a lightsaber and almost kills him, at which point they realise they don't hate each other at all.' The boy stopped and looked embarrassed again. 'I told you it was a dumb idea.'

'That's not dumb at all, it sounds like the perfect enemies-to-lovers story. And tell me, do they get together in the end? Because one rule of romance novels is they always have to have a happy ending.'

Ash grinned. 'Not quite. Rey dies killing Emperor Palpatine, and then Kylo Ren, who by this point is called Ben, transfers his life essence into Rey, sacrificing himself to save her. Then they kiss and Ben dies.'

'What? That's horrible!'

Ash laughed. 'Sorry, but *Star Wars* isn't exactly a romance.'

'Clearly not,' Arthur said, chuckling too. 'These new ones sound good though.'

'Yeah; I mean, *The Rise of Skywalker* is average but the other two are excellent. *The Force Awakens* might actually be my favourite of all the films, even better than *The Empire Strikes Back*. I can lend it to you on DVD, if you like?'

Arthur was taken aback by the offer. 'Thanks . . . that'd be grand. But one thing you said there made me think back to *Much Ado About Nothing*. Did you get to the bit where Claudio dumps Hero at the altar?'

'Because he thinks she's been having an affair, right?'

'Yes. There's this strange old friar guy who comes up with a daft plan to fake Hero's death to make Claudio feel bad. As if Romeo and Juliet didn't teach them that faking death is a bad idea!'

Arthur chuckled but the reference clearly went over Ash's head as the boy looked blank.

'Anyway, the plan works: when Claudio thinks Hero's dead, he realises what an idiot he's been, and he actually loved her all along. And from what you said just now, it sounds a bit like when your Rey almost kills Ben Kylo, or whatever he's called, and it takes his near death for the two of them to realise they love each other.'

'Like when Kate has the carriage accident and Anthony Bridgerton finally tells her he loves her?'

'Yes, lad!' Arthur laughed and Ash laughed, too, clearly delighted at having made the connection. 'Who'd have thought it: Willy Shakespeare, George Lucas and Julia Quinn all had the exact same idea.'

'Well, sadly I'm not sure I'm going to be able to use any of that in my English lesson,' Ash said. 'My teacher would think I'd lost the plot if I started comparing Shakespeare to Star Wars.'

'Oh, but you never know. And maybe Dan's a fan too?'

At the mention of the other boy's name, Ash's face grew serious.

'I don't know why I'm bothering with any of this, Arthur. Even if I do manage to say a coherent sentence in class, it's not like Dan would ever like someone like me.'

'Why ever not?'

'You've seen him. He's captain of the school football team, a prefect and one of the most popular kids in school. And I'm just a loser who likes science fiction and computer games.'

'So, haven't you ever heard of opposites attract? Just look at Anthony Bridgerton and Kate Sheffield.'

Ash smiled, but it was a half-hearted one this time. 'Sadly, this isn't a romance novel; we're not guaranteed a happily ever after.'

'Maybe not, but let me tell you a true story. The first time I plucked up the courage to talk to Esi, it quickly became clear she was totally out of my league. She wasn't just beautiful, she was the smartest person I'd ever met. Her father had been a successful Ghanaian businessman who'd sent her to this fancy English boarding school, and when he died, she and her mother moved here permanently. Esi was well-read and well-travelled, whereas I'd barely left St Tredock my whole life and smelled of manure. I didn't stand a chance.'

Ash didn't say anything, but Arthur could tell he was listening.

'All my friends told me to forget about her and find myself a local lass who'd be happy with the simple life I could give her. But I couldn't get Esi out of my mind. And so instead of giving up, like everyone told me to, I focused on the one thing I had in my favour.'

'Which was?'

'*Books*. I knew that however different we were, we could have books in common. And here we are, almost sixty years later, happily married and still arguing about books every single day.'

Ash smiled. 'That's a lovely story, Arthur.'

'Well, all I'm saying is that you shouldn't give up on this Dan just because he's different from you. Sometimes, these differences are the very things that make a relationship work.'

'Do you really think so?'

'I'm living proof of it, lad. Now come on, let's see if we can make sense of this *Much Ado About Nothing* malarkey together.'

Chapter Fourteen

Phyllis

The funeral dragged on for what felt like hours. Phyllis was desperate to slip out to try and find the man, who she was now sure must have been Michael, but she was trapped in the pew next to the silver-haired man and couldn't escape without drawing attention to herself. So instead, she sat there, kicking herself for getting distracted and allowing her chief suspect to get away for a second time.

Finally, the service drew to a close and the congregation stood up to leave. Immediately, Phyllis pushed past the posh man and hurried out of the church. As she'd feared, Michael was nowhere to be seen; he'd probably be miles away by now. But still, the fact he'd come to the funeral was very interesting indeed. For one, it proved Phyllis's theory that Michael running off with a lover was nonsense, as he and Cynthia had looked pretty cosy in the church. And it showed that the man was getting overconfident, willing to take risks; a classic mistake that had been many a fictional murderer's undoing. Yet there were still many questions left unanswered, and it was these Phyllis pondered as she walked away from the church.

'Hello! Yoo-hoo, wait up!'

Phyllis glanced over her shoulder. The silver-haired man was hurrying after her, waving his order of service in the air like a flag.

'I was wondering if you'd like a lift to the wake? I've got my car parked round the corner.'

'No thanks, I'm not going.'

'Why not?' The man had reached her, panting a little. 'I saw the caterers going in this morning, the afternoon tea looks like it's going to be quite a spread.'

Phyllis opened her mouth to say she had to get home, but stopped. It would be highly risky to go in case Cynthia recognised her as the woman from the book club who'd been sniffing around about Michael. But equally, this wake gave her the perfect opportunity to investigate the house and look for clues. Phyllis paused, weighing it up. And then she remembered *4.50 from Paddington*, where Miss Marple gets herself invited for afternoon tea at Rutherford Hall so she can pretend to choke on a fish paste sandwich in order to entrap the killer. Although Phyllis hoped she wouldn't have to go that far, the invitation to visit the scene of the crime was too tempting to turn down. Besides, like Miss Marple, she was rather partial to a fish paste sandwich.

'Very well. Thanks for the offer.'

It was only a ten-minute drive from the church to Mountfort Close, during which Phyllis gently pumped the silver-haired man – whose name was Richard – for more information on Michael and his mother. It turned out that Eve had lived in the house for forty years, and Michael and Cynthia had moved in with her nine months ago, after they were forced to sell their own home in Bristol.

'Michael was very secretive, but from what Eve could work out, he'd made some bad investment decisions and got himself in a spot of financial bother,' Richard said, as they drove along the coast. Last week's storms were long forgotten, and a low autumn sun hung over the glistening sea. 'Eve and I were friends, and she confided in me that Michael had not only lost his home but all his and Cynthia's savings too. And from the sounds of their argument last week, I imagine there were other debts Eve had only just found out about.'

'And so Michael wanted his mother to sell her house?'

'That's right, he was putting a lot of pressure on Eve, but she refused. She loved that house: it was where she'd lived with her beloved husband up until his death, and she'd put a lot of time and effort into the garden. But it wasn't just that. Between you and me, she told me that she was worried if she sold the house and gave Michael his inheritance early, he'd just squander it like he had his own money. Eve loved her son very much, and she wanted to protect him from himself.'

'And so he killed her to get his hands on the inheritance,' Phyllis said. Just like in *Ordeal by Innocence*.

'I keep thinking: if only I'd rung on the doorbell when I heard them arguing, maybe I could have saved her. I'll live with that regret for the rest of my life.'

Phyllis glanced at Richard and saw him staring out of the front window, his face creased with sorrow. Then he shook his head and turned to look at her.

'Sorry, I've waffled on and rudely asked you nothing about yourself. How did you know Eve?'

'Oh, eh . . .' Phyllis wracked her brains for a cover story, then realised it only risked complicating things. Better to tell the truth; or a version of it, anyway. 'I actually never met her. But I was in a book club with Michael, and I've met Cynthia before, so I felt I should come and pay my respects today.'

'How kind of you,' Richard said, smiling at her. 'Now tell me about this book club. I've always been interested in joining one.'

'We meet at St Tredock Community Centre on the third Wednesday of the month.'

'And what sort of books do you read?'

'A mixture. Most of them are pretty poor, if I'm honest, but that always makes for a good discussion.'

Richard laughed, and Phyllis felt herself flush again. What was going on with her today? She was behaving like a silly school girl.

'And are you open to new members?' Richard asked. 'I've only lived in the area for eighteen months and still not met many people, so perhaps a book club would be a good way for me to make new friends?'

'New members are welcome,' Phyllis said, staring out the passenger window so Richard wouldn't see her pink cheeks. Thankfully, they were pulling into Mountfort Close, cars already parked up along the pavement. Phyllis was relieved to see a large crowd of people filing into number eight; with this many guests at the wake, she should be able to have a snoop without Cynthia spotting her.

'Here you go.' Richard held Phyllis's door open for her and she didn't move, momentarily flustered.

Once she was out of the car, Richard offered Phyllis his arm, but she pretended not to notice and walked straight to the door of number eight. Her whole body was vibrating with excitement as she stepped inside. Here she was, Miss Phyllis Hudson, about to sneak into the prime suspect's house and find the vital clue to incriminate the killer. It was enough to make Agatha Christie proud.

'Let's go to the living room, that's probably where the food is,' Richard said, and Phyllis allowed herself to be steered left into a large, airy room.

There was a huge three-piece-suite in the middle, the biggest Phyllis had ever seen, and a conservatory off the back looking out over a sprawling mature garden. Phyllis thought of her own sparse living room and swallowed.

'That's Cynthia's sister over there,' Richard said, nodding at a small, birdlike woman twitching by the fireplace. 'And the pair she's talking to are Cynthia and Michael's daughters, Caroline and Elinor. They rarely visited their grandmother, although they've both been playing the part of the grieving granddaughters *very* convincingly this week.'

Was the whole family involved in the plot to kill Eve and get their hands on the inheritance? It would explain why Cynthia's sister was looking so jumpy, and why the two daughters were trying to impress everyone. Phyllis studied the three of them, but their faces gave nothing away. She scanned the rest of the guests, but didn't recognise any of their faces, apart from . . . Phyllis quickly turned away when she saw Beryl from the community centre chatting to an elderly couple. The last thing she needed was that woman seeing her here; Beryl was a notorious gossip.

'They must have set up the buffet in the dining room,' Richard said. 'How about you stay here and I go and get us both a plate?'

'Thank you.'

He gave a small bow and then disappeared in search of sustenance. As soon as he was gone, Phyllis turned and headed back towards the front hall, keeping her face tilted away from Beryl. If there were any clues to be found, they wouldn't be on show down here in the living room. There was a staircase leading up from the hall and Phyllis began to climb it. With every step, she expected to hear someone shouting for her to stop, but no one said a word and she got to the top unnoticed.

There were five doors leading off the upstairs landing, and Phyllis scanned her eyes across them before heading to the one on the far right, at the front of the house. It was a bedroom, and from the raised guards on either side of the bed, Phyllis guessed that it must have been Eve Watkins's. Was this where Michael and his mother had argued before he killed her? If so, the crime scene had long ago been cleaned up: the bed had been stripped of all linen and the strong smell of bleach suggested the whole room had been disinfected, removing any evidence of foul play. To the right of the door were several boxes of books and some black bin bags, and Phyllis pulled one of the bags open to see it was full of women's clothes. Eve's family were clearly wasting no time in casting her belongings off. Phyllis abandoned the bags and moved on to the next door.

This room appeared to be some sort of an office: there was a bookcase along one wall and a desk under the window. Phyllis crept into the room, pulling the door shut behind her as she tiptoed across to the desk. It was tidy, with only a computer, a pen pot – from the golfing images on the front, Phyllis assumed it belonged to Michael – and a paper diary. She opened it and began to flick through the pages to the most recent dates, but there was nothing about murdering a mother or running away to Bodmin in there. She put the diary aside and turned her attention to the desk drawer. Phyllis expected it to be locked, but when she pulled on the handle it opened to reveal a pile of papers. She took them out of the drawer and hastily flicked through. They seemed to be mostly household documents: electricity bills, insurance policies and some old receipts. But halfway through the pile, Phyllis stopped and drew breath. In front of her was a credit card statement addressed to Mr M. Watkins. And there, in red, was a number the size of which Phyllis had never seen.

£165,449.

Was that how much Michael owed? Richard had mentioned the man was in financial trouble, but this debt was bigger than anything Phyllis had ever imagined. No wonder he'd looked so stressed the whole time; just the thought of it made Phyllis feel sick. Was this what Eve had discovered and she and Michael were arguing about before he killed her? If so, the police had missed a key piece of evidence.

Phyllis stuffed it into her bag and began to move around the rest of the room. She was sure there must be another clue in here, but what was it? Not a stopped clock, like in *The Murder at the Vicarage*, or a frayed lamp cord, as in *A Murder Is Announced*? Phyllis mentally kicked herself; if Miss Marple were here, she'd know what to look for.

And then she spotted it.

Under the desk, a small wastepaper basket which, by the looks of things, hadn't been emptied for a while. Phyllis hurried back to the desk and picked up the bin. It contained the usual random assortment of rubbish: a few empty crisp packets – Michael had clearly been a fan of Monster Munch – several discarded tissues, and some ripped-up bits of paper. It was these Phyllis was most interested in, and she scooped out the contents of the bin and stuffed them into her handbag. She would go through these later, when she was in the safety of her own home.

A clock chimed, causing Phyllis to jump. She really needed to get back downstairs before Richard returned from the buffet and started wondering where she was. At the thought of him, Phyllis's stomach gave a small dip. It was ridiculous, a woman of her age fawning like a silly teenager. But still, it had been more than sixty years since a man had smiled at her in the way Richard had.

'And just look how that ended,' Phyllis muttered to herself, shaking all thoughts of romance out of her head. With one last glance around the office, she opened the door and stepped back into the hall. She began to make her way towards the stairs and then stopped. To her left was another door, slightly ajar, and through it she could see a double bed, fully made. Was this Cynthia and Michael's room? If so, it might well contain clues. Glancing around her to check the coast was still clear, she slipped inside.

It was indeed the principal bedroom. There was a large double bed, fitted wardrobes along one wall and a dressing table overflowing with pots and bottles. In the far corner was a door, which Phyllis assumed led into an en suite bathroom; she'd read about those in books but never seen one in real life. For a second, she considered having a look but resisted. To the right of the bed was a chest of drawers and she crossed to that and opened the top drawer. It was filled with men's underpants, and she quickly closed it. The next one contained socks; and the one below, T-shirts and sweaters. Wherever Michael had gone, he hadn't taken much with him.

On top of the dresser were two framed photos. The first was of Michael and Cynthia on their wedding day: she was wearing a puffy wedding dress, and he was in top hat and tails, both with the look of rabbits caught in the headlights. The second photo was black and white and clearly much older. Phyllis picked up the frame to take a closer look. It showed a woman and a small boy standing in front of a stone cottage, the sea stretching out behind them. The cottage looked vaguely familiar, like the ones that used to stand on the coastal path to St Piran's, until the erosion got so bad they had to be pulled down. Phyllis immediately recognised the woman as Eve Watkins, as she had the same eyebrows and jawline as the photo in the order of service. The child looked about five or six, with dimpled cheeks and pudgy legs sticking out from his shorts. This must be Michael outside his childhood home. Both he and his mother were looking at the camera, grinning at whoever had taken the photo as the wind whipped their hair. There was something about their happy, carefree faces that made Phyllis's chest ache, and she was about to put the photo down when she heard a creak from outside the bedroom door.

Someone was coming up the stairs!

Phyllis's heart started to pound, and she looked around for somewhere to hide. There was the en suite, but what if this person wanted to use the toilet? The footsteps were getting louder, and Phyllis opened the nearest wardrobe door and climbed inside, pulling it shut behind her. A second later, she heard the bedroom door click open.

Phyllis held her breath so as not to make a sound. She could hear footsteps moving round the room and the opening and closing of drawers. It must be Cynthia, looking for something. After a minute or so, Phyllis heard the footsteps moving back towards the door. She allowed herself to breathe again; this must mean Cynthia was going downstairs. And then there was another creak and a male voice.

'Ah, here you are, love. I was wondering where you'd snuck off to.'

From her position in the wardrobe, Phyllis let out a silent gasp. Michael was here!

'What are you doing up here?' Cynthia said. 'Did anyone see you?'

'Of course not, I crept up. Besides, everyone's too busy fighting over the buffet.'

'It's still too risky. Imagine if word got out? Everyone's gossiping enough as it is.'

Phyllis inched forwards and pressed her eye up against the crack in the wardrobe doors. There were only a few millimetres of space, but it was enough to see Cynthia standing by the bed next to the man. His back was to the wardrobe door, but it was definitely the same person as in the church. So, Michael really had dared to return to the scene of the crime, and on such a public occasion! Phyllis felt a flicker of admiration, before she remembered that he'd murdered his mother and stolen ten thousand pounds from the community centre.

'Relax, they're just a bunch of bored pensioners,' Michael said. 'What are you doing up here, anyway?'

'Hiding from my sister. She's been trying to get me on my own all day and I know *exactly* what she wants to talk about.'

'You think she's panicking?'

'Of course she is. That Goody Two-shoes is terrified someone will work out I wasn't really at hers on Wednesday night.'

'You don't think she'll tell the police, do you?'

'No, she's not that stupid.'

Aha, so Cynthia hadn't been at her sister's the night of the murder! Phyllis had known the woman was lying about her alibi. For a second, she was tempted to burst out of the wardrobe and tell the pair she'd caught them red-handed, but Miss Marple would never have done something so brash.

'I just want this all to be over so we can get out of here,' Cynthia said, her voice weary.

'Not long now, love. Once the house has been cleared, you'll never have to come back here again. I was thinking, maybe we should go somewhere hot? We both deserve a bit of sunshine after all of this.'

Phyllis felt a stab of panic. Michael and Cynthia were fleeing the country! Perhaps they were going to hide out in the Caribbean? Miss Marple had gone to St Honoré in *A Caribbean Mystery*, and it sounded wonderful, serial killer aside.

Phyllis heard feet moving across the carpeted floor, and the pair stepped out of her line of vision.

'I know this past week has been hideous, but it might all work out for the best in the end.' Michael had dropped his voice to almost a whisper. 'With Mike out of the way, we can finally be together.'

Wait, what? Had she just misheard that? Phyllis leaned forwards and very gently pushed the door ajar to get a better view.

Few things shocked Phyllis Hudson. But the sight of Cynthia Watkins being kissed passionately in the arms of a man – a man who was most definitely *not* her husband, Michael Watkins – took her breath away. She recoiled, and as she did her head knocked against a coat hanger, causing it to clatter against the rear of the wardrobe.

'Did you hear that?'

Phyllis pushed herself into the coats and dresses, trying to disappear, but it was no use. A second later, the door was yanked open and there stood Cynthia and the man who wasn't Michael, both glaring at her.

'Who the hell are you and what are you doing in my wardrobe?' Cynthia demanded, as the man grabbed Phyllis's arm, pulling her out. She stumbled but his grip was strong, and she didn't fall.

'Were you just spying on us?' His face was red.

'I wasn't, I swear.' Phyllis didn't have to put on her fake 'little old lady' voice now; it was quivering for real.

'Oh my God, it's *you*,' Cynthia said. 'You're the woman who was here last week, aren't you? The one with the humping dog. She said she was in a book club with Michael.'

'Michael was in a book club?' The man still had hold of Phyllis's arm, but he turned to look at Cynthia, his face twisted in disbelief. 'He didn't strike me as the reading sort.'

'He isn't, she was lying.'

'I wasn't,' Phyllis croaked.

'Then what are you doing here?'

'I was . . .' Phyllis wracked her brain. What would Miss Marple do? But her mind was blank, because Miss Marple would never have been stupid enough to be caught hiding in a wardrobe.

'Right, that's it, I'm calling the police,' the man said.

'No!' Phyllis cried, at the same moment Cynthia said, 'Don't bother.'

'But she's clearly up to something,' the man said.

'Yes, but the last thing we need is the police turning up in front of those vultures downstairs, giving them something else to gossip about,' Cynthia said. 'Just get her out of the house without a fuss. I'll deal with this myself later.'

Cynthia's lover looked like he was about to say something else, then he nodded and pulled Phyllis towards the door. His grip was painful on her arm, but she was determined not to cry out as he led her down the stairs. There was a crowd of people milling around in the hallway, and their eyes turned to look at Phyllis as she descended.

'Nothing to see here folks!' Cynthia's lover said in an overly cheery voice. 'Just an old lady who needs some air.'

'Phyllis?'

She looked round to see Richard standing in the living room doorway, holding two plates piled high with food. His expression turned to confusion when he saw her being marched towards the front door. But before she could say anything, Phyllis was pushed outside and the door slammed behind her.

Chapter Fifteen

Nova

Nova was having a Very Bad Day.

The problems had started before she even got up. She and Craig were drinking coffee in bed when his phone buzzed. He read the message and his eyes went wide.

'What is it?' Nova asked.

He chewed his lip, and she could tell he was working out what to say.

'Craig?'

'Don't freak out, but it's an e-mail from the solicitors. Apparently Declan was released from prison last week.'

Nova's stomach plummeted. She'd known this was due to happen soon, but it still sent goose bumps rippling across her skin. Craig reached over and put his arm round her shoulder.

'It's okay, babe. You're 200 miles away now, he can't—'

'I'm not worried about that,' Nova said quickly. 'It's just a shock hearing the name again, that's all.'

'The terms of his parole mean that—' Craig was interrupted by a scream from outside the door. Nova jumped and a moment later Pamela came bursting into the bedroom, her face ashen.

'Nova, what did you *do*?'

'What's wrong?' Craig said.

'I just texted the photographer to see whether she wanted chicken or beef on Saturday, and it turns out Nova gave her the wrong date! She thought our wedding was on the 26th of *November*, not October, and she's got another wedding booked this weekend.'

Nova exhaled with relief – for a moment there she'd thought it was something genuinely bad – but Craig was looking at her in horror.

'How can you have got the date wrong for your own wedding?'

'I definitely told her October. This is the photographer's mistake, not mine.'

'It was your *one* job,' Pamela said through gritted teeth.

Nova tried to defend herself, but Pamela stormed out of the room and refused to talk to her for the rest of the morning.

Things didn't improve when Nova got to work for the start of her shift at midday and found Sandy and Lauren pulling the office apart.

'Where did you put the keys to the sports cupboard?' Sandy demanded as soon as she walked through the door. 'Tim's got twenty toddlers about to turn up for baby gym and we can't find them anywhere!'

'I put them back in the key cupboard last night.'

'Well, they're not there now. Are you sure you didn't forget again?'

'I'm sure I—' she started, but then stopped when Lauren caught her eye and mouthed the word *Derek*. Nova's heart sank. She'd been on her way to put the keys away yesterday when she'd been cornered by a community centre regular, Derek, who'd spent twenty minutes telling her in graphic detail about his prostate operation. By the time he'd finished, Nova must have put the keys in her pocket and forgotten all about them.

'I'm sorry, Sandy, I must have taken them home with me,' she said. 'Do we not have a spare set?'

'No, we lost those years ago.'

'I can go home and get them now if—'

'Never mind,' Sandy snapped. 'I'll have to tell Tim to run the session without any bloody equipment.' She stormed out of the office, slamming the door shut behind her, and Nova sank down into a chair.

'You okay?' Lauren asked.

'I just feel like Sandy's going to sack me at any moment, and I have this constant tightness in my chest.'

'Oh, sweetie,' Lauren said. 'Have you talked to Craig about how you're feeling?'

'I've tried but he thinks it's just pre-wedding nerves.'

'And what do you think?'

'I don't know.' Nova sighed. Was this what every bride felt like, four days before their wedding day; this horrible sensation of suffocating? But then she supposed most brides weren't mourning the recent death of their father, or the imminent loss of their job.

'I think you need to be more honest with him,' Lauren said gently. 'If you're feeling this stressed about the wedding then perhaps you should consider postponing it for a bit?'

'I can't do that. You know what Pamela's like.'

'But Pamela isn't the one who matters here. I'm sure if you explain to Craig how you're feeling, he'd understand. He adores you, and I know he wouldn't want to go through with the wedding if it's making you feel physically unwell.'

'It's fine; I'm fine.' Nova took a deep breath. 'I'm just tired. I need to get through the next few days without getting fired, and then my mum's coming over for the wedding and I have a week off work. I know I'll feel better after that.'

Her friend gave her a small smile, but Nova could tell she wasn't convinced.

The afternoon rumbled on without incident. Nova was determined not to make any more silly mistakes, and she double-checked every booking she put in the diary, and even made an effort to tidy her desk in case the sports cupboard keys were there.

At four o'clock she had a short break, but rather than sitting in the office with a glowering Sandy, Nova made herself a cup of tea and headed to Tintagel. As she turned the door handle, she heard a shuffling sound on the other side. Nova stepped in to see Arthur and Ash sitting at one of the tables, Ash trying to stuff something in his bag.

'What's going on in here?' Nova asked, looking between their guilty expressions.

'We were just having a little chat,' Arthur said. 'Lovely weather we're having today, isn't it?'

Nova frowned and was about to press further when the door behind her flew open again, crashing into her back. She yelped in pain as Phyllis came bowling into the room, followed closely by Craddock. They were both panting.

'Are you okay?' Nova asked, as Phyllis leaned on a table to catch her breath.

'We . . . were . . . wrong . . .' The older lady gasped. 'Everything . . . we thought . . . is wrong.'

'What on earth are you talking about?'

Phyllis straightened up, and Nova saw a strange intensity in her eyes. 'We thought it was Michael who killed his mother, but it was Cynthia! *She's* the murderer . . . and I think she's behind Michael's disappearance too.'

It was such an absurd statement that Nova couldn't help laughing.

'Phyllis, I'm sorry, but you really need to stop reading so many murder mysteries.'

Phyllis wrinkled her nose. 'Laugh all you want. Miss Marple was used to people laughing at her and dismissing her as a silly old lady too.'

'I don't think you're silly, Phyllis, just—'

'Greed was the motive, just like I said it would be!' Phyllis interrupted. 'Michael lost all their money, so Cynthia killed Eve to get her hands on the inheritance. And she's the one having an affair, not Michael. My guess is that after killing Eve, Cynthia and her lover kidnapped Michael to frame him for the murder and get him out of the way so they could be together.'

'People do all sorts of crazy things when they're in love,' Arthur said with a knowing nod of his head.

'Hang on, I don't think Michael was kidnapped,' Nova said. 'PC Khan told me that they found his car abandoned in the middle of Bodmin Moor, so it sounds like he drove down there after the book club.'

'No!' Phyllis slammed her hand on the table, making them all jump. 'The abandoned car must be part of Cynthia's plan, to make it *look* like Michael ran away. I have to give it to the woman, that's an excellent touch.'

'How did you find all of this out?' Nova asked.

The older woman looked away. 'That's not important.'

'Phyllis, tell me.'

'You'll just make a fuss.' She crossed her arms and let out a long sigh. '*Fine*. Earlier today, I went to Eve Watkins's funeral.'

'What?'

'I suspected that Michael might attend in disguise, so I went to try and catch him red-handed. And then I learned some new information at the funeral – don't ask me to reveal my source – that led me to attend the wake at Michael's house. And while I was there, I learned that Cynthia has a lover, and they plan to flee the country now that Michael's out of the way.'

'Phyllis!' Nova burst out when the woman finally stopped speaking. 'What the hell were you thinking? Do you have any idea how dangerous that was?'

'Oh nonsense, I was never in danger.'

'What if Cynthia had recognised you from when we went round there last week?'

'Well, thankfully she didn't,' Phyllis said, rubbing her left arm and not catching Nova's eye.

'I wish you'd told me about your plans, I'd have come too,' Arthur said with a chuckle. 'It's like something out of one of Esi's books.'

'This isn't funny,' Nova said. 'You could have been arrested for gate-crashing a funeral and trespassing on private property.'

'Oh, stop being such a drama queen,' Phyllis tutted. 'I was merely paying my respects to an elderly member of the community.'

'Did you find anything else at the house?' This was the first time Ash had spoken, and Phyllis looked startled at seeing him there.

'I did, as a matter of fact.'

She made a big show of reaching into her handbag and pulling out a sheet of paper. She laid it down on the table with a grand flourish.

'Is this a credit card bill?' Arthur asked.

'It is. Michael owed over one hundred and sixty-five thousand pounds, and by the looks of things, this was a final demand. He and Cynthia were running out of time to get the money.'

'This proves they were in financial difficulties, but it doesn't prove either of them killed Eve,' Arthur said. 'We'd need more than this to go to the police.'

'Be patient, there *is* more!'

Phyllis reached into her bag again, and despite herself, Nova found she was holding her breath. Then Phyllis withdrew her hand, and Nova exhaled in disappointment when the woman placed what looked like the contents of a rubbish bin on the table.

'Did you steal all of this?' Nova said, not really wanting to know the answer.

'It wasn't theft. I was simply doing some recycling.'

'Is that a used tissue?' Arthur said, his nose wrinkled.

'Ignore that. It's these we're interested in.' Phyllis pushed several pieces of paper towards Arthur.

Nova stepped forwards to get a closer look. 'Is that a torn-up envelope?'

'Exactly!'

'How does that help us?'

'At the wake, my source told me that on Wednesday, shortly before Eve was murdered, he heard Michael and his mother arguing about a letter. Initially I thought they might have been fighting about the credit card bill, but then I found these ripped up in the bin.'

'But what good is this to us?' Nova said. 'We can't even see who the envelope was addressed to, half the pieces are missing.'

'It's not who the letter was *to* we're interested in,' Phyllis said. 'It's who the letter was *from*.'

She picked up another scrap of paper from her pile and passed it to Nova, who glanced at the words on it and frowned.

'Ham pie . . . pudding. Phyllis, this isn't a clue, it's a bit of old shopping list.'

'No, I believe it's a return address on the back of the envelope. Look, you can see a bit of the sealed flap here. And look again at what it says next to pudding.'

Nova reread the scrap. 'It says 3 Pudding, but I can't read anything else as it's been ripped.'

'Do you see now?' Phyllis's face was alight.

'See what?'

'It's an address,' Ash said, and when Nova looked over at him, he was staring at his phone, his thumbs moving fast across the screen. 'According to this there are two Pudding Lanes in the UK, one Pudding Street and one Pudding Road.' He looked up from his screen. 'One of the Pudding Lanes is in Port Gowan.'

'I knew it!' Phyllis crowed. 'Whoever that letter was from, this is where they live. My guess is it's someone Michael owes money to, perhaps a dodgy loan shark. Either way, I believe if we trace this—'

'It's not a loan shark,' Ash interrupted, and Nova saw his eyes were bright with excitement too. 'It's a man called Graham Pierce who owns a company called Pierce Security.'

'*Ham pie*,' Arthur said, smiling in admiration at Ash's detective skills. 'But why would Cynthia and Michael need security?'

'It's not just security. Here, look at the website.'

Ash held out his phone and they all crowded closer to see.

'Read it aloud, I haven't got my glasses on,' Arthur said.

Ash cleared his throat, clearly embarrassed at having to speak in front of them all.

'Graham Pierce has worked in security for ten years, following a career in the British Intelligence Service.'

'British Intelligence Service!' Phyllis interrupted. 'You know what that means? The man's a spy, a trained killer.'

'He can provide a range of services from personal security to surveillance and private investigation work,' Ash continued. 'If you're interested in using his services then call the number below to arrange a meeting. Competitive rates, discretion guaranteed.'

Phyllis was bouncing up and down, barely able to contain her excitement. 'Cynthia must have employed this private investigator to help get her hands on Eve's money. Maybe Eve found the letter and told Michael what Cynthia was up to, and that's what they were arguing about? And then Cynthia realised her secret was out, so she killed Eve and made Michael disappear!'

'You know, something like this happened in a book I read Esi,' Arthur said. 'Only in that one, the assassin ended up falling in love with the woman he was meant to kill and then—'

'For the hundredth time, Michael doesn't have a lover,' Phyllis said, cutting him off mid-flow. '*Cynthia* is the one having the affair.'

'Okay, let's just think about this calmly for a moment,' Nova said, although her heart was racing in a not particularly calm way. 'If we think Cynthia might have hired a private investigator then maybe it was perfectly innocent? People sometimes use them when they're getting divorced, especially if they think their ex is hiding money from them.'

'You're not looking at the facts,' Phyllis said. 'There's been a theft, a murder and a missing person, and now we find out an ex-spy is involved too. There's nothing innocent about any of this!'

'I think we should take this information to the police,' Arthur said.

'Absolutely not,' Phyllis snapped.

'But if you think Cynthia might be behind Eve's death, not Michael, then you have to tell them.'

'I am not going to the police, and that's final,' Phyllis said, crossing her arms.

'But—'

'They won't listen to me.' Phyllis was staring at her feet. 'In fact, if I tell them it was Cynthia, then they'll actively dismiss it.'

'But why?' Nova asked.

The older lady paused before she answered, and Nova wasn't sure she'd ever seen her look so uncomfortable. 'The police and I have a bit of a history, as a result of which they've made it clear that they're no longer open to my assistance . . .'

She trailed off, but she didn't need to say anything else; Nova understood perfectly. Phyllis had obviously taken her amateur investigations to the police one too many times.

'But it's different this time,' Arthur said gently. 'There's been an actual murder, and you have important information that could help them.'

Phyllis let out a long sigh. 'Six months.'

'What?'

'That's the maximum prison sentence you can get for wasting police time. And the North Cornish constabulary have made it clear they'd press charges if I ever got involved in one of their investigations again.'

'Ah, I see,' Arthur said, catching Nova's eye behind Phyllis's back and raising his eyebrows.

'So, what do we do now?' Nova asked. 'We can't just go barging into this Graham Pierce's office asking questions about Cynthia, he'd get suspicious straightaway.'

'No, we need a cover story,' Arthur said. 'We have to pretend we need his services to get a meeting, and while we're there we do some digging.'

'Fine, well I'll call and get an appointment, then.' Phyllis pointed at Ash. 'Give me the phone number and I'll call now.'

'I don't think you should do it, Phyllis,' Arthur said.

'Why not?'

'For one, Cynthia might be onto you, especially if you've been sniffing round the funeral and wake. What if she's already told this PI about you, and he recognises you? What if she reports you to the police?'

Phyllis opened her mouth to argue, then obviously thought better of it. 'Who'll go, then?' She looked at Nova.

'No way, I can't risk it. Honestly, I'm in enough trouble as it is, without getting involved with some dodgy private investigator.'

'I don't mind going,' Arthur said. 'No one will suspect an old Cornish farmer so I can probably ask a few questions without him getting suspicious.'

'I can go too,' Ash said, and they all looked at him in surprise. He blushed but carried on. 'I know I'm not very good at talking, but people often don't notice me, which might be helpful?'

'It's true, I didn't spot you when I came in here,' Phyllis said, then frowned. 'Are you sure I shouldn't come too? I've spent a lifetime studying one of the best detectives in the world. I'm sure Miss Marple would get all the information she needed and have time for a cup of tea.'

Arthur smiled at her. 'We'll still need your help, Phyllis. If this plan is going to work, you've a vital role to play.'

Chapter Sixteen

Arthur

At 10:59 a.m., Arthur stood outside the tall, nondescript building on Pudding Lane, staring at the names on the buzzer. In between Ros Stewart: Psychodrama Psychoanalysis and Top Thai Massage was a faded handwritten label for Pierce Security. Arthur's stomach churned.

It had all been very well volunteering yesterday, when he was full of bravado having listened to Phyllis's spying exploits at the funeral. But now he was standing here, about to meet a possible contract killer, Arthur felt considerably less confident. He was a farmer, not some bloody amateur sleuth.

'Maybe we should just have a phone chat with him instead?' he said to Ash.

'We'll never discover anything on the phone. We need to get into his office so we can have a look around,' the teenager said, and before Arthur could stop him, he leaned forwards and pressed the bell.

For about ten seconds nothing happened, and Arthur sighed with relief. 'I knew he'd be unreliable; he must have forgotten about our—'

He was interrupted by a click as the door lock opened. Bugger.

'Okay, remember our plan?' Ash whispered as he stepped inside.

'I think so,' Arthur said, although in truth he was so nervous he could barely think straight. What if he got something wrong and the private investigator worked out who they were? Esi's historical romances often featured assassins and spies, and they were all volatile, dangerous men able to kill a person with their bare hands. What if this Graham Pierce was the same?

Pierce Security had their office on the fourth floor, and Arthur spent the slow climb running over their cover story in his head. After much deliberation, he and Ash had decided to go with a story inspired by another of Esi's much-loved Bridgerton books, *On the Way to the Wedding*. It was a slightly far-fetched plot, but Arthur hoped that it would be unusual enough to catch Pierce's attention and get him talking. Still, his heart was hammering, and not just because of the stairs. When he reached the fourth floor, he saw Ash standing in front of a grey door. He glanced over his shoulder at Arthur.

'Ready?'

Arthur grabbed hold of the banister to stop his legs from shaking. 'Ready.'

Ash knocked, then moved back to stand next to Arthur. A moment later the door opened to reveal Graham Pierce.

Arthur wasn't sure what he'd been expecting from an ex-British intelligence officer; perhaps someone tall and dark, with an angular jaw and brooding eyes. But the man standing in front of them looked like a middle-aged accountant, with balding hair and sandwich crumbs in his moustache. He didn't look like he was capable of tying his own shoelaces, let alone killing anyone.

'Come in, come in,' the man said, stepping aside and holding the door open.

Arthur walked through to find himself in a small, cramped office, in the middle of which was a desk covered in piles of papers and old newspapers. Shelves ran along the back wall, crammed with files, and a dirty window on the right wall looked out over the street below.

'Sorry, remind me of your names again?' the man said as he ushered them in.

'I'm Gregory Benedick. And this is my grandson, eh . . .'

Christ, what name had they come up with for Ash? Arthur wracked his brain, aware Graham was staring at him.

'Eh, Ben,' he said, throwing out the first name that came into his head.

'Ben Benedick?' Graham blinked in surprise and Arthur kicked himself. 'Well, please take a seat.'

Graham indicated two chairs, one of which had an empty McDonald's bag on it. He hastily scooped the rubbish up and retreated behind his desk.

'Do you mind if I take notes?' he said, nodding at his computer.

'No, go ahead.'

'Thanks. So, how can I help you both?'

Arthur opened his mouth to speak but his mind had gone blank again. What was he supposed to say? His skin was getting clammy and he felt nauseous. Oh God, was he going to be sick? If only Esi were here, this would all be so much easier. Everything had always been so much easier when his wife was by his side.

'We're here about my mum.'

Arthur looked at Ash in surprise. The teenager had insisted he didn't want to do any talking in the meeting, and yet here he was now, his voice calm and steady.

'She's getting married to this guy, Ricky Haselby, who my grandpa and I don't trust at all. He's much older than her and super sleazy and we think something weird is going on.'

'Eh . . . yes . . . we're concerned about why she's marrying him,' Arthur said, picking up the thread of the story. 'She doesn't seem to love him, or even like him very much, so we're worried something dodgy is going on. Like maybe he's blackmailing her to marry him . . . or something.'

Graham was tapping away on his keyboard. 'What makes you think it's blackmail?'

'Well, it just doesn't make sense why she'd go ahead with this marriage. They barely know each other. And we think she might actually be in love with someone else, which is what makes her engagement to Haselby all the stranger.'

Pierce looked up from his computer. 'Is this Mr Haselby very rich?'

Arthur gulped. Had Pierce read the Bridgerton books and recognised the story, and now he was toying with Arthur before he hurt him?

'Erm, yes,' Arthur said, carefully.

Pierce nodded. 'I thought as much. Do you think it's possible that your daughter is marrying him for his money? I see it all the time, women settling for men far below them just because the guy offers financial security. Maybe it's nothing more sinister than that?'

'I don't think it's that. My daughter isn't short of money, you see; she's very wealthy.' Arthur saw the PI take in his frayed jumper and ancient trousers and added, 'She's done well for herself in business, she's one of those entrepreneurs.'

'And I assume you've tried asking her if there's anything untoward going on?'

'We have but she won't tell us what's wrong. She just keeps saying she knows what she's doing, but we can tell something's up.'

'I see. And how would you like me to help?'

'We were wondering if you could do some digging and find out more about Ricky,' Ash said. 'And also, maybe find out if there's anything in my mum's life that she might be being blackmailed about.'

'I can certainly try,' Graham said. 'I'd suggest that with a case such as this, you'd want to start with some surveillance work of the two of them, both physical and digital. Depending on how that goes, we can then consider other approaches. Is there a date for the planned wedding?'

'Eh yes, next February,' Arthur said.

'Okay, so that only gives us a couple of months,' Graham said, typing another note.

Arthur glanced over at Ash and caught the boy's eye. This was going well so far; the PI didn't seem to be suspicious. But now was the trickier part.

'If you did manage to find evidence that Ricky has been black-mailing my Lucy, what would be the next steps?' Arthur hoped this question sounded more innocent than it felt.

'Well, I suppose I'd suggest you confront your daughter with the evidence and see how she reacts,' the PI said. 'If that still doesn't make her change her mind about the wedding then you'd have two choices: either take the evidence to the police, assuming it was enough to get him prosecuted, or let the wedding go ahead.'

'We don't want the wedding going ahead,' Arthur said. 'That man is a scumbag, and I know he'll make Lucy unhappy. Are there any other ways we could stop it happening?'

Arthur didn't dare look at the PI as he asked this. Phyllis had been adamant about this line of questioning; once they'd got Pierce to believe their story, they had to try and get him to open up about his other services, those he didn't advertise on his website. The same services he might have offered Cynthia Watkins to deal with Eve and Michael.

'I'm sorry, I'm not sure what you mean, Mr Benedick,' Graham said.

Arthur clenched his hands together in his lap to stop them shaking. This was his big moment; if he got this next bit wrong then Pierce might realise they were here under false pretences, tie them up and interrogate them until they confessed the truth. And Esi always joked that someone only had to tickle Arthur and he'd give up his life secrets.

'Well, say we didn't have enough evidence to go to the police, but we knew Ricky's been blackmailing Lucy,' he said carefully. 'Are there any other ways we could stop the wedding happening? Any ways we could make Ricky . . . go away?'

Graham didn't answer and Arthur felt the question hang in the air. He glanced at Ash and could see the boy's face was pale. The seconds ticked by, and Arthur waited for the moment Graham pulled out a gun and pointed it straight at Arthur's head. Or worse, at Ash's. He closed his eyes, waiting for the inevitable.

A loud noise shattered the silence and Arthur leaped in his chair. He opened his eyes, terrified of what he was about to see.

'Is that . . . "Blaze of Glory" by Jon Bon Jovi?' Ash asked, as music blasted out from somewhere on the desk.

'I'm sorry, it's my phone's ringtone,' Graham said, rummaging around to try and locate it. 'I thought it was on silent.'

The music continued to blare out.

'I think it might be here,' Ash said, and he pushed aside some paper and produced a buzzing mobile, handing it to Graham.

'Thanks, let me just turn that o—'

'No!' Arthur shouted. 'I mean, please feel free to take the call. It might be important.'

The PI shrugged but then pressed answer and the music abruptly stopped. 'Hello, Pierce Security.'

The room fell silent as the person on the other end of the line spoke and Arthur found he was holding his breath.

'Calm down, please, and say that again. You think someone has done what?'

Arthur could make out the sound of a voice on the phone but not what they were saying.

'Hang on a second.' Graham moved the phone away from his ear and turned to Arthur and Ash. 'I'm sorry, gentlemen, do you mind if I take this call in private?'

'Go ahead,' Arthur said.

Graham looked between the two of them, clearly waiting for them to leave his office.

'Oh, you want us to go out?' Arthur began to push himself up from his chair, making grunting and groaning sounds.

'Here, let me help you, Grandpa,' Ash said, jumping to his side.

Graham was watching them impatiently.

'Be careful. Take it slowly so you don't hurt yourself,' Ash said, as Arthur puffed and panted.

'Don't worry, I'll take this outside,' Graham said, and he stood up and strode towards the office door. 'Sorry, madam, please start that again,' he said as he stepped out.

A moment later, Arthur heard the office door click shut. Immediately, he jumped to his feet as Ash rushed round to the far side of the desk.

'Yes, he left his computer unlocked!' the teenager said.

Arthur started to shuffle through the mess on the desk, grabbing pieces of paper at random. Most of it seemed to be old receipts and bills. Giving up on the desk, he moved to the shelves on the back wall, running his eyes along the files, looking for Cynthia Watkins's name. Like with the desk, there seemed to be no obvious order or system here, with some files labelled by date and others by name.

'Anything on the computer?'

'I've searched his e-mail and there's nothing coming up with Cynthia Watkins's name,' Ash said. 'I'm doing a search of the files now.'

'This is chaos, it's like looking for a needle in a bleedin' haystack,' Arthur said, turning from the shelves in dismay.

'Try these drawers,' Ash said, nodding to the desk without taking his eyes off the screen.

Arthur pulled the first one open to be confronted by a mass of discarded KitKat Chunky wrappers.

'This man needs a better diet, or he'll die of a heart attack.' He tried to open the drawer underneath, but it was locked. He was about to start looking for a key when he heard a gasp from Ash.

'I've found something!' the boy said. 'There's a folder with Michael's name on it.'

'Blimey, Phyllis was right!' Arthur hissed.

Ash reached into his pocket and pulled out a memory stick, then bent down to slot it into the computer.

'I'm not sure I'm the best person to help you.' Graham's voice floated in through the door. 'Perhaps you'd have better luck with the police.'

'Quick, it sounds like he's finishing up.'

'I'm trying!' Ash's feet were tapping urgently on the floor. 'It's copying now.'

'Madam, this really isn't my line of business. Now if you'll excuse me, I'm in the middle of a meeting.'

Arthur gave up on the locked drawer and hurried back round to the other side of the desk. 'Ash, you have to come now!'

'One more second!'

'If you're going to talk to me like that then I definitely won't help. Good-bye!'

Arthur heard the sound of the door handle creak. At the same moment, Ash jumped up and charged back round the desk, collapsing into his seat the second the door swung open.

'I'm so sorry about that,' Graham said as he strode back in. 'That was some crazy woman who claimed eight people are stuck on an island off the south coast of Devon and are about to be murdered one by one. She said she knows who the murderer is and wants me to help her prove it.'

Arthur stifled the smile that was threatening to emerge as he recognised the plot from *And Then There Were None*, an Agatha Christie novel Phyllis had described in detail at a previous book club meeting.

'You wouldn't believe the number of weirdos I meet in this line of work, conspiracy theorists who want me to investigate the strangest things,' Graham continued. 'Thankfully, after ten years in this business, I've got pretty good at weeding out the time-wasters early on. Now, you were asking me if—'

'You know what, you've given us plenty to think about,' Arthur said. 'Ben and I will have a chat about how we'd like to proceed and be back in touch soon.'

He pushed himself up, giving a quick groan for effect, and Ash leaped up too.

'Would you like to discuss my price structure before you leave?'

Graham asked. 'I'm willing to offer discounts if you use more than one of my services.'

'Thanks, but we can chat about that next time,' Arthur said as he moved towards the door. 'We appreciate your time, Mr Pierce.'

'Okay, well you know where I am if you need me,' Graham said, but Arthur didn't wait to hear any more as he was out of the door and moving down the stairs as fast as his eighty-one-year-old legs would carry him.

Chapter Seventeen

Phyllis

'**N**ow close your eyes and breathe . . . that's it, slowly in and out, in and out . . . Feel nature's healing calm fill your body with every loving breath.'

Phyllis gritted her teeth, resisting the temptation to shout at the stupid man to shut up.

It had been Nova's suggestion that she come to the meditation class. Phyllis had been storming round the community centre, berating herself for letting Arthur and Ash go to visit the private investigator without her. What chance did a bumbling old farmer and a mute teenage boy have of getting information out of a member of the elite British Secret Service? Even though Phyllis had played her part by ringing the man and keeping him on the phone so they could investigate the office, she knew the chances of those two managing to find anything was tiny. And without any evidence that Cynthia had hired the PI to help kill Eve or get rid of Michael, there was nothing to stop the woman getting away with her crimes. In her rage, Phyllis had kicked a bucket, sending it skidding down a corridor and almost taking out a toddler. It was at that point that Nova had intervened and suggested Phyllis distract herself with some meditation while they waited for Arthur and Ash to return. Not that she was finding any of this nonsense remotely relaxing, or distracting.

'Oh my God, what *is* that smell?'

Phyllis opened her eyes. Several people sitting around her were pinching their noses and looking like they might be sick. Phyllis took a sniff and immediately knew the culprit.

'Is it that damn dog again?' said Neil, the bearded man who was taking the class. 'I'm sorry, but I told you, you can only bring him in here if he doesn't disturb anyone.'

'He's not disturbing anyone, it's just some flatulence.'

'I can't relax with that stench,' said a woman sitting to Phyllis's right.

'I'm afraid you'll have to take him out.'

'This is discrimination! You wouldn't throw out a human for farting, would you?'

'Phyllis, either he goes, or you both do.' Neil's face was looking distinctly lacking in nature's healing calm.

'Fine, this was rubbish anyway,' Phyllis said, standing up. 'Come on, Craddock, let's go.'

She grabbed the dog's lead and marched towards the door. As they reached it, Craddock let out another ripper, and Phyllis smiled.

She knew from experience he'd need to do his business soon, so she led him out into the car park and over to some small bushes at the edge. In his old age, the dog had become rather inefficient at emptying his bowels, so Phyllis looked around for something to keep her occupied while she waited.

There was a game she liked to play sometimes, where she'd pick a random stranger and try to imagine what observations Miss Marple would make about them. There was a youth across the road now, leaning against a low brick wall, smoking a cigarette, and Phyllis studied him closely. He was dressed in a tracksuit – a fashion item that would no doubt have horrified Jane – and had the hood pulled up to conceal his face. He wasn't local by the looks of the large rucksack next to him, and his right foot was bouncing up and down on the pavement with nervous energy as he stared at the community centre. A car drove in front of him, turning into the community centre car park and blocking Phyllis's view. She leaned sideways to keep the youth in vision, then stopped and turned her attention to the car.

It was a red MINI Cooper, a familiar face sitting behind the wheel as it reversed into a parking space. What the hell was Cynthia Watkins doing here? Phyllis turned her back so the woman wouldn't recognise her. Craddock had barely begun his business, and by the time he'd finished, Cynthia might be long gone.

'I need to go inside and see what's going on,' she said, wrapping Craddock's lead round the nearest fence post. 'I'll be back soon.'

Securing the lead in a knot, Phyllis hurried into the centre to see Cynthia striding down the corridor. Phyllis followed, keeping at a safe distance.

'I want to see the manager,' Cynthia demanded, barging into the office with the entitlement of a person who was used to getting her own way.

'That would be me, Sandy Reynolds. How can I help?'

'My name's Cynthia Watkins, and I want to make a formal complaint against members of your staff,' Cynthia said. 'They've been harassing me.'

'My staff?' Phyllis could hear the surprise in Sandy's voice. 'Goodness . . . What's happened?'

'Yesterday, a woman who claimed to be from the St Tredock Community Centre invaded the private wake of my mother-in-law and then hid in a wardrobe to spy on me.'

'What?! I'm so sorry to hear that.'

Even without being able to see her, Phyllis knew Sandy's face would be going bright red and her eyes starting to water. That woman was as limp as a lettuce leaf.

'Can you describe this person to me? Only I can't imagine any of my staff would do something like this.'

'She was an old lady: fat, blue hair.'

'Ah, right,' Sandy said, the relief evident in her tone. 'The person you're talking about isn't an employee here, she's just a woman who comes to the centre. Between you and me, she's a rather sad character. I don't think she has any family or friends so she's quite lonely, and as a result, she can let her imagination run a bit wild. I can have a gentle word with her, but I'm afraid she's not my responsibility.'

'It wasn't just her,' Cynthia snapped. 'Last week, she came with two others, and they harassed me on my doorstep, only twenty-four hours after I discovered my mother-in-law had been killed and my husband went missing.'

'Hold on, did you say your name is Cynthia Watkins?' Sandy said. 'Are you any relation of Michael Watkins?'

'He was . . . is my husband.'

'I see. And you said there were two others; can you remember what they looked like?'

'There was an old man with a big white beard, and a younger woman in a horrible furry red coat, plus a foul-smelling English bull-dog. They said they were from a book club here and accused Michael of stealing something.'

'A woman in a red coat?'

'Yes, it was an old, cheap-looking thing. She didn't say much, but she was clearly trying to intimidate me into revealing goodness knows what.'

'Oh dear . . .' Sandy said slowly. 'I'm afraid she might be a member of my team. Can you leave me your contact details and I'll investigate this and get back to you?'

'I want your assurances that these troublemakers will be dealt with. It's completely inappropriate that they should have repeatedly turned up at my house, harassing me while I'm going through a very traumatic period. I've brought this to you first as a common decency, but if you don't take action then my next port of call will be the police.'

'Yes, of course, I understand. Thank you.'

There was a noise in the office, and Phyllis just had time to dart through the open door of an empty room before she heard Cynthia step into the corridor, her heels clicking on the floor as she marched out.

Phyllis sank into a chair, her chest tight.

No friends or family . . .

Quite lonely . . .

Lets her imagination run wild . . .

Is that what people really thought of her? She'd always known she was seen as something of an eccentric: people were deeply suspicious of unmarried, childless women, plus the fact she still lived in the house she was born in always raised some eyebrows. But still, she had a family in Craddock, and she never let her imagination run wild; she was extremely rational and methodical. *Rather sad character*, Sandy had called her, each word landing like a punch.

Phyllis wasn't one for emotions – her mother had knocked them out of her at a young age – but it was still several minutes before she was able to breathe properly again. As soon as she could, she left the meeting room and headed towards the exit. Nova was walking out of the main hall, carrying a large box, but she stopped when she saw Phyllis's face.

'Are you okay?'

Phyllis pushed past her without answering. As she reached the door, she heard Sandy's voice calling out.

'Nova, I need to see you in my office.'

'Okay, but can I just check on Phyllis, she seems—'

'No! We need to talk. Now.'

Phyllis hurried outside. Never in her life had she been so desperate to get away from people. She turned and began to stagger towards where Craddock was tied up, and then she ground to a halt.

Ahead of her, Craddock was lying sprawled on the ground.

Phyllis ran towards the dog, dropping painfully to her knees. His eyes were closed but his whole body was shaking, as if he was having some kind of seizure, and she saw vomit dribbling out of his mouth.

'Craddock!' Phyllis cried, and for the second time in her life, she felt her heart break.

Chapter Eighteen

Nova

Nova walked into the office and placed the box of crafts on her desk. 'Has something happened with Phyllis? I saw her running out just now looking—'

'Nova, sit down.'

Sandy's face was grim, and Nova swallowed. Was Sandy about to tell her she was being sacked? Or worse, had the council already decided to close the community centre? She sat in her chair, waiting for Sandy to speak again.

'A lady has just been to see me and made some very serious allegations. She said that you went to her house after her mother-in-law died, accompanied by Phyllis and what sounds like Arthur Robinson, and accused her husband of theft. Is this true?'

Nova felt a wave of sickness wash over her. No, no, no, this couldn't be happening.

'Sandy, I can explain. I never meant for—'

'I don't want excuses, just tell me. Did you or didn't you visit Michael Watkins's house?'

Nova felt her cheeks burn. 'I did.'

'Shit!' Sandy reached for the worry beads round her wrist and began clicking them. 'What were you thinking? You knew the police were investigating the missing money, so why did you stick your nose in?'

'I didn't mean to get involved. We only went to the house because Phyllis said that Michael had died, and I wanted to pay my respects. But then when we got there, Phyllis started asking questions about him.'

'You realise this is a breach of our data protection policy?' Sandy said, lowering her voice. 'The three of you used a visitor's private address from our records, which I think is almost definitely illegal.'

'Oh God, I'd not thought about that.'

'No, clearly you didn't think about anything.' Sandy sank back in her chair and pulled off her glasses, rubbing her eyes. 'I thought things couldn't get any worse after the incidents with Beryl, but then the roof money was stolen, and now this. You realise you might have just driven the final nail into the community centre's coffin?'

'I'm so sorry.'

'I took a chance on you, Nova. Even after your old boss told me what had happened in London, I still gave you a go here. And this is how you repay me.'

'Sandy, I'm—'

'I need to report this to the council, but in the meantime, you're suspended with immediate effect.'

'No! Please, can't we find another solution?'

'You haven't left me with any other choice!' The woman's voice had risen. 'Tina wanted me to sack you for gross misconduct when you left the office unlocked, but I defended you. And within twenty-four hours, you broke data protection and upset a grieving woman so much that she's making a formal complaint against you.'

'I was trying to help recover the money,' Nova said, although she realised how pathetic that sounded.

'I've got to call Tina now and tell her what's happened. I'll let you know the outcome in due course, but I think you need to prepare yourself for the worst.'

'Please, Sandy . . .'

'You need to leave, Nova. And for Pete's sake, quit this amateur detective nonsense and try not to do anything else that might put the centre at risk.'

Nova opened her mouth to try and make one last defence, but tears were pricking at her eyes, so she grabbed her coat and bag and hurried out of the centre.

Her car was parked outside, but rather than getting into it, she headed out onto the main road and down the hill. The grim reality of Nova's situation hit her with every step. She'd known it was risky going to Michael's house, but she'd never considered what she was doing was illegal. What was Craig going to say when he found out? Plus, Pamela and David would no doubt be furious with her causing more problems before the wedding. And then there was the community centre. Had Nova really just put the final nail in its coffin? How could she have been so stupid? For a second, Nova wanted nothing more than to call her dad and get his advice, and then she remembered and the tears started to fall.

Nova's phone vibrated in her pocket, and she pulled it out. Arthur's name flashed up on her screen, and Nova's stomach curled. If Sandy found out she'd been involved in a pensioner and a teenager going to visit a potentially dangerous private investigator . . . Well, the consequences weren't worth thinking about. She stuffed the phone back into her pocket without answering.

Nova wasn't sure where she was walking, her vision blurred by tears, but eventually she found herself at the beach. What she needed more than anything was some space so she could clear her head and think straight. But as she walked down the steps onto the sand, she saw a familiar hunched figure standing on the shoreline, facing out to sea. At the sight of Phyllis, Nova felt a flash of anger. If the old woman hadn't acted like a crazed amateur detective, then none of this would have happened.

'Phyllis!' she shouted.

The woman didn't turn around and Nova marched towards her.

'Do you have any idea the trouble your snooping has caused me? Cynthia has made a formal complaint to Sandy and now my job is . . .'

Nova stopped.

'Phyllis, where's Craddock?'

She still didn't answer, staring out at the crashing waves.

'What happened? What's wrong?'

'He's sick . . .' Phyllis's voice was a croak.

'Oh my God, I'm so sorry. Is he at the vet's?'

The older woman nodded, her eyes glistening.

'Did they say what might be wrong with him? Is it his age or—'

'He's been poisoned.'

'Shit!'

'It was *her*.' Phyllis turned to look at Nova, her face hard. 'Cynthia was at the community centre just before it happened. She must have poisoned him on her way out.'

'Look, I can see why you might think that, but I'm sure Cynthia wouldn't have done anything that awful, especially not in broad daylight.'

'Of course she would! This is a woman who's killed her mother-in-law and made her own husband disappear. She's more than capable of trying to . . .'

Phyllis trailed off, clearly unable to say the words. Nova watched her take a deep breath.

'She's sending us a message. She knows we're onto her and this is her way of telling us to back off.'

'Phyllis, I know you're upset right now, but do you think that maybe there's another explanation? Perhaps Craddock ate something dodgy?'

Phyllis shook her head. 'Trust me, I know this isn't accidental. The vet is doing a toxicology test, but I bet you it's either strychnine, which would explain the tremors, or cyanide, which is fast acting. Arsenic's unlikely as it needs to be dissolved in hot liquid.'

Nova was about to ask how she knew so much about poison, then stopped. Of course: Agatha Christie. 'Look, it's freezing out here, let's get you home. Is your house far?'

'I'm not going back there without Craddock,' Phyllis said. 'I *can't* go back without him.'

Nova heard a tremble in the woman's voice, despite her determined words. 'Okay, I understand. We can wait here.'

Phyllis turned back to the sea and Nova stood next to her, staring out at the churning grey water. For a few minutes neither of them spoke, and the only sound was the crash of the surf and the scream of seagulls. Then Phyllis turned to look at Nova again.

'I know you all think I'm a sad, lonely old lady with an overactive imagination, but you need to be careful. If Cynthia's coming after me then she might come after you too. None of us are safe until we can prove what she's done.'

Chapter Nineteen

Nova

For the next two hours, the pair stood in silence on the beach, being battered by icy wind and, at one point, driving rain. Nova was wearing her red coat and a beret, both of which were soon soaked through, causing her teeth to chatter. She was beginning to worry that she and Phyllis might catch pneumonia when the vet finally called to say that Craddock was stable but still very unwell. As far as Nova could hear, the vet was waiting for the full toxicology report, but his best bet was poisoning by something called theobromine. He wanted to keep Craddock in overnight and told Phyllis he'd call her in the morning with more news.

Nova worried that Phyllis might insist on staying on the beach all night, but thankfully she came off the phone and immediately walked off the beach, without so much as a thank-you or good-bye. Still, Nova was concerned about the poor woman. She didn't know much about Phyllis's personal life, but she suspected she was quite isolated, and so goodness knows what she'd do if Craddock didn't pull through.

It was gone six by the time Nova got back to the house, freezing and desperate to sink into a hot bath. But no sooner had she walked through the front door than she found Craig waiting for her in the hall.

'Hey, where have you been? Why are you soaking?'

'It's a long story.'

'Well, I'm afraid it's going to have to wait, as Mum wants us to leave in fifteen minutes.'

'Where are we going?'

Craig tapped Nova's forehead affectionately. 'It's pub quiz night, remember? Your last before you officially become a Pritchard!'

Nova's heart sank. 'Oh love, I've had a hideous day. Can't we just stay at home, there's something I need to—'

'I hope you're not trying to wiggle out of it again,' Pamela said, sweeping into the hall. 'Come on, lazybones, you have to come tonight, it's going to be a special one.' She gave Nova a dramatic wink. 'You might want to get changed and brush your hair first though.'

Nova ran a self-conscious hand through her wet, windswept hair.

'I think you look sexy, like a wild Cornish mermaid,' Craig said, smiling and kissing her. 'But I'm afraid we do have to go: Mum's been plotting something.'

Nova soon learned what Pamela's plot was when they walked into the Anchor thirty minutes later to a roar of 'surprise!' and pink confetti being thrown in her eyes.

'I know you didn't want a hen do but you have to do *something* to celebrate your last days as an unmarried woman,' Pamela said. 'So, I invited a few ladies along to celebrate.'

'A few ladies' turned out to be about fifteen of Pamela's friends, most of whom Nova had never met before, plus a couple of Craig's old schoolmates. She was relieved to see Lauren's face among the crowd.

'Sorry, I wanted to warn you, but Mum swore me to secrecy and you know what she's like,' Craig whispered, putting his arm round Nova's shoulder. 'Although I did make her promise no penis straws.'

'You're not deserting me here, are you?' Nova said and Craig laughed.

'Of course not. Just put up with the fuss for a bit and then it's the pub quiz, and everyone will be so focused on winning that you can escape and join me.'

Nova was handed a glass of prosecco, and before she knew it, she had a 'Bride-to-be' sash thrown over her and a bright pink veil on her head.

'I know you refuse to wear a veil at the wedding, but you have to wear it tonight,' Pamela said, and Nova thought she saw a glint of victory in the woman's eyes.

Nova fixed a smile on her face and launched into small talk about wedding menus (smoked salmon to start, beef or chicken and then a trio of desserts), flowers (Pamela was in charge) and honeymoon plans (on hold, as they were saving up for a house). After half an hour, she made her excuses and slunk off to the toilet. Nova's head was thumping, not helped by the two glasses of prosecco she'd downed in quick succession, and she'd still not warmed up from her freezing afternoon on the beach with Phyllis. Nova was therefore relieved to step into the relative quiet and solitude of the loos. Yet no sooner had the door swung closed behind her than it opened again. Nova returned the rigid smile to her face, then relaxed when she saw it was Lauren.

'Thank God it's only you.'

'How are you holding up?'

'I don't mean to sound ungrateful, but this is literally my idea of hell.'

Lauren chuckled. 'I did try and tell Pamela, but she wasn't hearing any of it.'

'I was going to say it's sweet of her to go to all this effort, but I'm starting to think she's done it on purpose to get her revenge over the stupid wedding photographer mess up.'

'Oh yeah, I heard about that,' Lauren said, wincing.

'I don't even know anyone here, it's all Pamela's friends.'

'When are your London mates coming down for the wedding?'

'I only invited a handful, and they're getting the train down on Saturday morning. We're planning to have a celebration party in London in the spring, which will be more my style than Pamela and David's.'

'Good idea. And when's your mum arriving?'

'On Friday,' Nova said, feeling a swell of warmth at the thought. 'She's got two internal flights, then she's flying from Bogotá to Barcelona overnight on Thursday, then from Barcelona to Bristol on Friday morning.'

'You must be so excited to see her.'

'I really am.'

Lauren paused for a moment, chewing her lip. 'Look, I didn't want to have to bring this up tonight at your hen do—'

'Unofficial hen do,' Nova interrupted with a smile.

'Sandy told me about what happened today with Michael Watkins's wife.'

'Ah, yes,' Nova said, the smile disappearing from her face. 'I'm sorry, Lauren. I realise it was stupid of me to go to her house, but I honestly had no idea it was a data protection breach.'

'You don't have to apologise to *me*. I just can't believe Sandy suspended you.'

'I really messed up.' Nova shook her head and then winced at the thumping pain.

'Sandy had another meeting with Tina at the council this afternoon,' Lauren said. 'She came back with a face like thunder.'

'Did she tell you what Tina said?'

'No, but when I said I was coming here tonight, she asked me to tell you that you need to go in for a meeting at nine a.m. tomorrow.'

'Shit,' Nova said, running a hand through her hair and knocking the stupid veil off. 'This is it, Lauren. She's going to fire me.'

'Christ, I'm so sorry.'

Nova gave a small, dry laugh. 'Sacked two days before my wedding. That must be some sort of record.'

'What did Craig say?'

'I've not had a chance to tell him yet, we've not been alone all day.'

'Nova, you have to tell him soon. You know how fast gossip travels round St Tredock, and he'll be upset if he hears about it from someone else.'

Outside the door, Nova could hear the landlord on the microphone, telling people to get their drinks in before the quiz started.

'You're right, I'll talk to him now.'

'Okay, good luck. I'll get us both another drink.'

Nova headed back out to the pub. It was packed now, people taking their seats for the quiz. One of Pamela's friends signalled for Nova to join them, but she pretended not to notice and headed towards Craig, who was standing at the bar with Sam, Lauren's boyfriend.

'Can I have a quick word, Craig?'

'Now? I'm just getting a round in, we're starting in a minute.'

'Please, it's important.'

'Okay, let's go outside where it's quieter.'

'You two off for a quickie, are you?' Sam said, and there was a burst of raucous laughter from the lads standing around them.

Nova grabbed her coat, and they headed outside. It was a clear evening, bitterly cold, and the sky was alive with stars. Behind them, she could hear the waves crashing against the harbour wall.

'What is it?' Craig asked. 'Are you okay?'

'No, not really.' Nova cleared her throat. 'I've been suspended from work, and I think they're going to fire me.'

'What? Those bastards!' Craig exploded. 'They can't sack you for leaving the office unlocked, there's no proof you even—'

'It wasn't just that,' Nova interrupted. 'I did something else.'

'What?' Craig was staring at her, his hazel eyes intense on her face.

'You know the Michael guy I told you about, the one who disappeared from the book club and went missing?'

'The murder suspect?'

'Yeah, him. Well, I went to his house with a few members of the book club—'

'You did *what*?'

'And then we ended up speaking to his wife about Michael, and she's reported me to Sandy for harassment.'

'Bloody hell!' Craig swore, his cheeks flushing red. 'Why would you go to the house of a suspected murderer?'

'I didn't know he was a suspect at the time, and I thought we could help get the money back for the community centre. Plus, I had Phyllis, Arthur and Craddock with me.'

'Two pensioners and a decrepit dog? Nova, anything could have happened to you.'

'I wasn't in danger, I promise,' she said, but Craig was pacing back and forth, not listening.

'After everything that happened with Declan, you promised me you'd be more careful and not take any risks at work, and yet here we are again. I just don't understand, Nova; it's like you *want* to create drama.'

'I wasn't trying to create drama,' Nova said, hearing an unfamiliar hardness in her voice.

'Really? Because it's less than seventy-two hours until our wedding and you've just been suspended from your job for, what, spying? That feels like drama to me.'

There was a long moment of silence, as chilly as the October night air.

'Look, I'm sorry about the suspension,' Nova said, trying to keep her voice calm. 'But I won't apologise for trying to help the community centre. My parents always taught me to fight for what matters.'

Craig let out a long sigh, and Nova saw the anger deflate with his shoulders. 'I just don't want anything else bad to happen to you. After everything in London, when you nearly . . .' He stopped, his voice catching with emotion. 'I love you so much, Nova, and I just want to keep you safe.'

'I *am* safe here. This wasn't like last time, I promise,' she said, as Craig opened his arms and pulled her into a hug.

She pressed her head against his chest, feeling his arms wrapped tightly around her. It was the most wonderful sensation, like she was insulated against the problems of the world.

'I'm sorry you're having to go through all of this at work, but please just try and avoid any more drama between now and Saturday, okay? I really want to get you down the aisle in one piece.' Craig gave a soft laugh and then released her from the hug. 'Come on, let's get back inside.'

He moved towards the door, but Nova stayed where she was.

'Do you mind if I slip off home? I've got a pounding headache, and I have to meet with Sandy first thing tomorrow.'

Craig looked back to her. 'Really? I know my mum can be a lot sometimes, but she's gone to a load of trouble arranging tonight for you.'

'I know she has, but I'd made it very clear I didn't want a hen do.'

She could tell Craig wanted to say something else, but he just shrugged. 'Fine, whatever you want. Text me when you get home, okay?'

He turned and pulled open the pub door, disappearing inside without looking back.

Chapter Twenty

Arthur

On Thursday morning, Arthur arrived at the community centre at ten for his weekly Carers Support Group coffee morning. He'd been coming every week since Esi first started losing her eyesight and was always grateful for the hour spent chatting with others who understood the challenges, frustrations and rewards of being a full-time carer. But this morning, as he walked into the centre, he found his fellow group members milling round the lobby.

'Morning, Arthur, how are you?' asked Dill, another regular. 'How's Esi?'

'I've left her listening to a Beverly Jenkins audiobook so she's grand. How's Mick?'

Dill smiled and shrugged, an expression familiar to anyone in the support group, and one that held a hundred emotions. Arthur nodded.

'What's going on here?'

'They're running late setting up. Understaffed, apparently.'

Arthur put his head through the door of the main hall and saw it was empty.

'Sorry, excuse me, coming through.'

He turned round to see Nova staggering down the corridor, carrying the tea urn.

'Sorry for the delay, we'll be ready in a tick.'

'What's going on?' he asked her, following her into the hall.

'Sandy hasn't turned up.'

'That's unlike her, is she ill?'

'I don't know, I can't get hold of her.' Nova put the tea urn down and plugged it in. 'I'm not even meant to be working today; I've been suspended.'

'Suspended! But why?'

'Long story. Do you mind helping me get the chairs out?'

'Of course.'

Nova gave him a grateful smile as they headed towards the store cupboard. 'How did it go with the private investigator yesterday? Sorry I didn't call you back, but I had a full-on day.'

'It was interesting. Ash found a file on his computer labelled "Michael Watkins".'

'Oh, wow! What's in it?'

'Turns out it's password protected, so we can't open it. Ash is trying to get in though; that boy is a whiz with computers.'

'I wonder why Pierce had a file on Michael?'

'My guess is Phyllis was right and Cynthia employed him to do some digging into Michael. Maybe that's how she found out he was having an affair?'

'I suppose,' Nova said, but she didn't sound convinced. 'Either way, we need to stop our investigation into Michael and Cynthia.'

'Why? We're just getting somewhere, especially if Ash can hack into this file.'

'It's too risky. Cynthia made a formal complaint to Sandy about us; that's why I've been suspended. Plus, yesterday Craddock was really sick, and Phyllis thinks Cynthia poisoned him.'

'What?' Arthur almost dropped the chair he was carrying. 'Why would Cynthia poison Craddock?'

'Phyllis thinks she was trying to warn her off and she'll be coming for us next. Personally, I'm not so sure. You know what Craddock's like, he'll steal any food he can get his paws on, so he might have poisoned himself.'

'But still, if Cynthia's complained about us then we've obviously spooked her. She's clearly trying to hide something, which is all the more reason to keep investigating her.'

'No, Arthur. Whatever's going on, we need to leave it to the police. I've promised Sandy I'll stop.'

Arthur wanted to argue, but Nova had a determined expression on her face, so he kept quiet. Still, if they backed off now then Cynthia would elope with her lover, and they might never find out what had happened to Michael and the missing money.

'Is Nova Davies around?' a voice called out from the lobby.

'I'm in here. Hang on a . . . Oh, hi Yusaf.'

Arthur looked round to see PC Khan and another uniformed police officer walking into the hall.

'Is this about the stolen money?' Nova asked. 'I'm afraid Sandy isn't here yet so—'

'This isn't about the money,' Yusaf said. 'I need you to come down to the station with me and answer a few questions.'

Nova's face had gone pale. 'Is this about the data protection breach? I swear, I didn't realise it was illegal, it was a genuine mistake.'

'Data protection? No, it's not that either,' Yusaf said, looking impatient. 'This is about Sandy.'

'Sandy? Why, where is she?'

Yusaf took a moment before he answered. 'She's in the hospital. She was attacked last night at her home.'

'What? No!' Arthur had known Sandy for more than twenty years, and she always seemed like a nice woman: overly emotional and frequently stressed, but popular with everyone. Who on earth would want to attack her?

'Is she okay?' Nova asked.

'She's shaken, but she'll be fine.'

'My God, poor Sandy. Was it a robbery?'

Yusaf shook his head. 'It doesn't seem so. But if you can come to the station with us, we'll discuss this further.'

'I'd love to come and help but now's not a great time,' Nova said. 'Sandy isn't here, obviously, and Lauren isn't in yet. Can I wait until—'

'No, I'm afraid I need you to come with us now,' the other officer said, in a tone that stopped any argument.

'Why do you want to talk to her?' Arthur asked.

'One of the victim's neighbours said she saw an individual running away from Sandy's house around the time of the attack.'

'So, I still don't understand what that has to do with Nova.'

'The neighbour said the person was wearing a bright red coat.'

For a second, none of them spoke and Arthur saw Nova's eyes go wide.

'You think it was . . . me?' she stuttered. 'I'd never hurt Sandy.'

'Where were you between 10:50 and 11:20 p.m. last night?' the second officer asked Nova.

'I was at home, asleep in bed.'

'And do you have an alibi for that time period?'

'No, Craig and his parents were at the pub quiz.'

'And why weren't you with them?'

'I left early, I had a headache,' Nova said, her voice rising in panic.

'Nova, we need you to come to the station with us,' Yusaf said, his tone gentle but insistent. 'It would be much easier if you came willingly, *please*.'

'Okay, fine.' Nova looked around her, flustered. 'I just don't know what to do about this place, I can't leave everyone here unsupervised.'

'Don't worry, I can hold the fort until Lauren arrives,' Arthur said.

'Are you sure? She should be here soon.'

'Come on, let's get going,' the second officer said, taking Nova's arm.

The young woman allowed herself to be led towards the exit, but as she reached the door, she turned back to Arthur.

'You need to speak to Phyllis. Tell her that her theory might be correct after all.'

Chapter Twenty-One

Phyllis

Phyllis sat on the sofa, an embroidery needle motionless in her hand, her eyes fixed on the telephone. The vet had said he'd call her landline with an update this morning, and so Phyllis had been sitting by the telephone since five a.m. She was gasping for a cup of tea and her bladder was uncomfortably full, but she wouldn't, couldn't, dare move in case the phone rang while she was out of the room.

Phyllis had never been so aware of the deafening silence of her home. She may have lived here her entire life, but for the first sixty-five years she'd had her mother as a companion, a woman who either prayed loudly or complained loudly from the moment she woke to the moment she went to sleep. Even on her deathbed, Eliza Hudson had barely drawn breath between criticising Phyllis and demanding water. When she finally passed away, Phyllis had spent a week echoing round the empty cottage, and then the day after her mother's funeral, she'd gone to the dog shelter and found a small, neglected English bulldog puppy. Phyllis had been accompanied by Craddock's wheezes, snorts and farts ever since. But today, the only sound was the agonising tick of the carriage clock on the mantelpiece, tormenting Phyllis with its slow progress.

The clock said it was 10:35. This was well and truly mid-morning so why hadn't the vet rung yet? Was the fact he hadn't bad news? Did that mean . . .

Phyllis closed her eyes to try and block out the questions, but that was no help. All she could see was Craddock yesterday: his laboured, ragged breaths, the tremors that shook his whole body and the convulsions as he vomited. Phyllis opened her eyes and returned her attention to the mutinous phone.

There was a ringing sound, piercing the silence, and Phyllis's hand shot out to grab the handset.

'Hello?'

Her word was met with the dead tone of the phone line. Then the ring sounded again and she groaned. It was the damn doorbell, not the phone. For a moment, Phyllis considered ignoring it, but what if it was the vet, coming to tell her the bad news in person? She got to her feet and hurried to the front door. Through the frosted glass she could make out a single dark silhouette on the other side. Her hand was shaking so much she could barely pull back the chain and turn the lock. She took a deep breath, bracing herself for the moment when the bottom fell out of her world. But when she pulled the door back, she saw not the fresh-faced young vet, but the weathered mug of Arthur Robinson.

'What do you want?' Even in the midst of her grief, Phyllis knew that wasn't a particularly polite welcome, but she didn't have time for social callers right now.

'Morning, Phyllis,' Arthur said. 'I was wondering if I could pop in and—'

'Now's not a good time.' Phyllis stepped back and shut the door in his face. The phone was still silent, but it could ring at any moment and what if she didn't get there in time?

'It's about Nova,' Arthur called through the glass. 'She's been arrested.'

Phyllis paused in the hallway. Her eyes flicked towards the living room, but then she turned and pulled the door open again. 'What are you talking about, man?'

'Just now, at the community centre. Sandy was attacked last night, and the police think Nova did it.'

'What? That girl's terrified of her own shadow; she couldn't hurt a fly. Why do the cops think it was her?'

'Someone wearing a red coat was seen outside Sandy's house around the time of the attack. Nova said I needed to speak to you. She said, "Tell Phyllis her theory might be right."'

'Of course I'm bloody right,' Phyllis muttered. 'Okay, you'd better come in. But take your shoes off, I don't want your filthy boots all over my carpet.'

Phyllis hurried back to the phone. Arthur was so large that he had to stoop to get through her door, and then he stood in the middle of the room, his eyes surveying the ancient furniture and bare walls, with nothing but a large wooden crucifix as decoration. Phyllis's mother had made no secret of the fact she regretted getting married and having a child as opposed to becoming a nun, which she believed was her true calling, and so she'd decorated her home as if it were a particularly austere convent.

'It's a . . . lovely place you have here,' Arthur mumbled.

'It does me fine.'

Phyllis supposed she could have redecorated after her mother died, but given she never had visitors, she'd not seen the point.

'You can take a seat.'

Arthur began to move towards the chair by the gas fire that Craddock liked to sleep in.

'Not that one!'

Arthur nodded and came to sit next to her on the hard sofa. Phyllis shuffled along so she didn't have to touch him.

'I'm sorry to hear about Craddock,' he said gruffly.

Phyllis looked away so he wouldn't see the anguish that she knew was creasing her face at that name.

'Is he still with the vet?'

'Yes.'

'Nova told me you thought Cynthia Watkins might have something to do with it.'

Phyllis turned back to look at Arthur. 'That woman poisoned him. I saw her at the community centre, and the minute she left, Craddock got ill.'

She waited for Arthur to tell her she was being paranoid, as the vet and Nova had done yesterday, but he just shook his head. 'It isn't right, hurting a defenceless animal like that. Craddock never did anyone any harm.'

'I told Nova that Cynthia was sending me a message to back off and stop investigating. I told her she had to be careful, that Cynthia would come after her too. And now look what's happened.'

Arthur nodded, taking it in, and as he did, Phyllis remembered his mission yesterday.

'What happened with the private investigator?'

She listened as Arthur told her about his meeting and Ash finding the Michael file on the computer, and despite her grief over Craddock, Phyllis couldn't help but feel a flicker of excitement about the latest evidence. Surely this proved that Cynthia had employed

Graham Pierce to investigate Michael, and potentially even more than that?

'We have to find out what's in that file,' she said when Arthur had finished. 'It could contain the evidence we need to show Cynthia's a murderer and a kidnapper.'

Arthur wrinkled his nose. 'Graham Pierce struck me as more of a sitting-in-the-car, taking-photos-and-eating-KitKats kind of private investigator, as opposed to a murdering-and-kidnapping one. My guess is Cynthia employed him to find out about Michael's lover. But I agree we need to get into the file, and if we can find out where this mistress lives, I reckon we might be able to find Michael too.'

Phyllis snorted. 'How many times do I have to tell you, Michael's not with his mistress! There's not a scrap of evidence to suggest a lover exists; that was just Cynthia trying to frame him for the murder.'

'But there's no real evidence to back up your theory either,' Arthur said. 'I know you want to prove Cynthia's a murderer, but do you think, perhaps, you've got a bit carried away with it all?'

Phyllis let out a long sigh. More than ever, she now knew how Miss Marple must have felt when people repeatedly underestimated her, dismissing her theories as mere gossip and conjecture. But dear Jane knew that if you had a theory that fits every fact, then it must be the correct one.

'Let's look at the facts again, shall we? Fact one: we know that Michael was in huge debt and had been forced to sell their house and move in with his mother, something that can't have delighted Cynthia. Fact two: we know that Cynthia's been having an affair with a man she's planning on leaving the country with.'

'I told you it always comes down to love,' Arthur muttered.

'Fact three: we know that she lied about being at her sister's the night her mother-in-law was killed. Fact four: we now know, thanks to you and Ash, that she'd employed the services of a private investigator who has a folder dedicated to Michael on his computer, and now Michael has gone missing and maybe even worse. Fact five: we know that, after discovering me at the wake, Cynthia threatened to "deal with me later", and within twenty-four hours Craddock was poisoned.'

'Did she really say that?'

'And fact six: we know that Cynthia was given confirmation by Sandy that Nova was her employee at the community centre, and that same day, Sandy was brutally attacked by a person wearing a coat like Nova's. All of these things are concrete facts, and they all suggest that Cynthia is behind the recent series of crimes.'

Phyllis leaned back on the sofa, waiting for Arthur to finally admit defeat and tell her she was correct. But the man was still frowning.

'One thing I don't understand is how the missing money fits into it all.'

Phyllis bit her lip; she'd been wondering the same thing, and she had a theory, even if there were no facts to back it up. *Yet*.

'I think the theft of the money might be the only part of the whole affair that wasn't planned and executed by Cynthia. It's my suspicion that the text Michael received during our book club meeting was somehow alerting him to the fact that Cynthia had killed his mother and she or Graham Pierce were coming after him, and so Michael decided to run away. As he was leaving the centre, he saw the office door was unlocked, took a chance and grabbed the petty cash tin, hoping it would contain some money to help him escape. Unfortunately, that wasn't to be. Whether Graham and Cynthia captured him in St Tredock and then dumped his car in Bodmin to confuse the police, or whether Michael made it as far as the moor before they caught up with him, I don't know. But either way, I think if we're to have any chance of recovering that money, we have to work out where Michael is.'

It was a moment before Arthur spoke again, and Phyllis could see him processing everything she'd just said.

'Suppose you're correct,' he said eventually. 'Suppose Cynthia did commit all the other crimes, including attacking Sandy and—'

Arthur didn't get any further as he was interrupted by a shrill ring. This time Phyllis knew it was the phone and she snatched the handset up. 'Hello?'

'Hi Phyllis, this is Sheldon from Port Pets.'

'How is he? What's the news?' The words tumbled out of her.

'I'm pleased to say Craddock's doing much better; he's more alert this morning and has eaten breakfast.'

'Really?' Phyllis heard herself gasp.

'We got the toxicology report back and it confirmed my suspicion. Craddock must have eaten chocolate, possibly with caffeine in it, too, and he had theobromine poisoning. But thanks to your quick reactions in getting him here so fast, we managed to treat him before there was any permanent damage. He's a very lucky dog.'

Phyllis hadn't realised she'd been holding her breath, and she released it slowly. 'Thank you.'

'I want to keep him in for a bit longer, until he's had a normal bowel movement, but you should be able to collect him at the end of the day.'

'End of day . . . okay . . . Bye.'

Phyllis hung up the phone. Her heart was racing at one hundred miles an hour and she closed her eyes.

'Phyllis?'

She startled and opened her eyes to see Arthur looking at her with concern.

'He's going to be all right,' she said, her voice a whisper. 'The vet says he's going to be okay.'

'Oh, Phyllis, I'm so relieved.'

She felt a tear sting the corner of her eye and squeezed them shut again. Phyllis was not a crier. She hadn't cried when her mother died, or at the woman's funeral. In fact, the last time she'd cried was almost sixty years ago, on the day she—

'It's all right, Phyllis. You can let it out.'

Arthur's voice was soft, and she felt more tears pressing behind her eyelids. She lifted her hand to her face and found her cheeks were wet. For a moment, she considered shouting at Arthur, demanding he leave her alone and never come back. But instead, Phyllis leaned forwards and allowed herself to sob.

Chapter Twenty-Two

Nova

Nova walked out of the police station with her head low, a silent Craig at her side. He'd arrived several hours ago with his parents' solicitor, Bob, a balding man with halitosis who had stared at Nova's chest but got her released without charge, although Yusaf had made it very clear she was still a person of interest. Even though Nova knew she was innocent, she felt as if she had a guilty sign hanging above her head as she followed Craig to the car.

'Jeez, Nova,' he said, once the doors were closed, his voice more weary than angry. 'I thought we'd agreed no more drama?'

'This isn't my fault, Craig. I didn't attack Sandy.'

'I know you didn't,' he said as he started the engine and reversed out of the space. 'I just don't get the coat thing. From what Bob told me, it sounds like this neighbour described your coat exactly. And it's not like there are loads of people walking round St Tredock in a bright red furry coat.'

'I wasn't even wearing that coat to the pub last night. I left it at home, as it was soaking wet. Maybe someone broke into the house and stole it?'

Craig raised an eyebrow. 'And then broke back in to return it before I got home at half eleven? I think that's pretty unlikely; unless you left the door unlocked again?'

Nova heard the slight accusation in the word *again* and looked out the window. She wished with all her heart that her parents were here right now, to hug her and tell her everything was going to be all right.

'Mum's completely freaking out, as you can imagine,' Craig said. 'She spent the morning checking the wedding insurance documents to see if it covers "bride being arrested for assault".'

'I'm sorry.' Nova knew it sounded limp, but she'd said the word so many times lately, it had started to lose its meaning.

They were turning left at the roundabout, heading away from St Tredock, and Nova frowned.

'Why are we going this way? I need to get back to the community centre, Lauren's going to be having a nightmare on her own.'

'The centre's closed. Lauren texted me earlier and said the council have shut it down until further notice.'

'What? They can't do that!'

'Sandy's in hospital and you've been suspended; Lauren can hardly run the place on her own.'

'Oh my God,' Nova said, putting her hands over her face. 'This is all my fault.'

'No, it's not, babe. The fate of the community centre doesn't sit on your shoulders. It was struggling long before you moved here.'

'But still, if I hadn't been stupid enough to get suspended then we could have kept it going until Sandy was well enough to return. What's going to happen to the food bank tomorrow? And where are people like Phyllis and Arthur going to go?'

Next to her, she heard Craig sigh. 'Is that seriously your biggest worry right now?'

She turned to look at him sharply. 'What do you mean?'

'You've just spent hours at the police station being questioned about an assault, and yet you're more concerned about a couple of pensioners not being able to go to their coffee mornings.'

'The community centre is there for a lot more than just hosting coffee mornings, Craig. There are people in this town who can't afford to heat their homes and come to keep warm; people who are lonely and isolated and have literally nowhere else to go.'

'There are plenty of cafes in St Tredock.'

Nova glared at him, not quite believing she had to explain this to her own fiancé, of all people. 'Cafes cost money; money lots of people don't have. The community centre is free.'

Craig must have heard the anger in her voice, as he shrugged. 'Sure, and obviously I don't want it to close. All I'm saying is that right now, we have more pressing things to think about, like the fact we're getting married in less than forty-eight hours. Assuming you still want to get married, that is?'

His question hung in the air for a moment before Nova answered. 'Of course I do.'

'Are you sure? Because you've been completely distracted for the past few weeks.'

'I'm just stressed, Craig. If you hadn't noticed, there's been a lot going on for me at work.'

'Is that all it is? Because Mum said when you went to your final dress fitting last weekend, you looked like you were about to burst into tears. Please, tell me, are you having second thoughts?'

Nova remembered that moment in the wedding dress shop: standing in front of the mirror in that huge white blancmange and feeling like she couldn't breathe. Then she remembered what Lauren had said the other day about being more honest with Craig about her feelings.

'I'm not having second thoughts. But, if I'm being completely honest, there are moments when it feels like this wedding is more about what your mum wants than what *we* want.'

'Is this about the church thing?' Craig said. 'I told you, I'm sorry we had to give in on that, but it means a lot to my parents; they got married in St Piran's and so did my grandparents. I thought you said you were okay with it?'

'It's not just the church: it's also the reception and the flowers and my dress, and even my hen do, for God's sake. Your mum has made so many of the decisions for us and—'

'She's only made decisions because you wouldn't,' Craig snapped. 'My mum's worked her arse off to give us a once-in-a-lifetime wedding.'

'But a wedding of whose lifetime? Because it's certainly not the big day I dreamed of.'

'Well, then you should have been more proactive in organising it, shouldn't you? Because I think it's a bit rich you complaining now, given the only thing you've done is mess up the photographer and get yourself arrested right before the wedding.'

Nova felt the words like a slap. 'Is that really what you think?'

Craig groaned. 'No, of course not. Sorry, I'm just stressed too; I had a shit ton of work today and could have done without spending my afternoon sitting in the police station.'

Nova didn't reply, and they drove the last mile in silence. She was relieved to see neither Pamela's nor David's car in the driveway when they pulled up at the house. Nova opened her door, but Craig kept the engine running.

'Are you coming in?'

'I need to go back to the garage for a couple of hours and catch up on some work. I'll see you later, okay?'

Nova thought about asking him to stay then stopped herself. They needed a bit of time apart to calm down before one of them said something they'd regret.

'Okay, bye,' she said, and she watched as Craig drove off, his tires sending gravel flying.

As soon as she got into the house, Nova tried calling her mum, but there was no answer; she must already be on her first flight. Still, at least she'd be in Cornwall tomorrow; Nova couldn't wait to melt into her mum's arms for the longest hug.

She had a shower and was getting dressed again when she heard the doorbell ring. When she opened the door, Lauren was standing on the doorstep, brandishing a bottle of wine.

'I thought you could do with this,' she said.

Nova smiled and ushered her through to the kitchen. 'Thanks for coming over. Have you heard any more news on Sandy?'

'I've just been to see her in the hospital.'

'How is she?'

'In remarkably good spirits, all things considered. You should see how many bunches of flowers she's got; I think she's quite enjoying all the fuss.'

'Can she remember anything about the person who attacked her?'

Lauren shook her head. 'Unfortunately not. She says she was going upstairs to bed when she heard a noise at the front door, and when she opened it, someone pushed her and she fell backwards. But she said she couldn't see their face, as it was dark outside and they were wearing a hood.'

'The poor woman,' Nova said, pouring wine into two glasses and handing one to Lauren. 'Does she really think it could have been me?'

Lauren took a sip before she answered. 'She doesn't *want* to think it was you.'

'But?'

'Sandy did say you were the only person she could think of who might have a motive to hurt her, given she'd just suspended you. Plus, her neighbour saw your red coat.'

'It wasn't my coat, Lauren; mine was here at the house, with me.'

'I know, that's what I told her. But I think after everything that's happened recently, with the missing money and now this . . .' She winced. 'You have to admit; from the outside it does all look a bit suspicious.'

Nova chewed her lip. Should she tell Lauren the book club's theory about Cynthia? But where to even begin. The whole thing would sound deranged, and the last thing she needed was Lauren thinking she'd lost the plot. Still, for a second, Nova allowed herself to ponder the idea that Cynthia might have attacked Sandy in order to frame her. It seemed far-fetched, but *if* the woman was capable of killing her own mother-in-law, getting rid of her husband and poisoning Craddock, maybe she was capable of hurting Sandy too?

'Is Craig not here?' Lauren asked, jolting Nova from her thoughts.

'No, he's at work. We just had an argument in the car, so we need a bit of space from each other right now.'

'Shit, I'm sorry to hear that. Wanna talk about it?'

Nova took a swig of wine. 'There's not much to say. I think Craig is pissed off at me for getting suspended, although he hasn't said it outright, and he asked if I still want to go ahead with the wedding.'

'Wow,' Lauren said, and Nova saw her eyes widen. 'What did you say?'

'I told him that I wanted to, of course. But I don't know if he's the one having second thoughts now.'

'Oh, love,' Lauren said, coming round to stand next to Nova.

'You've been through so much lately, and now this on top of every-thing else.'

'I just really wish my mum was here. And my dad too.'

'I get it. And I'm sorry Craig's being a knob. He should be sup-porting you now, not making you feel even worse.'

'It's not all his fault. I *have* been distracted lately, and I've not been focusing on the wedding like I should have been.'

'Do you want me to speak to him? I could have a gentle word and tell him how stressed you are, so he backs off a bit? Or I could have a not-so-gentle word and kick his arse for being an insensitive bastard?'

Nova laughed. 'Thanks for the offer, but we'll be okay. He's just stressed about everything too. Once Saturday is out of the way, I'm sure everything will calm down.'

'If you're sure?' Lauren said, and Nova nodded.

'I am. Now let's drink this wine and you can help me write my wedding speech.'

Chapter Twenty-Three

Nova

On Friday morning, Nova ate breakfast with Craig and his mum. The mood in the house had been tense last night, with Pamela barely able to look at Nova over dinner. Nova had made an effort to talk enthusiastically about the wedding, and had even managed to feign interest in a discussion about the groomsmen's boutonnieres, all the while reminding herself that soon she and Craig would move out to their own place and she wouldn't have to eat every meal with her mother-in-law.

'We're all set for the rehearsal later,' Pamela said, as she served seconds of bacon onto Craig's plate. 'I'm going to be setting up the flowers in the church from three, so you both just need to get there by six.'

'Dad and I have to finish up some urgent jobs at the garage, but we should be there around five-thirty,' Craig said. 'Nova, remember you've got to collect your mum from Bristol airport at one o'clock.'

'As if she'd forget her own mum!' Pamela said.

'I dunno, I wouldn't put it past Ditsy—'

'Don't call me that,' Nova interrupted. 'I'll get my mum.'

'Before you do, I've got some important jobs for you,' Pamela

said. 'Please can you finish making up the favours for me? It's ten sugared almonds per bag – five pink and five ivory – and then the orders
of service need folding. I'll pop back at lunchtime to collect them.'

'Consider it done.'

'Well, in that case I'd better be off. See you kids at the church
later.' Pamela headed out of the kitchen, leaving Nova and Craig
alone.

'I should get going too,' Craig said, eating the last bit of bacon on
his plate and standing up. 'Will you be all right on your own this
morning?'

'Of course. I've got plenty to be getting on with. Those sugared
almonds won't sort themselves.'

Craig smiled. 'Just as long as you keep out of trouble. I could do
without another trip to the police station today, so no more Nancy
Drew nonsense, okay?'

'I promise, my troublemaking days are over.'

Craig leaned down to kiss her, pinching the last piece of toast
from her plate as he left.

An hour later, Nova was sitting on the floor in the living room,
surrounded by sugared almonds and two hundred small silk bags,
each monogrammed with her and Craig's initials. Her mum was going to have an absolute field day when she saw these, Nova thought
with a smile. Maddy should be in Barcelona by now, waiting to catch
her flight to Bristol. The thought made Nova's stomach flip with excitement.

From outside, she heard the sound of footsteps on gravel. Surely
that wasn't Pamela back to collect the favours already? Nova sped up
her work, then heard a ring on the doorbell. She got up and walked
to the hall, pulling the door open.

Phyllis, Arthur and Ash were standing on the doorstep, while behind them Craddock was trying to eat Pamela's rhododendrons.

'What are you all doing here?'

'We wanted to check you're okay,' Arthur said.

Nova was taken aback. 'Thank you, that's very sweet. But how did you get my address?'

'I have my sources,' Phyllis said, tapping her nose. 'Are you going to invite us in? We have a complex case to discuss.'

Nova was about to say yes when she remembered her words to Craig just an hour ago. 'I'm afraid it's not a good time, I've got loads to do and—'

She got no further as Phyllis barged past her into the hallway.

'Okay, you can come in for a few minutes, but can you leave Craddock outside, as Craig's mum doesn't like—'

'I can't leave him, he's still recovering from being poisoned,' Phyllis said.

She was clearly not going to be dissuaded, so Nova might as well get this over with quickly, before Pamela returned.

'Come on through,' she said, leading the mismatched group into the living room. Craddock headed straight for the sugared almonds and managed to scoff several before Nova was able to pull him back and move the tubs out of the way. 'Please, take a seat.'

Ash and Arthur sat on one of the large sofas, while Phyllis took David's armchair, Craddock settling at her feet.

'So, how are you all—' Nova started, but Phyllis brushed the pleasantries aside.

'We need to discuss our next steps. Nova's been suspended, Sandy's in hospital and the community centre has been closed. Unless we can find the missing money, and fast, it may never open its doors again.'

'Phyllis, I—'

'Arthur and I had a long chat yesterday, and we agreed our best plan to find Michael and prove Cynthia's behind the crimes is to focus on the private investigator angle.'

'I don't remember agreeing to that,' Arthur said, but Phyllis ploughed on.

'The computer file is key to everything, so it's vital we get into it ASAP.' Phyllis turned her intense gaze on Ash, who sunk back into the sofa.

'I told you, I'm trying,' he stuttered. 'I've just downloaded a new piece of software; it's not strictly legal, but it might help.'

'Good boy,' Phyllis said, her eyes flashing with satisfaction at the words 'not strictly legal'. She turned her attention back to Nova. 'We also need to work out how to clear your name. Has Sandy remembered any more about her attack?'

'Apparently not; it was dark outside, and the figure pushed her as soon as she opened the door.'

'Hmm, that's most inconvenient.'

'How is Sandy?' Arthur asked.

'Okay, I think. No serious injuries, but it sounds like it was a nasty shock.'

'Cynthia's crafty, I'll give her that,' Phyllis said, absentmindedly stroking Craddock's head. 'She'd give Mr Symington a run for his money.'

'Who?' Arthur asked.

'Richard Symington, from *The Moving Finger*. One of Agatha Christie's most perfect works, and all about adultery. I've been scouring it looking for useful tips for our case.'

'Does that mean you're finally admitting that love was the motive?' Arthur said, and Nova saw a twinkle in his eye. 'I've said all along, people will commit all sorts of crimes for love. In this one book I read Esi, *Devil in Winter*, this woman, Evie, marries a known scoundrel to get her awful family off her back but then—'

'One thing I've learned from *The Moving Finger*,' Phyllis said, speaking over Arthur, 'is that the criminal will often go to elaborate measures to distract Miss Marple from seeing the true intention behind their—'

'And then this disturbed assassin comes after Evie and so Sebastian is forced to—'

'Oh my God, listen to the pair of you!' Nova spoke louder than she'd intended to, and they both stopped mid-sentence. 'You're both talking about books, *fictional* books, but this is my real life. I'm getting married tomorrow, and in the past forty-eight hours I've been suspended from my job, and someone has framed me for attacking my boss. So, I'm sorry, but I don't care about Evie or Miss Marple. I have to focus on my own situation.'

'Of course you do, and that's why we're here,' Arthur said. 'We want to prove Cynthia is behind the crimes so we can clear your name.'

'And I appreciate that, but it's not really working, is it? So far, every time we try and prove Cynthia is behind a crime, something even worse happens. And I can't risk anything else going wrong and ruining my wedding tomorrow.'

'This isn't just about you,' Phyllis said. 'If we can't work out what happened to the stolen money then the community centre will close, and that affects us all.'

'I'm very aware of what will happen if the money isn't found. But scouring the plots of novels to find a solution isn't going to make the money magically reappear. The only way it'll be found is if the police can trace Michael.'

Phyllis snorted. 'Oh, then we'll be waiting forever and the centre will close.'

'Maybe it will,' Nova said quietly. 'But I can't waste any more time trying to solve this crime. Now, if you'll excuse me, I have wedding favours to sort.'

'This is outrageous!' Phyllis said. 'You should be—'

'Phyllis, let's go and leave Nova be,' Arthur said. 'She's right; maybe we have let ourselves get a bit carried away with it all.'

'Miss Marple never walked away from a case, especially not so close to the end,' Phyllis protested, but Arthur and Ash were already standing up. The older woman looked like she was about to complain again, but then she let out a grunt and stood up too.

Nova led them back through to the hallway and opened the door.

'I hope you have a wonderful time at your wedding tomorrow,' Arthur said as he stepped outside.

'Yeah, good luck,' Ash said, following the older man out.

Nova waited for Phyllis to step outside, too, but there was no sign of the woman. She turned round to see her standing by the stairs, rummaging through a box on the floor.

'What are you doing?'

'Is this the stuff you got in that charity shop last week?'

'Yes, why?'

Phyllis didn't answer. She was holding the framed painting Nova had bought, the one of a pretty cottage against an azure-blue sea. Phyllis was staring at the painting through narrow, critical eyes.

'Come on, we should head to the bus stop,' Arthur called from outside.

Phyllis put the picture down, opened her handbag and pulled out a smaller frame. 'Here, look.'

She thrust it at Nova, who stifled a sigh as she took it and looked at the picture inside. It was an old black-and-white photograph, a holiday snap by the looks of things, showing a woman and a young boy.

'What am I looking at, Phyllis? I don't recognise either of these people.'

'That's Michael and his mother.'

'What?' Nova looked at her in horror. 'Where the hell did you get this from? *Please* tell me you didn't steal it?'

'Of course I didn't steal it,' Phyllis said, sounding insulted at the accusation. 'I just happened to be holding it when I heard Cynthia coming upstairs and so I jumped into the wardrobe to hide, and then put it into my handbag without realising. It was a high-pressure situation.'

'If Cynthia realises it's missing, she could report you to the police for theft,' Nova said, thrusting the photo back at Phyllis; the last thing she needed was her fingerprints on stolen goods.

'What's going on?' Arthur said, stepping back inside.

'Phyllis has stolen—'

'It is not stolen! And anyway, you're missing the point. Look at the photo again.'

She held it back out and both Nova and Arthur leaned forwards to study it.

'Who's the lady?' Arthur asked.

'Ignore the lady. *Look.*'

Phyllis grabbed Nova's framed painting and held it up next to the photo. Nova's eyes flicked between the two, and then she let out a gasp.

Chapter Twenty-Four

Nova

'The first time I saw this photo, I knew there was something vaguely familiar about the cottage,' Phyllis said. 'But it wasn't until just now I realised where I'd seen it before. It's the same one as in this horrible painting of yours.'

'It's not horrible, Esi quite likes this sort of thing,' Arthur said. 'But I'm sorry, I'm not sure I understand the relevance of it.'

'Remember the first time we spoke to Cynthia, the day after Michael disappeared?' Phyllis said. 'She complained about how much Michael had left her to deal with, including sorting out all of Eve's things. And when I went to the wake, I saw boxes of books and bags of old clothes in Eve's bedroom.'

'What, so you think this painting belonged to Michael's mum?'

'Cynthia must have taken some of Eve's belongings, including this painting, to the Cancer Research charity shop in Port Gowan, where Nova bought it. From the looks of this photo, my guess is the cottage is a holiday house they used to go to when Michael was a child. And the fact Eve owned a painting of it suggests it wasn't just somewhere they rented, but a place that belonged to them. Maybe it still does.'

'Good lord, so you think—' Arthur said, but Phyllis got there first.

'Assuming he's still alive, this might be where Michael is. If we can find this cottage, maybe we can find him and the missing money.'

There was a moment of silence as they all took in what this meant.

'This cottage could be anywhere,' Arthur said. 'It might not even be in the UK.'

'Let me have a look at that photo,' Nova said, and Phyllis handed her the frame. Nova turned it over and began to unclip the back. 'My dad loved photography; he had this old SLR camera he took with us whenever we went travelling. He used to develop the photos himself when we got home and then . . .' She stopped, lifting the old photo out of the frame with a smile. 'He always used to write on the back where the photo was taken and when. Just like Michael's parents did.'

'What's it say?' Phyllis said, as Nova raised the photo closer to her face. It must be at least fifty years old and the pencil writing was faded, but she could just make out two words and a date.

'Chy Pysk, 1969.'

'Fish house?' Arthur said. 'That's a funny name for a place.'

'We need to search for it online,' Phyllis said.

'Already on it.'

They all turned to see Ash tapping away on his phone.

'It looks like there are seven—no, eight—Chy Pysks in Cornwall,' he said after a moment.

'We don't need eight, we just need the one on Bodmin Moor,' Phyllis said.

Ash shook his head, not taking his eyes off the screen. 'There isn't one coming up near Bodmin. All of these are on the coast.'

'Makes sense, what with the name,' Arthur said.

'Give me a minute and I'll get them up on a map,' Ash said.

'We need to go to these houses and look for Michael,' Phyllis said, reaching out and grasping Nova's arm. 'Michael's going to be in one of them, I know it. The only question is whether he's there of his own volition, or if he's being held against his will.'

'Ash did suggest he might have been abducted, didn't you, lad?' Arthur said, but the teenager didn't reply, his attention fixed on his phone.

'Here.' He turned it round so they could all see the screen. There was a map of Cornwall, and marked on it were eight red dots.

'Oh no, they're all over the place,' Arthur said with a groan. 'Look, there's one near Looe, there's one up by Padstow, and another all the way down near Lizard Point. It would take us days to visit all of these.'

'We don't have days,' Phyllis said with a growl of frustration.

Nova tried to zone out their conversation. Something was tugging in the back of her brain, something small and faint but insistent. Something about . . .

'Lizards!'

The other three all stared at her.

'What are you talking about?' Phyllis demanded.

'There was a bookmark in Michael's copy of *Where the Crawdads Sing*, the one he left at the book club. It was an old leather National Trust one and the lettering was really faded, but I remember seeing the word *lizard*. I thought it was about the reptiles, but I think it might have said Lizard Point. What if that's the Chy Pysk we need?'

'My God, we've got him!' Phyllis's face was flushed with excitement. 'We need to get down there now.'

'Awesome,' Ash said, grinning.

'Actually, not you, Ash,' Phyllis said. 'You need to keep trying to get into that Michael file; I still think it contains vital evidence against Cynthia.'

The boy's face fell, but he nodded.

'I'll stay and help Ash,' Arthur said. 'Besides, I can't disappear off and leave Esi all day.'

'Fine, well it's just me and Nova. Come on, let's go.'

Phyllis grabbed Craddock's lead and moved towards the door, but Nova stayed where she was.

'Why are you dawdling, we need to get going. It's at least a four-hour round trip and—'

'I'm sorry, Phyllis, but I can't come.'

'Why not?'

'I told you, I'm getting married tomorrow. My mum's landing in a couple of hours and I have to collect her from the airport, and then we have a church rehearsal at six.'

'We'll be back by then, and surely you can get someone else to collect your mum?'

'I promised Craig I wouldn't risk getting into any more trouble. If he found out I'd driven all the way to the southernmost tip of Great Britain to find a murder suspect, he'd call the wedding off on the spot.'

'Well, then you don't have to tell him you've gone.' Phyllis's voice had risen in exasperation. 'This is your chance to clear your name and hopefully get the stolen money back. Isn't that more important than some silly rehearsal?'

'I'm sorry, Phyllis, but I can't go.'

'But you're the only one with a car. Ash and I don't drive, and Arthur's only got his old tractor, which isn't going to get us very far. Without you, I can't get there and this whole thing is over.'

Nova faltered, and then she remembered Craig's words. *No more Nancy Drew nonsense.* 'I really am sorry.'

She couldn't look at the older lady, but she could sense her eyes boring into her. There was a long, drawn-out silence, the only sound Craddock's huffing breaths.

'Come on, Phyllis, let's go,' Arthur said.

'But Michael . . .' Phyllis muttered.

'I can call the police and tell them what we know; I won't mention your name,' Arthur said. 'Maybe they'll send someone down to the cottage to check.'

The three of them shuffled outside. Nova waited for them to say good-bye, but none of them turned round as they headed down the driveway towards the road.

She shut the front door and returned to the living room, where the silk bags were waiting for her on the floor. She'd done the right thing, hadn't she? Craig had been adamant Nova shouldn't get involved in any more amateur sleuthing, and she couldn't lie to the man she was about to marry. Besides, she needed to head off to the airport soon.

At the thought of her mum, Nova picked up her phone from where she'd left it on the floor with the silk bags. As she turned it over, she saw two missed calls from her mum. Nova clicked on her name and listened to the dialling tone.

'There you are!'

'Hey Mum. Sorry, I was just busy with something. How are you? How was the flight?'

'Darling, have you listened to my voice-mail?'

'Not yet. What did it say?'

'Oh love, it's been a nightmare. My internal flight to Bogotá was cancelled so I'm still in Colombia.'

Nova felt a cold flash of panic. 'What?'

'I'm so sorry, Nono. I didn't tell you sooner because I didn't want to worry you until I'd sorted out an alternative. But I'm taking a flight to Bogotá this afternoon and then I'll fly to London overnight and get the train down to Cornwall first thing tomorrow. It's going to be tight, but I'll be there in time for the wedding, I promise.'

'Bloody hell.' Nova sunk back on the sofa, exhaling slowly.

'I'm really sorry. There are terrible storms here so everything's in chaos.'

'That's all right.'

'How are you doing? You sound stressed.'

'Oh Mum, you have no idea,' Nova said with a tired laugh.

'Is it pre-wedding nerves?'

'That and the fact I've been suspended from work and questioned by the police for assault.'

'What? Nono, what happened?'

'Sandy was attacked in her home the other night.'

'Oh God, is she okay?'

'Yes. But a witness saw someone wearing a red coat like mine near her house at the exact time she was attacked, so I'm the prime suspect.'

'But what does that mean? Do you think someone tried to frame you?'

'I think it's possible.'

'Why would anyone do that? You're hardly the kind of person who makes enemies. Unless . . . you don't think this has anything to do with Declan, do you?'

'Declan? No, I don't think so. Phyllis, this lady from my book club, is convinced it's all connected to the stolen community centre money I e-mailed you about the other day. She has this theory involving the wife of the man we think stole the money and his dead mother, which is too complicated to even explain. But whatever's going on, my life has pretty much imploded in the last forty-eight hours.'

'Oh sweetheart, I'm so sorry I've not been there for you,' Maddy said quietly. 'Has Craig been helpful?'

'Yes, but you know how much he worries. He just wants me to focus on the wedding and not get distracted by everything that's going on at work.'

'Easy for him to say! This is your job, the career you love and have worked so hard for. If I were you, I'd be fighting to clear my name too.'

'Well, instead of doing that I'm sitting here, making up monogrammed bags of sugared almonds as gifts for the wedding guests tomorrow.'

Maddy laughed and then stopped when she realised Nova wasn't joking. 'Sweetheart, I don't want to come between you and Craig, but you're not the kind of person who sits back and does nothing. Remember at school, when that awful teacher tried to get you thrown out of the drama club because she thought you'd stolen some costumes? You took up a one-woman crusade to clear your name and get yourself back into that club.'

'Yeah, but this is a bit more serious than a stolen brocade jacket, Mum. A woman's been murdered, money's been stolen, and Sandy's been attacked. The police are involved, so shouldn't I just stay out of it?'

'Okay love, if you think that's best. But just remember what your dad always used to say.'

Nova knew immediately what her mum was referring to. She

could picture her dad sitting cross-legged on her old bed, reading one of their many favourite stories. *You have to get out there and seize life with both hands, Nono,* he used to say when he closed the pages and kissed her goodnight. *After all, no one writes books about characters who sit around waiting for life to happen to them.*

Nova glanced at the clock on the wall and took a deep breath.

'All right, Mum. I'll see you tomorrow.'

Chapter Twenty-Five

Phyllis

Phyllis smiled to herself as the car bombed down the A39. She couldn't remember the last time she'd been this far from St Tredock. Her mother hadn't believed in holidays and so the furthest they'd ever ventured was Weston-super-Mare for a few joyless weekends. When her mother died, Phyllis had considered going on a proper holiday and had even got as far as picking up passport forms from the post office, but something had always stopped her. It was the same thing that had stopped her selling the wretched house and moving out of St Tredock altogether. The *what if?*

'We'll have to stop halfway and let Craddock out for a pee,' she said, but Nova didn't respond. The girl hadn't said a word since she'd almost run over Phyllis half an hour ago. Even when she'd stopped the car, all she'd done was open the passenger door and indicate for Phyllis to get in. They'd driven in silence ever since, Nova hunched over the steering wheel as if she were Michael Schumacher in the Grand Prix. Still, Phyllis didn't mind; she was on her way to find Michael Watkins and finally get to the bottom of the case.

She glanced out the window and saw a signpost for Bodmin Moor, and the smile disappeared from her face. This was one detail

Phyllis still needed to work out. Why had Michael abandoned his car in the middle of the moor, sixty miles from his final destination? Two possible explanations presented themselves. One – and Phyllis hated to admit this even to herself – was that Arthur had been correct, and Michael had arranged a rendezvous with a mysterious stranger on the moor, at which point he'd abandoned his car and travelled the remaining distance in an alternative vehicle. If that was the case, it would suggest that his whole 'disappearance' had been both voluntary and premeditated, and Michael was currently shacked up in the cottage with his lover and ten grand in cash.

The second explanation, and the one Phyllis's instincts told her was nearer to the truth, was her original theory that Michael's disappearance was neither premeditated nor voluntary. Cynthia and/or Graham Pierce had finally caught up with Michael on Bodmin Moor, where they forced him out of his vehicle and into theirs. They'd then driven him to Lizard Point, where he was being held hostage while Cynthia no doubt emptied their bank account and eloped with her lover. In which case, Phyllis and Nova's road trip might be about to turn into a full-blown rescue mission.

A loud ringing noise filled the car and Nova grimaced.

'That'll be Craig.'

'You don't have to answer it,' Phyllis said.

Nova leaned forwards and pressed the screen. 'Hi, Craig.'

'Hey babe, where are you?' His voice filled the car on loudspeaker. 'Mum said she just got home and you're not there.'

Nova didn't immediately reply, and Phyllis watched the young woman chew her lip. It felt obtrusive to be listening to a private conversation, but at the same time, one could tell so much about a person by the way they spoke to their loved ones.

'Have you gone early to collect your mum?' Craig said, when Nova still hadn't answered.

'No, her internal flight got cancelled so she missed her connection. She's getting a new one, but she won't be here until tomorrow morning.'

'Oh no, that's awful for her! But that means she'll miss the rehearsal too? Shit, my mum really wanted everyone there tonight to practise their parts.'

'It's all right, Craig; all my mum's got to do is walk me down the aisle and do a reading, I'm sure she can handle that,' Nova said, and Phyllis could hear an edge of irritation in her voice.

'Where have you gone, then? It sounds like you're in the car.'

Phyllis saw Nova's hands gripping the steering wheel tightly. 'I've just gone for a little drive. I needed to get out of the house for a bit.'

Craig sighed, louder than was entirely necessary. 'Mum said the favours are only half-finished and you've not folded any of the orders of service. You could at least have done those before you went out.'

'I'm sorry, but I can do them later.'

'It's not like she's asked you to do much, Nova. It's just two tiny jobs, and you can't even be bothered to do those.'

Phyllis scowled at the man's tone. She was no expert on relationships – she'd never been married and had only ever courted one man, a very long time ago – but Phyllis was pretty sure you weren't supposed to tell your future wife off the day before your wedding.

'I just needed to clear my head, but you can tell your mum I'll—'

'I'm not your messenger, Nova. You should tell Mum yourself if you're going to let her down.'

'For goodness' sake, the girl said she's sorry so leave her alone.'

The words were out of Phyllis's mouth before she realised she'd said them. There was silence on the other end of the phone line. Next to her, Nova inhaled sharply.

'Nova, who's that?' Craig said.

'I'm Phyllis Hudson, a member of your fiancée's book club. I'm helping Nova save her job.'

'For Christ sake's, Nova, what is wrong with you?' The man's voice was so loud it made Phyllis jump. 'You promised me you'd keep out of trouble, but here you are, pissing about with that bloody book club and putting yourself in danger *yet* again.'

'It's not dangerous, I've got Phyllis here with me,' Nova said.

'Is that the old busybody with the smelly dog? How the hell is *she* going to help protect you?'

'How dare you!' Phyllis said. 'Craddock isn't smelly.'

'"My troublemaking days are over," you said, Nova. Is this what our marriage is going to be like, you lying to me and then running off behind my back?'

'I wasn't lying to you when I said that. But then Phyllis and the others came to see me, and we had a breakthrough with where Michael might be. And Mum's flight was delayed, so I knew I had time to do this. If I can find Michael and recover the stolen money, it won't just save my job; it'll save the community centre too.'

'How many times do I have to tell you, if that centre closes it won't be because of you.' Craig snapped. 'And yet still you apparently think it's more important than our wedding.'

'Of course I don't think that.'

'Do you have any idea how embarrassing it is, having Mum call me up and say my fiancée's done a runner? You can't just—'

The line went dead. Phyllis sat back in the seat, crossing her arms in satisfaction.

'What did you do that for? You can't just turn off my phone, he'll think I hung up on him!'

'Well, you should have, quite frankly. And what's so wrong with being a busybody? Miss Marple was a self-professed busybody, and it helped her solve dozens of crimes.'

Nova groaned. 'For God's sake, Phyllis, turn it back on. I need the satnav.'

'I can direct us perfectly well with this,' Phyllis said, pulling an old AA road map out of the passenger door compartment. 'Does your fiancé always talk to you like that?'

'Of course not. He's just worried about me.'

'Why on earth is he worrying about you? You're a grown woman, not some helpless child who needs a man's permission to leave the house.'

'He's not treating me like a child. You have no idea what you're talking about.'

Phyllis swallowed down a stab of indignation. 'I might not have much personal experience of romantic relationships, but I know plenty about controlling ones, thank you very much.'

'Trust me, it's not how it looks. Something happened back in London, and ever since then Craig's been a little overprotective. It's only because he loves me.'

Phyllis sniffed. 'I've heard that excuse before, when I correctly deduced Sheila Clark's husband was hurting her on purpose. Sheila tried to defend him, too, but I had the evidence I needed to report him to the police. She left him eventually, and now she's happily married to the man who used to clean her windows.'

Nova let out a long sigh. 'Look, I realise you're just trying to help here, but I promise you that Craig isn't like that. As I said, it's only because of what happened in my old job. He just doesn't want me getting hurt again.'

'What happened in your job?'

Phyllis watched Nova's brow furrow as she weighed up whether to tell her or not. Then her shoulders sagged.

'Before we moved to St Tredock, I was a youth worker at a community centre in London. Although it wasn't easy and there were lots of complex issues to deal with, I loved the job and thought I'd do it forever . . .'

Nova trailed off, her eyes locked on the road ahead of them.

'So, why didn't you?'

'There was this one sixteen-year-old boy, Declan, who used to come to some of the sessions I ran. He'd had the crappiest start in life. His parents were addicts, he'd been in and out of care, and when I first met him, he'd been expelled from two schools and was on a final warning at a third. But he was a smart kid, really smart; he loved Manga graphic novels and used to read them faster than anyone I've ever known. And you should have heard the way he talked about them, he was so insightful.'

'It sounds like he'd have been a welcome addition to our book club,' Phyllis said.

'God, yes, he'd have given you a run for your money!' Nova smiled, but then her face fell serious again. 'Anyway, as a youth worker, there are all these strict rules in place to protect both you and the young people you work with, like no physical contact and you're never allowed to be alone with them. But I admit, I used to break the rules a bit with Declan, letting him hang out at the centre when I was doing boring admin jobs after hours. I knew I shouldn't have been on my own with him, and I'm not making excuses for what I did, but I was still reeling from the grief of losing my dad. And when I chatted to this kid about his books, I felt a million miles away from everything that had happened. But I was so naive.'

Nova paused again, and the only sound was Craddock's throaty snores in the back seat.

'You don't have to continue if you don't want to,' Phyllis said, because as much as she wanted to find out Nova's story, she could tell it was hurting the girl to retell it.

'One day, Declan came to see me at the centre. I was on my own locking up, but I let him in for a chat. I realised pretty quickly something was up. His pupils were dilated, and he was really agitated, like he couldn't stand still.'

'Drugs?' Phyllis asked, and Nova nodded.

'He kept going on about how everything was shit and unfair, and I eventually managed to get out of him that there'd been some incident at school, a fight with another kid, and he'd been expelled. I tried to calm him down and get him out of the centre, but I must have said the wrong thing because he just flipped. The next thing I knew, he'd pulled out a knife and was holding it against my throat.'

Despite herself, Phyllis inhaled sharply. She'd always known there must have been something bad in Nova's past, given how jumpy the girl could be, but she'd never imagined it was something like this.

'A passerby heard my shout and came running into the centre. Declan fled, but the police caught up with him pretty fast. It turned out he'd pulled the same knife on a lad at school who'd taken the piss out of his mum, and so the two offences meant he didn't stand a chance.'

From the back seat, Craddock let out a loud, protracted yawn. Nova shook herself, as if waking from a daydream.

'I'm sorry that happened to you,' Phyllis said.

'It was my fault. I should never have allowed myself to be alone in a vulnerable position with him, and I rightly got fired for breaking the safeguarding rules.'

'Fired? That hardly seems fair; the whole thing must have been terrifying for you.'

'To be honest, I think it scared Craig more than it scared me. It was one of the reasons we moved down here, because he was so worried something like that might happen again if we stayed in London. And that's why he overreacted just now, because he's scared I'll put myself in a dangerous situation again, and this time the outcome will be worse.'

'What happened to the boy?' Phyllis asked.

Nova sighed again. 'He ended up getting six months in a youth offenders unit, although I heard he got released recently.'

'Does that worry you?'

Nova shook her head. 'I don't think he ever meant to hurt me, he was just high, confused and scared. If anything, I'm more worried *for* him. It can be hard to move on from something like that. One mistake at the age of sixteen can define your whole life, especially if those around you won't let you move on.'

Phyllis felt suddenly cold, despite the car heater blasting out, and she pulled her coat around her shoulders.

'It sounds like it was very traumatic, but I still don't think this should be an excuse for your fiancée speaking to you like that.'

'He—'

'I understand what happened must have been a shock for him, but that doesn't mean he can wrap you up in cotton wool. You have to be allowed to carry on living your own life.'

'I know, and I don't think he wants to wrap me in cotton wool,'

Nova said. 'I guess just with all the stress of the wedding, he's feeling particularly sensitive at the moment. I'm sure it'll all be much easier once tomorrow is out of the way.'

Phyllis had never heard a bride talk about their wedding as something to get out of the way, but she decided not to say any more. As Miss Marple knew, sometimes it was better to say nothing at all. And so they drifted back into silence as the car drove on west, carrying them towards Michael Watkins.

Chapter Twenty-Six

Arthur

It was gone eleven by the time Arthur and Ash got back to St Tredock.

'Are you heading home now?' Arthur asked as they disembarked from the bus at the harbour.

'I thought I might work in the Lobster Pot for a bit. Our Wi-Fi is playing up and I want to have another go at using this password-cracking software. I'll call you if it works.'

'I can stay and help, if you like?'

'Don't you need to get back to your wife?'

Arthur glanced towards the cafe. 'She'll be all right without me for a bit longer; her friend's visiting today.'

They found a table in the corner, and Arthur ordered them coffees while Ash set to work on his laptop. Watching him hunched over the screen, Arthur couldn't help wondering what it would have been like to have a grandson like Ash. He and Esi had never been blessed with children, despite many years of trying, and as only children themselves, there were no hordes of nephews and nieces round the table at Christmas either. Arthur had made peace with this long ago, although Esi had always found it harder, and her pain still cut Arthur like a knife. She would have been a wonderful mother, and he reckoned he wouldn't have been too bad a pa either. And maybe one day there would have been a teenager like Ash, shy and bright and kind, sitting at their kitchen table eating Esi's scones.

'Stop staring at me, Arthur, it's putting me off.'

'Sorry, lad. I just wish there was something I could do. I don't like sitting twiddling my thumbs while Nova and Phyllis drive to see Michael and you do all the work here.'

'You can always try and think of more password suggestions,' Ash said. 'I've tried all the obvious ones – variations on his name, important dates – but maybe you can come up with other ideas?'

'Right you are.' Arthur closed his eyes and tried to concentrate. What kind of password would a private investigator have? Something flashy, no doubt, like *Danger0* or *JamesBond69*. No, that was ridiculous; Graham Pierce was as unlike 007 as you could get. His password would be something more boring, like the name of his childhood dog or his favourite food. *Big Mac? Guinness?*

'Have you tried KitKat Chunky?'

Ash looked at him over the laptop screen. 'Why would that be his password?'

'He had a drawer full of their wrappers, so I wondered if he might have used his favourite snack.'

The boy shrugged but typed it in. 'Nope, that didn't work.'

'What about Jon Bon Jovi? That was his ringtone.'

'Good idea.' Ash tapped away and sighed. 'Not that either.'

'Fair enough. Sorry, I'll carry on thinking.'

Arthur tried to picture the man's office. What else had been in there that showed Graham's interests? But there had been nothing to give any clues about the man's life, apart from the fact he was clearly single, unhealthy and unhappy.

'Oh my God, that's it!'

Arthur looked over to see the teenager's face alight.

'Did you do it?'

'No, *you* did it. Blazeofglory1965, his favourite Jon Bon Jovi song and his year of birth. Arthur, we're in!'

Ash angled the laptop round so they could both see the screen. There was only one file in the folder, labelled '27.06.24'. He double-clicked on it and Arthur held his breath as he waited for the file to open.

'The Wi-Fi speed is ridiculously slow here,' Ash said. 'It should be any second.'

A moment later, the screen was filled with a large colour photo of a very ordinary-looking terraced cottage. There was something vaguely familiar about it and Arthur stared at the image, trying to place where he'd seen it before, but Ash was already scrolling down to the next one. This photo showed the door of the house open but not the person inside. Ash flicked on and a figure emerged in slow motion. Their head was tilted down so Arthur couldn't see their face, but there was no mistaking who it was.

'Oh shit!' Ash whispered next to him.

He scrolled on and the two of them watched in horrified silence as Phyllis emerged from her house with Craddock on his lead, shut her front door and walked down her path onto the pavement. It was clear she had no idea she was being photographed as she didn't look at the camera once.

'Why the hell was the private investigator taking photos of Phyllis?' Ash said.

'I have no idea. But it must mean Cynthia was . . .' Arthur stopped as something occurred to him, and he let out a gasp. 'Oh my God, we've been such idiots!'

'What?'

'All along, we've assumed Cynthia was the one who'd hired Graham to investigate Michael. But what if this had nothing to do with Cynthia? What if Michael was the one who hired the PI?'

'Oh no!' Ash said, his face suddenly pale. 'The file's not named Michael because it's *about* him. It's because he's the client who paid for the photos.'

'But why would Michael want photos of Phyllis? She never mentioned that she knew him.'

Neither of them spoke for a moment, and Arthur could sense Ash's brain was whirring like his own. Then the teenager jumped in his seat, grabbing Arthur's arm.

'What if Michael's some creepy stalker who's got it in for Phyllis? And now she and Nova are driving straight into his hands?'

'We need to get in touch with them.' Arthur reached into his pocket and fumbled for his phone. His hands were trembling as he flicked to Nova's number and pressed dial.

'Damn, it's gone straight to voice-mail,' he said as he heard Nova's cheery voice. He waited for the bleep. 'Nova, this is Arthur. You need to turn around and come back now. It's too complicated to explain, but we think Michael might have bad intentions for Phyllis. Please, call me as soon as you get this.'

'Do you have a number for Phyllis?' Ash asked as he hung up.

Arthur shook his head. 'What if they're already there, Ash? What if Michael has deliberately lured them into a trap?'

'There's more photos of Phyllis on here,' Ash said, nodding at his laptop screen. 'Graham followed her into the village and around the shops. There are even photos of her going into the community centre.'

'I'll try calling again,' Arthur said, but it still went straight to voice-mail. 'We need to go after them. Do you know anyone who can drive us?'

'My dad's away for work with the car so I can't ask my parents. And none of my mates have driving licences yet.'

'A cab would cost a fortune, I can't afford one on my pension. Oh, I wish I still had a car.' Arthur wracked his brains for someone, anyone, they could ask, but most of his friends had given up driving long ago.

Then a thought occurred to him, and Arthur found himself smiling for the first time since they opened the computer file.

Chapter Twenty-Seven

Nova

Phyllis was clearly not an experienced map reader, and she sent Nova the wrong way four times before they made it to the small village of Landewednack, just northeast of Lizard Point. Once there, she directed them down a narrow farm track, which she claimed would take them to Chy Pysk. Nova had never been this far south-west before, and as the car rumbled down the bumpy lane, she really did feel like she was at the end of England. Fields lined the lane, but beyond them Nova could see the Atlantic glistening in the autumn sunshine.

'Are you sure we've not gone the wrong way again, Phyllis? We've been on this lane for half a mile now and there are no houses anywhere.'

'Keep going. It should be at the very end, when we get to the coast.'

'This would have been so much easier with satnav,' Nova grumbled. Although in truth, she was dreading turning her phone back on and seeing the no doubt dozens of voice-mails and messages from Craig.

They rounded a corner, and Nova saw the track come to an end ahead of them at the edge of the cliff. She glanced around, but there was no sign of a house anywhere.

'This can't be right, it should be exactly here,' Phyllis said.

Nova reached for her phone to switch it back on and check the map, but Phyllis was already out of the car and striding towards the edge. Nova climbed out and ran to follow her. The wind was strong here, whipping her curls into her face, and the only sound was the roar of the waves crashing against the rocks below. Phyllis was standing on the cliff edge, looking down at the sea. Nova joined her, her stomach plummeting with vertigo as she peered over. She was expecting to see nothing but rocks and water, but to her astonishment, she saw a small stone cottage balanced on a narrow ridge about thirty metres down from where they stood.

'How is that place still standing?' Phyllis said in wonder.

'It doesn't look like anyone's lived there for years,' Nova said, as she took in the crooked stone walls and the slate roof, which made the St Tredock Community Centre's look positively modern. 'This can't be the right place. I must have made a mistake with the Lizard Point bookmark.'

Phyllis didn't reply, and when Nova turned round the woman was gone. For a horrible moment, Nova wondered if she'd toppled over the edge and fallen into the sea a hundred metres below, but then she heard a throaty bark and saw the short, squat figure of Phyllis scrambling down a narrow path towards the cottage, Craddock following behind.

'Phyllis, come back!' Nova shouted into the wind, but the woman ignored her.

Cursing, Nova set off after her. She'd always hated heights, and she clung to the rocky cliff face as she edged after Phyllis, not allowing herself to glance down at the precipitous drop below. The path was barely wide enough for her feet, and at one point Nova heard the sickening sound of rocks tumbling down the cliff. She glanced back to see a good two metres of the path had broken away and crumbled into the sea. How the hell were they going to get back up now?

Phyllis seemed to have no such concerns and had already reached the cottage, disappearing round the back of it. Finally, Nova arrived at the flat rock, too, and hurried to join her.

'My God, you're like a mountain goat,' she said, her legs trembling as she gasped to catch her breath.

The older woman didn't answer, studying the photo in her hand, and Nova moved next to her to see it too. This was definitely the same cottage as the young Michael and his mother were standing in front of, although the rest of the scene was unrecognisable: the pretty garden had long ago disappeared into the sea and now all that was left was rocks and the cottage itself.

Phyllis walked to the front door and gave the rusty handle a twist.

'Phyllis, stop!' Nova commanded, and to her surprise, the woman glanced back at her. 'You can't go in there; the whole thing looks like it might topple into the sea at any moment.'

'I've not come all the way down here to turn back now,' Phyllis said. 'Michael might be inside.'

'Oh, come on, he's not here; the place is derelict. Plus, there's no car parked anywhere nearby.'

Phyllis looked down at Craddock, who was sniffing around at her feet. 'Do you think anyone's in here?'

Nova's eyebrows shot up. *Had Phyllis really just asked her dog a question?* 'Come on, let's go. There might be traffic on the way back and I don't want to cut it too fine for my rehearsal.'

'Craddock thinks someone's been here recently,' Phyllis said, reaching for the door handle again.

'No Phyllis, you can't—'

But before Nova could finish her sentence, Phyllis had twisted the knob. With an almighty creak, the door swung open, and the old woman stepped inside, followed by her dog.

Nova took a deep breath. This was ridiculous; she should never have allowed herself to be talked into coming here. But she couldn't let Phyllis wander round the old house alone; God knows how rotten things were in there, and she or Craddock might hurt themselves. Nova hurried to the door and followed her inside.

The room Phyllis was standing in appeared to have once been a kitchen, but mother nature had long ago taken over. The floor was covered in seagull droppings and there was lichen growing on the damp walls. There was an old range on the far side of the room, under a window, its glass smashed so that the wind whistled through, filling the air with a salty mist. Small clues as to its previous life littered the room; a few mugs still sat on a crooked shelf and a broken table lay collapsed in the middle of the room.

'No one's been here in decades.'

'Then why are you whispering?' Phyllis asked as she moved across the room.

Nova held her breath in case the rotten floorboards suddenly gave way. 'This isn't safe. We should leave now.'

'I knew it!' Phyllis was standing by the sink and she turned round, holding something in her hand. 'He's been here!'

Nova stepped closer and saw what looked like an empty crisp packet.

'Monster Munch,' Phyllis said. 'Michael's favourite.'

'That could have been from years ago.' But as Nova said this, she saw a bin bag lying by what must have once been the back door. She bent down and opened it to see more empty crisp packets, sandwich cartons and plastic water bottles inside. Those definitely didn't look years old.

Phyllis had moved to the far end of the room and was peering through another doorway. Nova knelt down and opened the cupboard under the sink, then regretted it when a foul smell hit her. She tried the tap, but unsurprisingly no water came out.

'Maybe he's been here recently but he's clearly not here now,' she said, turning round, but Phyllis had left the room.

Nova moved to the door and peered through. There was a small hallway leading onto a second room, a narrow, dark staircase in between. Jesus, had Phyllis gone up there?

'For God's sake, this staircase is rotten with damp. What are—'

But Nova never got to finish her sentence, as she was interrupted by a bark and then a bloodcurdling scream.

Chapter Twenty-Eight

Nova

Nova began to charge up the creaking stairs, the scream still echoing in her ears.

'Phyllis, where are you?' she shouted as she reached a small hallway at the top. There were two doors, one open and one closed, and Nova crossed to the open door and peered inside.

The curtains were drawn, and the room was so dark she could make out little more than vague shapes inside. There was what looked like a single bed at the far side of the room and a figure was standing at the end of it, their back to the doorway, but in the gloom, Nova couldn't tell who it was. They had an arm raised above their head, as if they were about to strike something or someone on the other side of the bed. Nova ran across the room.

'Stop!' she shouted as she grabbed the raised arm.

Immediately, the person swung round and Nova saw it was Phyllis.

'What are you . . .'

Nova stopped as Phyllis's eyes swung back towards the bed. When Nova followed them, she saw a man cowering on the floor on the other side, his hands raised to protect himself from Craddock, who appeared to be trying to lick him to death.

'What the hell did you do to him?'

'I didn't touch him!' Phyllis snapped. 'I just walked in here and he took one look at me, screamed and jumped behind the bed.'

Nova leaned forwards and grabbed Craddock's collar, hauling him off.

'Michael, are you okay?' she asked, but he didn't look up. 'It's all right, it's only us: Nova and Phyllis from the St Tredock Book Club.'

At the mention of their names, the man let out a low whimper.

'For goodness' sake, we need some light in here.' Phyllis strode to the window, pulling back the thick curtain.

Sunlight burst in through the broken pane of glass and Nova could finally see Michael properly. He didn't appear to be injured, but when he raised his head, she saw his face was pale, a layer of greying stubble over his chin. His eyes flicked between Nova and Phyllis, wide with alarm.

'Michael, are you here alone?'

He nodded but didn't speak.

'What on earth happened to you? Are you okay?'

'I'm a bit hungry.' His voice was a rasp, as if he hadn't used it in days.

'I've got some biscuits.' Phyllis rummaged in her bag and pulled out a packet of Rich Teas, which she held towards Michael. The man tentatively reached out, not looking at Phyllis as he took them. He opened the packet and stuffed a biscuit in his mouth, barely chewing before he swallowed it and took another one. Craddock shuffled nearer to eat the crumbs that fell on the floor.

'Slow down or you'll be sick,' Nova said.

'I have some water too,' Phyllis said, producing a plastic bottle.

Michael grabbed it and took several long gulps until the thing was empty. Then he leaned back against the wall behind him, closing his eyes as he caught his breath.

'Right, now you've had something to eat, it's time to start talking,' Phyllis said. 'The police think you committed murder and then ran away with the stolen money, but we know that's not the truth. Is this all Cynthia's doing, and she's been holding you here against your will?'

'What?' Michael croaked.

'There's no point trying to lie to us. You can't protect Cynthia now.'

'Phyllis, slow down a minute,' Nova said, elbowing the woman before she could launch into any more accusations. 'Michael, did you come here alone, or did someone bring you?'

'Alone.'

'So, you weren't kidnapped, then?' Phyllis interjected.

'No!' Michael looked at Nova. 'Why would she ask that?'

'So, you're saying you came here willingly,' Phyllis said, and Nova could see the woman recalibrating her theory as she spoke. 'Are you hiding out here because of the murder?'

'What murder?' He looked at Nova imploringly. 'What the hell is she talking about?'

'Don't play naive,' Phyllis said. 'You know as well as I do that either you or Cynthia killed your mother the night you ran away.'

Finally, Michael looked at Phyllis, his face twisted with confusion. 'My mother?'

'Was it you? You clearly have mummy issues, given your rant in the book club. Or was it Cynthia in order to get her hands on the inheritance?'

'My mum . . . Mum's dead?' Michael blinked several times and then Nova watched as his face slowly crumpled. A second later, a rumbling moan escaped from his mouth.

'Oh God,' Nova hissed, turning to Phyllis. 'He didn't know!'

Phyllis was staring at him, her nose wrinkled. 'He's acting.'

Nova looked back to Michael, whose head had dropped onto his knees, his whole body racking with sobs.

'Michael, are you okay?'

In response, he let out another wail of grief. Nova crouched down so she was at his level, but didn't say anything else, allowing the man to cry. This wasn't an act, surely? He seemed genuinely distraught at the news. Up close, Nova could smell a strange, sour odour coming off his body. Was he having some kind of mental health episode, and he'd completely blanked out killing his own mother? If so, they should treat him with extreme caution, as goodness knows what he might do. Behind her, she could feel Phyllis's toe tapping on the floor, and Nova glared at her.

Finally, the man's sobs subsided, although he kept his face buried in his knees.

'Michael?' Nova said gently, and he jolted, as if he'd forgotten they were there. He looked up at her, his face wet from the tears.

'Is she really dead?'

'I'm so sorry.'

'When?'

'Last Wednesday; the day you came to our book club.'

'And what day is it today?'

'Friday, October 25th.'

She watched Michael do the mental calculations and then fresh tears started to stream down his cheeks. 'She died nine days ago?'

'Do you really expect us to believe you didn't know? When you were overheard having a raging argument with your mother just minutes before she died?' Phyllis's voice was hard, and Nova saw Michael blanch.

'I swear I didn't know,' he whimpered. 'And you said . . . murdered?'

'That's what the police think. They also think you're the prime suspect.'

'What?' His eyes were wide again.

'You're in debt, aren't you, Michael?' Phyllis said. 'And you were trying to force your mum to sell her house and give you the money. Is that why you killed her?'

'Oh my God, of course I didn't!'

'So, are you telling us that Richard's lying, and you didn't fight with your mum about money the night she died?'

'He's not lying, but it's not what you think. I'd never kill my mum; I love her!'

He looked so desperate that Nova truly wanted to believe him. 'I'm sure you did, Michael, but you have to admit it doesn't look great. You were overheard arguing, you ran out of the house around the same time the police believe she was killed, you came to our book club covered in blood and then you disappeared for nine days.'

'Oh Jesus,' he said with a groan. 'It's not how it looks.'

'Then how is it, Michael?' Phyllis demanded. 'What possible explanation can you have for what happened?'

For a moment he didn't reply, rubbing his hands over his exhausted face, and Nova found herself willing Michael to have a decent explanation for the events of last Wednesday.

'My mum and I did have an argument,' he said eventually. 'She'd just learned something – something I'd been trying to protect her from – and she was furious with me. It was a horrible fight and we both said some terrible things. Things I deeply regret, especially now . . .'

He trailed off, and for a moment Nova thought he was going to start crying again. He ran a hand over his face before he carried on.

'I've been having a difficult time lately, and that argument was the last straw. I knew I needed to get away for a bit, so I threw some things in a bag and ran out of the house. But my mum was alive when I left, I swear.'

Phyllis let out a loud snort. 'So, tell me, if that's true, then how do you explain the blood on your shirt when you came to our book club?'

'I had a nosebleed. I get them when I'm stressed.'

'Then what about the fact you ran out of the meeting after ten minutes and haven't been seen or heard from since?'

Michael visibly swallowed. 'I received a text message with some news – bad news – and it was all too much. I jumped in the car and came straight here.'

'Except you didn't come straight here, did you?' Phyllis said. 'You drove to Bodmin Moor and then abandoned your car in order to hide your whereabouts from the police.'

'My car broke down! The gear box has been playing up for ages and I kept meaning to get it fixed, only with everything that was going on I never got round to it. It finally gave up near Bodmin, so I walked to the nearest town and then caught a bus, a train and then two more buses.'

'And you're trying to tell us you've been – what? – having a nice little holiday here ever since, completely oblivious to the fact your mother's been murdered and you're the prime suspect?'

Michael let out a long sigh. 'When you put it like that, I know it sounds suspicious. But I just really needed to get away from it all: my mum and Cynthia and all the pressures at home. I've barely left this cottage since I arrived and there's no electricity so I couldn't charge my phone. I only intended to stay for a few days, but I guess I lost track of time.'

As he said this, Michael looked around him at the bedroom, its stone walls slick with moss and a layer of salt on every surface.

'I used to come here every summer with my parents. It was so idyllic, just us and the sea. It was like something out of that book.'

'What book?' Nova asked.

'The Crawdads one, from your book club. When I was reading about that girl living in the wild with nothing but nature, it reminded me of this place. I hadn't thought about it for years, but that night in the book club, I suddenly knew I wanted to come back again. I've even been trying to repair it a bit, so I could bring Mum again . . .' He trailed off, and Nova could see the realisation dawning on him that that would never happen.

'You must think we were born yesterday,' Phyllis said. 'You're going to need to come up with a considerably better story when the police come to arrest you. And we've not even started on the stolen money.'

'What stolen money?' Michael was looking at Nova again. 'Please, my head hurts and I have no idea what she's talking about.'

'Someone stole ten grand from the community centre the night you ran away. In your absence, you've become the number one suspect for that as well.'

'Oh shit!' He put his hands up to his face again, shaking his head.

'Why else did you come to the book club, if not to steal the money?' Phyllis demanded. 'And if you try to tell me it's because you like reading then I'll know for *sure* you're lying.'

'No, it wasn't that,' Michael said from behind his hands.

'Well, why did you come, then?'

Michael didn't reply, his whole body hunched over like a child trying to hide. The poor thing, it was clear he was having some kind of nervous breakdown. Nova glanced at Phyllis, but the woman's face was hard. From far below them, she heard the sound of a wave crash against the rocks.

'We need to get outside; this building's not safe. Can you stand up, Michael?'

He didn't move.

'Phyllis, can you help me get him up? I think we need to take him to a hospital, he's clearly in shock.'

Phyllis grunted and stepped forwards to take one of Michael's arms. But as soon as she touched him, he shrieked and recoiled.

'Come on, Michael. We need to get you out of here,' Nova said.

'You can't hide here forever,' Phyllis said. 'Either you or your wife killed your mother, and whichever of you it was deserves to go to prison for a very long time.'

'It wasn't either of us,' Michael moaned.

'I told you, there's no point trying to protect Cynthia,' Phyllis said. 'Are you aware your wife's been having an affair? She even hired a PI who's been investigating you.'

'What?' Michael looked up from his hands and his face had gone even paler. 'What private investigator?'

'A man called Graham Pierce. We thought Cynthia might have paid him to kidnap you, but now it seems that theory was incorrect. But she was certainly paying him to do something related to you, as the man has a computer file with your name on it.'

'Oh God!' Michael said with a low groan.

'We have a copy of the file back in St Tredock, so as soon as we can get into it, we'll know exactly what Cynthia's been up to.'

'Please, no . . .' The man had started to visibly shake.

'Michael, are you okay?' Nova said. 'You need to breathe, you're hyperventilating.'

'You can't see them!'

'See what?' Phyllis said.

'The photos.'

'What . . .' Nova stopped. 'Hang on, how do you know there are photos in the PI's folder?'

Michael's eyes were roaming the room now, looking everywhere but at her and Phyllis. 'It wasn't meant to happen like this,' he muttered to himself. 'Not here.'

'What are you talking about? What isn't meant to happen here?'

'I can't do it here . . . It's all wrong.'

Michael had a strange intensity in his eyes. An intensity Nova had seen once before, with Declan. She felt a cold stab of fear.

'Michael, please try to keep calm.' As she said the words, Nova began to slowly back away from the man, trying to nudge Phyllis towards the door. 'Just take deep breaths, you're going to be—'

But she didn't get to finish her sentence, as at that moment Michael leaped to his feet and hurled himself at Phyllis.

Chapter Twenty-Nine

Arthur

'So, let me get this straight,' Dan said, as they sped down the A39. 'We're driving eighty miles to rescue your friends, who've gone to find a missing man who you all think stole some money and was framed for murder. But now Ash has hacked into a computer file, and you've discovered this missing man might actually be some kind of dangerous stalker who wants to harm Phyllis. Is that correct?'

'Yep, that's about it,' Arthur said.

In the driver's seat, Dan shook his head. 'And there was me thinking you were just this quiet guy from my English class, Ash. I had no idea you were a secret hacker on the case of a suspected criminal with your grandpa!'

Dan chuckled, but in the passenger seat next to him, Ash was mute. The boy had been horrified when Arthur suggested they ask Dan for help, and initially outright refused to call him. He only relented when Arthur pointed out that Dan was the only person they knew with a car, and if they didn't ask for his help then Phyllis and Nova could be the next murder victims. When Dan had come to pick them up at the cafe, Arthur had subtly insisted on sitting in the back seat so Ash could sit up front and the boys could chat. Unfortunately, he hadn't accounted for quite how love-struck tongue-tied Ash really was. The lad could barely manage a grunt, and despite Dan's repeated efforts to chat, every conversation ended up sliding into awkward silence.

'So, do you watch many films?' Dan asked Ash, after a question about football hadn't elicited a response.

'Eh . . . sometimes,' Ash stuttered.

'What kind of stuff do you like?'

'All sorts.'

'Ash is a Star Wars fan,' Arthur interjected. He'd promised himself he'd stay quiet and leave the boys to it, but this was getting too painful to watch.

'Oh cool, I love them too,' Dan said. 'I think episode IV might be my favourite, which I know is an uncool take, but I just have such happy memories of watching it with my dad. Which is your favourite?'

Arthur knew the answer to this and waited for Ash to say *The Force Awakens*, but instead the teenager just shrugged.

'I like them all.'

Arthur inwardly groaned. 'I've not watched the new Star Wars films, but Ash is always telling me how much he loves them,' he said in a last-ditch attempt to get the conversation going. 'He was saying that the Kylo-what's-his-name and Rey love story is a bit like Claudio and Hero in *Much Ado About Nothing*, weren't you, lad?'

Arthur couldn't see Ash's face, but from the way the boy was sinking down in his seat as if he wanted it to swallow him whole, Arthur wondered if he'd said the wrong thing.

'That's cool, I hadn't made that connection myself,' Dan said. 'What made you say that?'

'Nothing, it was a stupid idea,' Ash mumbled, practically turning his back on Dan.

Arthur slumped back in his own seat, defeated. Esi had once told him that one of her favourite moments in any good romance novel was when a character realised their true feelings for their love interest and was forced to push themselves out of their comfort zone to win that person over. Like when Mr Darcy goes chasing after Wickham and Lydia to prove his love for Elizabeth in *Pride and Prejudice*, or when Gregory suddenly realises he's in love with Lucy and tries to stop her wedding in *On the Way to the Wedding*. Arthur had hoped this car journey to rescue Nova and Phyllis might be that moment for Ash, but clearly he'd been wrong: the poor boy made Evie from *Devil in Winter* look positively chatty.

They drove on in silence, and Arthur watched the scenery change outside the window as they pushed farther west. He'd been down here a few times on holidays with Esi, and he loved the wild ruggedness of this part of Cornwall. Esi loved it, too, and said she always hoped to find Ross Poldark striding over the fields towards her. At the thought of his wife, Arthur's chest contracted. He'd not been away from home for this long in years, and he felt her absence like a physical pain.

'Satnav says we're not far,' Dan said, as they reached a junction in the road, one way pointing to Lizard and the other to a place called Landewednack.

'I hope we've made it in time,' Arthur said, his thoughts swinging back to Phyllis and Nova. Had they already found Michael? Assuming the man was alone, Arthur hoped that the combined strength of Nova, Phyllis and Craddock would be enough to overpower him if he tried to hurt them. Unless he was armed, in which case . . .

'You need to drive faster, Dan. We have to get to them.'

'The house should be at the end of this road,' Dan said, turning onto a rough farm track that led towards the sea.

Arthur sat up in his seat, staring out the front window for any sign of the cottage from the photo. After about half a mile, Ash let out a shout.

'That's Nova's car!'

They pulled up behind the rusty yellow Fiat and all three of them climbed out. There was no sign of a cottage until Dan looked over the edge of the cliff.

'Bloody hell, it's like something from Ahch-To.'

Arthur hurried to join him. Diagonally below the road was a small derelict building, looking as if it had almost been carved into the rock face itself.

'That can't be it.'

'Maybe there's another cottage nearby,' Dan said.

Ash, who'd been staring at his phone, shook his head. 'According to Google maps, this is the only property round here.'

'How the hell did they get down there?' Arthur said. 'Look, that path has fallen into the sea.'

At that moment, a terrified human shriek sounded from the cottage below.

'Nova!' Arthur and Ash cried together.

'We need to find a way of getting there!' Arthur said.

'I've got some rope in my car, one of us could abseil down.' Dan rushed to the back of his car and pulled open his boot.

'Good idea. We should tie it round the car to anchor it.'

Dan pulled the rope out and hurried back to Arthur. Together they began to untangle it, Arthur's heart pounding in his chest.

'Wait, where's Ash?' Dan said.

Arthur looked up, but there was no sign of the boy. He ran back to the edge of the cliff and then let out a cry of his own. The teenager was halfway down to the cottage and had reached the point where the path disappeared. He turned to face the cliff and began to edge his way across the gap, using tiny crags in the rock as footholds.

'Jesus, he's going to kill himself!' Arthur groaned.

Dan had already taken off after Ash, almost slipping in his haste. Arthur began to follow them, taking it slower. He'd always been nimble; a lifetime spent working around cows taught you to stay light on your feet. But he was eighty-one now, with creaking hips and dodgy knees, and he'd never had a head for heights. Still, like Anthony Bridgerton chasing after Kate Sheffield's out-of-control carriage, he had to get to that cottage and save Nova and Phyllis from danger.

'Here, Arthur, take my hand.' Dan had reached the other side of the destroyed path, and clinging onto the rock face, he stretched out his arm towards Arthur. 'You're tall enough that you should be able to jump across.'

Arthur clasped hold of the teenager's hand and, muttering a prayer of love to Esi, he leaped across the gap. For a second his foot met with nothing but air, and he felt his stomach drop as he started to tilt forwards. But Dan had a tight grasp on his hand, and he pulled Arthur back until he was on the far side of the path.

'Thanks,' Arthur gasped, his voice shaking. 'Now get down there and help Ash.'

Dan scrambled on. Up ahead, Arthur could see that Ash had reached the flat rock by the cottage and was running towards the front door. But before he got there, the door burst open, and Michael Watkins came staggering out.

The man was almost unrecognisable from the last time Arthur had seen him at the book club. His clothes were tatty and he'd visibly lost weight, although he was still broader than Ash and could easily overpower him. Arthur held his breath, waiting for the moment Michael saw Ash and flattened him. But Michael seemed momentarily disorientated, squinting in the bright sunlight, and hadn't yet spotted the teenager. Ash had spotted him though, and Arthur watched as the teenager pulled back his right arm and threw a clumsy punch at Michael's head. The older man let out a shout of surprise and fell to the ground as Ash leaped on top of him. For a moment the two of them struggled, then Dan rushed to join Ash, dropping to his knees and pinning Michael's legs down. The man clearly realised he was defeated as he stopped struggling and went still.

Arthur felt his way down the last few metres of path and hurried over to the boys.

'Get inside and find them,' Ash shouted, and Arthur rushed past them into the cottage. It was dark in here, the air much cooler than outside, and there was a strong smell of salty rot.

'Nova! Phyllis!'

'Arthur?' Nova shouted back.

He followed the sound of her voice through the small kitchen and up a narrow flight of stairs to the top floor. A bedroom door was open, and he rushed inside, dreading what he was about to see.

Nova was kneeling on the floor, Craddock next to her. They were both leaning over a body.

Phyllis's body.

'Oh my God, no!' Arthur staggered and felt tears spring to his eyes. 'We tried to get here in time. I'm so sorry we're too—'

'For goodness' sake, what are you waffling on about?'

Phyllis's distinctive voice emerged from the body, and Arthur gasped.

'You're alive!'

'Of course I'm alive, you daft bugger. Now help me up, both of you.'

'I don't think you should move yet, you had a nasty fall,' Nova said, but the old woman waved her arms in the air until Arthur and Nova helped her up.

'What happened? Did Michael hurt you?' Arthur asked as Phyllis dusted herself down. 'We heard your shout, Nova.'

'He just took me by surprise,' Nova said. 'Michael clearly wanted to get out in a hurry, so he pushed past me and Phyllis. And in the confusion, I stepped backwards and tripped over Craddock.'

'Don't blame the dog, you were the clumsy one who landed on top of me,' Phyllis said with a tut. 'What on earth are you doing here, Arthur?'

'Ash got into the Michael folder. We think we were wrong, it wasn't Cynthia who hired Graham Pierce. It was Michael.'

'So that's why he knew it contained photos!' Nova said, looking at Phyllis.

'Well, what were the photos of?' Phyllis demanded. 'He seemed very concerned we didn't see them, so it's clearly something illegal or depraved.'

Arthur's heart was still pounding from all the adrenaline, and he took a deep breath before he answered. 'They were of you.'

'What?' The woman's voice shot up an octave. 'Why would he want photos of me?'

'I don't know, but that's why Ash and I rushed down here. We were worried you were walking into a trap.'

'Ash is here?'

'Yes. He's outside with his friend, Dan; they're restraining Michael.'

'Then I think we need to go and have another little chat with our newest book club member,' Phyllis said, and she pushed past Arthur and began to march towards the stairs.

Chapter Thirty

Michael

Michael lay pinned to the ground by two teenage boys, nursing his throbbing head and wondering how everything had gone so horribly wrong.

His throat was parched and he could smell an unpleasant, fishy odour, which he had a horrible suspicion might be coming from his own body. Had he really been here for over a week? It felt like only a few days since he'd fled his mother's house, three pairs of underpants and a copy of *Where the Crawdads Sing* hastily stuffed into his bag. And now apparently nine days had passed, and his mum was dead.

Dead. Another wave of grief crashed over him. He thought back to the last time he'd seen her and the bitter words he'd screamed. At the time, Michael had only wanted to hurt his mother, like she'd hurt him. And now she was gone, and he'd never be able to apologise; never be able to tell her how much he loved her. He squeezed his eyes shut and let out a moan of regret.

'Are you all right?'

Michael opened his eyes and squinted up at the teenage boy above his head.

'Not really. Could you please move? I have a bad back and this isn't helping.'

'No way, you'll just try and run away again,' the boy said, blowing his long fringe out of his eyes. He looked vaguely familiar, but Michael couldn't place where he'd seen him before.

'I can't believe you knocked him over like that,' the taller boy at his feet said. 'That was so cool!'

'I don't know what came over me. I just heard Nova's shout and the next thing I knew I was down here punching him,' the first boy said. 'I've never hit anyone in my life.'

'Well, you're clearly a natural. It's like when Rey defeated Kylo Ren, even though she'd never used a lightsaber before.'

'I wouldn't quite compare myself to Rey,' the punching boy said, and when Michael looked up at him, he could see the kid was blushing. My God, were they flirting over the top of him?

'Look, I promise I'm not going to run away. Just let me move before we need to get a chiropractor down here.'

The teenagers discussed it for a moment, and then Michael felt himself being hauled to his feet.

'Ouch! Shit, that hurts,' he winced, as pain shot through his lower back.

'Sit down here,' the taller boy said, and the two of them helped Michael limp to one of the rock seats his father had carved fifty years ago.

Michael lowered himself down and rested his head in his hands. What on earth was Phyllis Hudson doing here? Even back in the very earliest days, before he'd contacted Graham Pierce, it had never occurred to Michael that he might one day have to face her like this. But now not only was she here, but he'd gone and hurt her. Michael had wanted to stop and check she was okay when he saw her fall, but the flight instinct in his body had been so strong that he'd charged out of the room without even looking. My God, this was all such a mess.

He glanced up at the two teenage boys who were deep in conversation, the tall one inspecting the bruised hand of the shorter one, as if he was some kind of war hero. Was that the shy kid from the book club? And Michael had seen the old man who looked like a giant Father Christmas hobbling into the house too. How on earth had they all found him here? Michael closed his eyes again, trying to make sense of it all.

'Michael Watkins, I want a word with you!'

He opened his eyes and then wished he hadn't. Phyllis was marching out of the house towards him. She didn't look like she was injured, but the expression on her face was murderous.

'Why did you have a private investigator take photos of me?'

She stopped in front of him, so close he could smell her; a mixture of wool, dog and hair spray.

'It's not what you think,' he mumbled.

'And what do I think?'

'I don't know . . . that this is something sinister. That I want to hurt you.'

Phyllis let out a curt laugh. 'You couldn't hurt *me*. But you do owe me an explanation.'

There had to be some way to get out of this. Michael glanced towards the cliff path and saw it had all but disappeared, lost into the sea along with the front garden and his mum's flower beds. Besides, even if the path was still there, he wasn't sure he could outrun the five humans and one dog who were all staring at him, their eyes full of suspicion and contempt.

Michael looked down at his hands, shaking in his lap. There was nothing for it, he was going to have to tell them the truth. He glanced up at Phyllis and was struck once again by her bright green eyes; the same eyes he'd noticed the first time he saw a photo of her.

'Okay, I'll explain. But you might want to sit down.'

Michael had been an only child. His parents, Eve and Martin, were already in their thirties by the time he was born – our miracle baby, they used to call him – but they had adored him, and his childhood had been a happy one. He'd enjoyed school, gone to Exeter City football matches with his father on the weekends, and every holiday they'd come down to Chy Pysk, their tiny bolt hole by the sea.

At eighteen, Michael had gone to university, where he met Cynthia, and shortly after he graduated, they got married and settled in Bristol. But he'd remained close to his parents, coming to visit them regularly. And so when, last November, his father had suffered a massive stroke, Michael had rushed down and sat by the hospital bed for hours, holding his father's hand and willing him to wake up. The doctors had said to prepare for the worst, that the damage done to his father's body was too much for him to survive, but Michael knew something they didn't: that his father was the strongest man he'd ever met, and this was not how he was going to die.

Sure enough, after forty-six hours, Martin Watkins opened his eyes and looked at his son. Michael had been about to call out to the doctors with the good news, when his father had squeezed his hand, still powerful despite everything that had happened.

'There are things I need to tell you,' he'd said, his words slow and laboured.

Michael had shuffled his chair closer to the bed. 'What is it, Dad?'

He'd watched his father take a deep, painful breath. 'The money's gone.'

'What—'

'I lost it . . . Pension . . . Savings . . . The house . . . All gambled away.'

Michael had stared at his father in disbelief. Martin Watkins wasn't a gambler: he was a sensible, solid man, someone who mowed the lawn every Sunday and never forgot to put the bins out. But the look on his dad's face – the fear in his eyes – told Michael that he wasn't lying.

'Look after your mother,' Martin had said, wincing with the effort of the words. 'She has no idea . . . Protect her from the truth. *Please, Michael.*'

There had been so many things Michael had wanted to ask his dad: whys and hows and whens. But the look on the old man's face told Michael he didn't have time for that now, so instead he'd just nodded. 'I'll take care of her. I promise.'

Martin had let out a sigh of relief in response and closed his eyes, and for a horrible moment, Michael thought his father had taken his last breath. Then he opened his eyes again.

'There's something else,' he'd wheezed. 'You're adopted.'

It was such a ridiculous statement that Michael's initial reaction was to laugh. 'What?'

'We should have told you . . . years ago.'

'What are you talking about, Dad? I'm not adopted.'

'Through the church,' Martin said, his words barely more than a slur now. 'Reverend Platt at St Piran's . . . our miracle baby.'

'But—'

'You were all we ever wanted.' Martin took a deep, gasping breath. 'We loved you . . . so . . . much.'

'Who was my birth mother?' Michael had asked, the words spilling out of him like water from a broken pipe.

In reply, his father sighed and closed his eyes. He never opened them again.

The next few months were the worst of Michael's life. Navigating the shock and grief had been one thing, but doing that while trying to unpick the financial mess his father had left behind was quite another. Martin had done an extraordinary job of hiding his gambling addiction from his family, but once Michael peeled back the surface, he discovered debts everywhere he looked. With the fear of loan sharks quite literally turning up on his grieving ninety-one-year-old mother's doorstep, Michael and Cynthia decided to sell their own house in Bristol and use the money to settle as many of his dad's debts as they could. Cynthia had been furious at being uprooted from her home, and this had driven yet another wedge into their already crumbling marriage. But it was a price Michael felt he had to pay to honour the promise he'd made to his father. So, when Eve asked why he'd sold his house and moved in with her, Michael told her that he'd made some bad business decisions and lost all his money. When she tutted and told him he should have been more fiscally sensible, like his father, Michael had bitten his lip and stayed silent. And when he lay awake in bed at night, the word *adopted* swimming round his brain, Michael had tried to ignore it.

But, like an infection incubating in a body, over time the word grew stronger and more dangerous, until it became impossible to fight. Suddenly, little things began to make sense, like the fact Michael had green eyes when his parents' were blue, or his affinity for maths, when neither his mother nor father had the first clue about sums. These things had never bothered him before, but now Michael found himself consumed by them. So much so that one day, six months after his father's death, Michael sat down at the computer and searched for a local private investigator.

He hadn't had high expectations when he went to meet Graham Pierce in his cramped, messy office. After all, he had no information to go on apart from the name of a long-dead vicar who his father had said was involved. But Graham had told him that this kind of thing was more common than you might expect; that in the fifties and sixties, lots of private adoptions were arranged through the church and that in many cases the adoptive parents' details were put on the birth certificate, as had happened with Michael. The investigator hadn't made any promises but had said he'd do his best to find Michael's birth mother. After that, they'd agreed a price and Michael had returned to his own life.

He hadn't heard anything for the next six weeks. And then one day in late June, as he was eating an egg mayonnaise sandwich in the back garden, an e-mail had popped into his inbox. Michael had opened the message and dropped his sandwich on the patio. Because not only was the private investigator claiming to have traced Michael's birth mother, but the woman's address was in St Tredock, less than five miles from where he was sitting at that moment. His hands shook as he clicked on the attachment, and suddenly there were photos of a short, rotund woman with blue-tinted hair and green eyes.

His birth mother.

Phyllis Norma Hudson.

Chapter Thirty-One

Phyllis

Phyllis stared at Michael in mute shock.

This man was her son? She'd imagined him every day for the past sixty years: pictured what he might look like at six and sixteen. But at sixty? For some reason, she'd never allowed him to get that old in her head, and yet here he was, with grey hair and a beer belly. Phyllis searched his face for signs of herself but saw nothing apart from the eye colour. And yet the chin . . . that chin belonged to Michael's father, without a shadow of a doubt.

'I'm so sorry to spring this on you,' he said. 'Believe me, I never meant for you to find out who I was. I know it must be a huge shock.'

'Is that why you came to the book club?' Arthur asked, and Phyllis jolted at his voice; she'd forgotten anyone else was here.

Michael nodded, but his answer was to Phyllis. 'After Graham sent me your details, I didn't do anything at first. It was all such a lot to take in. Within the space of a few months, I'd not only lost my dad and learned I was adopted, but also discovered who my birth mother was. But after a couple of weeks, curiosity got the better of me, so I drove over to St Tredock and sat in my car outside your house until

I saw you come home. After that, I told myself I wouldn't go again, that it was too dangerous in case you spotted me, but I found I couldn't keep away. I started following you when you went out; not in a stalkerish way, I swear, but just to get a sense of who you were and what your life was like. And then one day, I followed you into the St Tredock Community Centre and Nova saw me and asked if I was there for the book club, and I panicked and said yes.'

Phyllis thought back to the first time she'd seen Michael at the book club; how he'd sat there silently, refusing to catch her eye. 'Is that why you came to the meeting last week; to see me again?'

Michael nodded slowly. 'That afternoon, my mum received a letter from their solicitor, telling her about Dad's gambling debts. I have no idea why the solicitor did that, but Mum was understandably furious that I'd kept it a secret from her, and we had a huge fight. I was so upset, and I knew that if I stayed in the house, I might end up saying something about the secrets she'd kept from *me* my whole life, so I ran upstairs and packed some things. I didn't know where to go, just that I had to get away. But then I saw my copy of *Where the Crawdads Sing* and realised you'd be at the book club that evening, and I suddenly wanted to see you again before I left . . .' He trailed off, staring at his feet.

'Why didn't you tell me who you were?'

'I thought about it, once or twice. But I kept thinking that if you'd given me up for adoption, that meant you wanted nothing to do with me.'

Phyllis felt a lump in her throat so huge that it took her a moment to speak. 'Did you really think I wouldn't want to see you?'

In answer Michael just shrugged, and for a moment he looked not like a sixty-year-old man, but like a six-year-old boy, scared of being rejected once again.

Phyllis's mouth was dry and she wished she hadn't given her water away. When she spoke again, her voice was hoarse.

'I owe you an explanation.'

'You don't owe me anything.'

'I do. After all this time, it's the very least I can do.'

'Truthfully, you don't have to. I—'

She raised her hand to silence him. 'Please, Michael. You've told me your story, now let me tell you mine.'

Phyllis had been fifteen when she met Billy Saunders, the day they both reached for the same copy of *The Mirror Crack'd from Side to Side* in the library.

Up until that moment, Phyllis had had virtually no contact with the opposite sex. The only child of a fierce, disapproving mother and an absent father who was never spoken of, she'd grown up in relative isolation. Her mother had homeschooled her, believing the only things a woman needed to know were how to read the Bible, write a shopping list and manage a house. Phyllis wasn't allowed to socialise with children her own age, and the only places she was permitted to go outside the house were to church and the shops, to a youth Bible studies class at St Tredock Community Centre, and to the library.

The library was the one beacon of light in Phyllis's small, dark world. Her mother allowed her to read the classics, as long as their subject matter was godly and there was no mention of romance, and so Phyllis would visit the library every week and come back clutching copies of The Chronicles of Narnia or *The Pilgrim's Progress*. And yet, what Eliza Hudson never knew was that inside her bag, young Phyllis would also bring home copies of the books she really wanted to read, smuggled to her by a kindly librarian who took pity on the shy, unworldly child.

Late at night, once her mother was snoring in the bed the two of them shared, Phyllis would creep downstairs and devour these illicit books. She got her first sense of social justice with Scout and Atticus in *To Kill a Mockingbird*, was swept away by Cathy and Heathcliff in *Wuthering Heights*, and sobbed her eyes out over the ending of *Anna Karenina*. But it was the mysteries that Phyllis loved the most. She devoured anything she could get her hands on by Arthur Conan Doyle, Dorothy L. Sayers, Josephine Tey and, above all others, Agatha Christie. It was in the pages of these books that Phyllis learned of the world outside her own small prison: a world of crime and scandal, freedom and adventure. And, above all else, a world in which anyone, including a woman who had barely left the confines of her small English village, could solve crimes and change people's lives, simply by using her curiosity, common sense and female intuition.

And so, it was entirely fitting that it was Miss Marple who led Phyllis to Billy. He laughed as she pulled the book off the shelf before him, revealing a dimpled chin and charmingly crooked front teeth, and told Phyllis she was welcome to borrow it first, as long as she lent it to him straight after. She'd been too embarrassed to speak and had hurried to the librarian's desk, her cheeks aflame. But the following Tuesday, when Phyllis returned *The Mirror Crack'd from Side to Side* to the library, Billy was there again, clutching a copy of *The Big Sleep* by an American author called Raymond Chandler, who he boldly told her was better than Agatha Christie. Phyllis agreed to read it, and so began their bookish courtship.

There was no way her mother would ever allow her to date a young man, especially one from a heathen family like Billy's, but such is the determination and cunning of young people in love that Phyllis and Billy soon found other ways to meet up. When Phyllis went to the butchers on a Wednesday, Billy would be waiting for her outside, and again at the fishmongers on a Friday. He even started attending her Bible studies class at the community centre, despite the fact he'd never been to church in his life. And although they didn't dare sit together in case the woman who ran it got suspicious, Phyllis would allow herself greedy glances at Billy throughout the meeting. Best of all, once they left at the end, they had a glorious ten minutes together as they walked from the community centre down the hill to Phyllis's road. And as spring turned to summer, that ten-minute walk stretched to fifteen and then twenty, and from holding hands to urgent kisses behind the community centre, and then a whole lot more.

Phyllis had never been taught about the birds and the bees, beyond her mother's vague mutterings about men and mortal sin. She therefore didn't think much of it when her monthlies were late. It wasn't until early winter, when she struggled to fasten her skirt and her brassiere no longer fitted, that she thought of poor Anna Karenina and realised what was wrong. Horrified, she told Billy the next time they met, and he got down on one knee and proposed to her there and then, in the mud behind the community centre. He was apprenticing to a local builder, but soon he would earn a small salary, and he told her he'd save every penny so that he could afford the rent on a cottage once they were married.

When she estimated she was about six months along and could no longer hide the growing bump under her clothes, Phyllis realised she had to tell her mother. She knew the woman wouldn't take the news well but hoped that once the initial shock died down, all her mother would care about was that her daughter and Billy got married as quickly as possible to minimise the inevitable scandal. But Phyllis had underestimated Eliza Hudson.

The next few days were a blur. Later, she wondered if the fact she couldn't recall the exact chain of events was because it had all happened so fast, or because she'd simply blocked the memories out. All she knew for sure was the locked bedroom door and the trays of food shoved through with rough hands. Of hearing Billy's voice outside the window and her mother's shouts at him to go away. Of Reverend Platt's brief visit and his cold, disapproving eyes, and then a night-time car journey, the reverend driving and her mother sitting in the front passenger seat, rigid with shame. Then there were black iron gates and a winding driveway leading to a tall, austere building, and a nun refusing to make eye contact as she led her into the building. It wasn't until Phyllis had been taken to a dormitory and seen the other girls in the same way that she had any inkling what was happening. By then her mother had already driven away, without so much as a good-bye.

Despite living in the mother and baby home for almost three months, nothing was done to prepare Phyllis for labour or birth, or for what was to come after. In fact, so naive was she that when her contractions started, she thought they were just indigestion and carried on working in the laundry. It was only when her waters broke all over the staircase, much to Sister Agnes's annoyance, that Phyllis learned what was happening. She asked if she could telephone her fiancé, just as she had done every day since she arrived at the home, but her request was ignored, as it always was. Instead, she was driven to a hospital where she was taken to a small, cramped room off the labour ward so as not to alarm the other mothers.

Phyllis remembered little of the labour itself. She was refused any pain relief, and when she cried out, she was told to keep the noise down so as not to give the midwives a headache. Finally, after seventeen hours without so much as a drink of water, Phyllis's baby was born in a rush of blood and hot liquid. For the briefest of moments, the swaddled baby was placed in her arms. Phyllis stared down at his tiny red face poking out above the blanket she'd knitted for him, and felt a surge of love so strong she thought it might lift them off the bed. She was vaguely aware of movement around her, of whispered conversations, and then a midwife took the baby out of her arms and carried him away, leaving Phyllis panting on the soiled bedsheets.

'My fiancé,' she finally managed to say to one of the midwives who was mopping the floor. 'Can someone call my fiancé and tell him our baby is here.'

The woman stopped her mopping and came to stand by Phyllis's bed.

'How old are you?' she asked.

'Sixteen.'

She heard the midwife inhale through her nose. 'It's for the best, pet. It really is.'

'What do you mean?' Phyllis asked, but the midwife resumed her mopping.

For the next two hours, Phyllis lay on the bed in agony, not daring to even get up to spend a penny in case she was needed for her son. Several times she called out for someone to come and tell her how her baby was, but no one came. Eventually, when Phyllis was about to climb out of bed and limp down to the nursery herself, the door opened. Phyllis felt a rush of relief, but the person who walked in wasn't a midwife with a baby but her mother, dressed in her church coat and hat. She didn't say anything as she came to stand at the foot of Phyllis's bed.

'Hello, Mother,' Phyllis said, for despite her anger at being sent away, Phyllis wasn't going to let those emotions ruin this magical day. 'Have you met my son yet?'

Her mother visibly recoiled at that word.

'Get yourself cleaned up. We've a long drive back to St Tredock.'

'But I don't have my baby yet. He's still in the nursery.'

'No, he's gone.'

Phyllis felt her stomach drop as if on a fairground ride. 'But that's not possible. The baby was healthy, I heard him cry.'

'He's alive. But he's gone already, with his parents.'

'But I'm ... Me and Billy are ...'

Phyllis stopped when she saw the expression on her mother's face: the narrow, almost squinting eyes and the hard line of her mouth. And then the realisation hit her, and she finally allowed herself to scream.

Chapter Thirty-Two

Nova

Phyllis stopped talking, and for a moment the only sound Nova could hear was the wind and the sea crashing below them. Michael had been silent throughout Phyllis's story, his hands clasped in his lap and his eyes glued to her face.

'So, you hadn't wanted to give me up?' His voice was so faint Nova could barely hear him.

'It had all been arranged behind my back,' Phyllis said. 'I later learned that the nuns usually insisted the babies spend a few weeks with their birth mothers back at the home before they were adopted, but my mother wouldn't allow it. She and Reverend Platt arranged to have my baby taken away within hours of birth.'

Michael shook his head, clearly too stunned to speak.

'It can't have been legal,' Arthur said, anger in his voice. 'Putting a baby up for adoption without the mother's consent must have been illegal, even back then.'

'Apparently I signed the papers when I first arrived at the mother and baby home. I had no idea what I was signing; nobody let me read them.'

Michael lifted a hand and ran it through his grey hair. 'I can't believe that my parents knew about this. They were good people, I swear. They'd never have adopted me if they'd known what was really going on.'

'I'm sure they didn't know,' Phyllis said. 'And anyway, things were different back then. Thousands of girls like me had their babies taken away from them in the fifties and sixties, and most of them were unregulated private adoptions.'

'What happened to you after that?' Michael asked.

Phyllis paused for a moment, and Nova could see her struggling with the memories.

'My mother drove me home in silence, and we never talked about what happened again. I'd turned sixteen while I was in the home, and so as soon as my bleeding stopped, she got me a job cleaning local houses. I wasn't allowed to go to the community centre or library anymore, so I didn't even have books as an escape. It was just me, Mother and church.'

'You must have hated your mum; why didn't you leave home?' Nova asked.

Phyllis sighed. 'Of course I resented her, but I was young and naive. My mother had always controlled every aspect of my life, and I didn't know it any other way. Besides, back then, I truly believed I'd done something terrible and deserved God's punishment. And that punishment was staying with my mother, a woman who hated me and never again believed a word I said.'

'What about Billy?'

Here Phyllis slowed for a moment. 'I'm not sure. A few months later, I heard he'd got a job in Plymouth and moved there, but I never saw or heard from him again.'

'Oh Phyllis, I'm so sorry,' Arthur said gently.

There was a pause as they all took in the enormity of Phyllis's story.

'Can I ask you one more question?' Michael said.

'Of course.'

'Why did you stay in St Tredock all these years? I understand why you stayed with your mother to begin with, but once you were older and more independent, surely you could have left?'

'Ah, now that's a good question,' Phyllis said, nodding. 'For a long time, I told myself I stayed because of my mother: first because I thought I had to and then, when she got older and her arthritis got bad, to be her carer. But that's not the real reason.'

'What is it?'

Phyllis looked up at Michael, and Nova saw her eyes were damp. 'I stayed for the baby. For you.'

He frowned. 'But why? You said yourself, you had no idea who'd adopted me or where I'd been taken.'

'I knew nothing about you or your parents, and I suspected you knew nothing about me either. But I suppose on some level, I always hoped that one day you might find out about me and come looking. And for that reason alone, I chose to stay in St Tredock, in the house I'd been born in, to make it easier if you ever tried.'

'And did you ever try to trace me?' Michael asked, and Nova heard a slight break in his voice.

'No, but only because I was too scared. What if you hated me for giving you up and wanted nothing to do with me? So, I decided that I'd leave it in your hands as to whether you wanted to find me or not.'

'But you wanted to be found?'

Phyllis smiled then, her eyes wet with tears. 'Not a day has gone by when I haven't dreamed of this moment, Michael. Admittedly, I never imagined it would happen on a cliff edge, but this is all I ever wanted. To finally get to see my son – to see *you*, Michael – and tell you how sorry I am that I never got to be your mother.'

Michael smiled, too, and it was such a tender, private moment that Nova turned away. Arthur did the same, and Nova could see tears in his eyes too. They both walked to join Ash and Dan, who were standing together by the cottage door.

'Bloody hell,' Arthur muttered. 'It's like something out of a novel.'

'With Phyllis's mum as the wicked witch,' Dan said. 'I can't believe she did that to her own daughter.'

'She makes Darth Vader look like Parent of the Year,' Ash said, and Nova saw the teenager blush when Dan smiled.

'What a day,' Arthur said. 'What time is it now?'

Nova pulled her phone out of her pocket, but it was still switched off. She hit the power button and waited for it to start up.

'It's 3:40,' Dan said, checking his watch.

'Oh shit!' Nova's stomach dropped. 'We need to get back or I'm going to miss my wedding rehearsal.'

'How are we going to get everyone back up that cliff?' Arthur said. 'Michael looks like he can barely walk, and that path isn't safe.'

'Maybe there's something in the cottage we can use to bridge the gap,' Ash said.

'Good idea, let's look inside,' Dan said, and the two boys disappeared in through the door.

Nova glanced at Arthur and saw he had a small smile on his lips. 'What are you looking so pleased about?'

'Oh, nothing. It just turns out that Ash had his Mr Darcy moment after all.'

Nova was about to ask what he meant when her phone buzzed into life. She looked down and saw message after message flashing up on her screen, all from Craig.

'I need to make a call,' she said, pressing dial and stepping away from the others.

Craig answered within seconds, his voice high with panic. 'Nova! Are you okay?'

'I'm completely fine. I'm so sorry, my phone was switched off, but I'm safe.'

'Oh, thank God, I've been worried sick. Where are you?'

'I'm near Lizard Point. We found Michael, the missing man, but then—'

'Lizard Point? But our rehearsal is in two and a half hours; you'll never make it back in time.'

'I'm sorry, Craig, I had no idea it would take this long. I'm going to leave soon, we just need to repair a cliff path so we can get back to the car.'

'Repair a cliff? I thought you said you were safe.'

'I am, it's just a bit of path fell away so we're a little trapped, but we're working on that as we speak.'

'Fucking hell, Nova!'

'I know I must have worried you sick by not answering my phone, but it's been full on down here. I'll explain properly later, but basically it turns out that Michael is Phyllis's son, and he had no idea his mum's been killed so—'

'Stop! Nova, listen to yourself. We're supposed to be getting married tomorrow and you're miles away, stuck down a cliff, getting caught up in some weird soap opera drama and missing your own rehearsal. What the hell is wrong with you?'

Nova bit her lip at the tone of his voice, and then imagined how she'd feel if the tables were turned and Craig was the one halfway down a crumbling cliff face.

'Have you even spoken to your mum yet?' he asked.

'Not since this morning, but she should be on her way to Bogotá by now.'

'Well, I'm afraid she isn't. There are still storms and her local flight wasn't able to take off.'

'What?' Nova felt a wave of vertigo and grabbed hold of the wall to steady herself. 'What does that mean? Can she fly later?'

'I've been talking to her and a travel agent all afternoon, trying to work something out, but there's nothing we can do. She's not going to make it back in time for the wedding.'

Nova let out a low moan.

'I'm sorry,' Craig said, his voice softening.

Nova's knees wobbled and she sunk down to the ground. Her mum wasn't going to be at her wedding: wouldn't be there to help her get ready or walk her down the aisle, or to make a speech. She was going to have to do it all alone.

'Do you want to cancel the wedding?' Craig asked.

'We can't just because of Mum.'

'I don't mean because of your mum, I mean because of you.' She heard him take a deep breath. 'Yesterday, I asked if you still wanted to get married and you promised me you did. And this morning, you swore you'd stay out of trouble; but look at you now.'

'I meant what I said, Craig; I do want to get married. I just really wanted to save my job and the community centre as well, and I thought by coming down here today I could do that.'

'And have you?'

Nova swallowed. 'No. Michael claims he doesn't have the money, so we're back at square one.'

'This is what I mean, Nova. You've let your search for this stolen money completely take over your life, to the point you're missing your own wedding rehearsal.'

'It's over now. I'll stop trying to find the money.'

'No, that's not enough.' Craig paused, and when he spoke again, his voice was quiet. 'I thought this job would be a good thing for you. After everything that happened with Declan, I thought it would help rebuild your confidence, but I was wrong. Clearly you're still traumatised by that attack and you're not ready to be back at work, especially not in a similar environment.'

'That's not true, I love this job.'

'Sure, but it's just five months in and you're once again breaking all the rules and repeatedly putting yourself at risk. This is not normal behaviour.'

'So, what are you saying?'

'I know your career is important to you, but you need to take a proper break. Allow yourself to grieve for your dad and get over your attack.'

Nova stifled a sigh; she really wasn't in the mood to have this conversation right now. 'You know I'll go stir crazy if I don't work. I've always had a job, and being a youth worker is such a big part of who I am.'

'I know, and I think you need time to work out who you are *aside* from your job.'

'Please can we talk about this after the wedding, Craig? I've had a hell of a day, and I really want to just get home and get some sleep, otherwise I'll look like a zombie bride tomorrow.'

'No. I'm sorry, but I can't keep doing this, Nova. I want to marry you tomorrow, I really do. But if that's going to happen, I need you to promise that you'll resign.'

'What? You're kidding me, right? You can't seriously—'

'I'm deadly serious. Your job at the community centre has caused nothing but problems over the past few months. If you want to get married tomorrow, I need to know you're willing to prioritise our relationship, and your own damn safety, by resigning.'

'You can't ask me to give up my career, that's completely unreasonable. I'm not some child who needs your permission to leave the house.'

'Then stop bloody acting like one. Now please just come home.'

Chapter Thirty-Three

Arthur

It took Ash and Dan half an hour to construct a makeshift bridge across the gap in the path, and another forty minutes to help everyone safely back up the cliff. Arthur watched the boys chatting and laughing as they worked, and couldn't help but feel a little proud of the part he'd played in bringing them together. It was exactly what Esi would have done if she were here.

By the time they all made it to the top it was almost five p.m., and clear that Nova was never going to get back to St Tredock in time for her wedding rehearsal.

'I'm sorry this all took so much longer than expected,' Arthur said to her, as they reconvened at the car. 'Was your fiancé understanding about the whole thing?'

'Yes, fine,' Nova said, but she wouldn't look him in the eye.

'Is it all right if I get a lift back with you? Three's a crowd and all that.' He nodded towards the teenage boys, who were deep in conversation over by Dan's car.

'Of course. I'm taking Phyllis and Michael, too, but we can all squeeze in.'

The journey back was more subdued than the drive down, all of them clearly exhausted by the drama and revelations of the afternoon. In the back seat, Michael fell asleep almost as soon as they hit the road, and Arthur could hardly blame him: in the space of a few hours, the poor man had learned he'd lost one mother and come face-to-face with another. Phyllis sat in the seat next to him, Craddock snoring between them. Arthur saw her stealing occasional glances at Michael, as if checking he was really there and not a figment of her imagination.

In the front, Nova drove in silence, too, her shoulders hunched and eyes locked on the road. Something told Arthur she'd not been completely honest with him about her fiancé's reaction, but he knew better than to ask again. Instead, he allowed his mind to wander over all the revelations of the afternoon. So Michael hadn't stolen the money nor killed his own mother. Arthur found himself inclined to believe the man's story; Michael had never struck him as the murdering sort. But if he was innocent, then who had killed Eve? Had it been Cynthia after all?

'That's my theory too.'

Phyllis's voice in the back seat made Arthur jump. 'What?'

'You said it must have been Cynthia, and I was agreeing with you.'

Arthur felt his cheeks flush; he hadn't realised he'd been thinking out loud. It was a habit he'd gotten into recently, but he'd never done it in public before.

'It's the only possible explanation,' Phyllis continued, her voice low so as not to wake Michael.

'But what about the money?' Arthur turned in his seat to look at her. 'If Michael didn't steal it—'

'Of course he didn't steal it,' Phyllis interrupted, and Arthur couldn't help but smile at her sudden maternal instinct to protect her son.

'But then who did? We have no other suspects; we always just assumed it was him.'

'Maybe that was Cynthia too?' Phyllis said, but she sounded unconvinced.

'What was that about Cynthia?' Michael had woken up and was rubbing his eyes.

Next to him, Arthur saw Phyllis squirm. 'I know you don't want to hear this, but we think that Cynthia might be behind your mother's death.'

'No, that's not possible,' Michael said. 'She loved my mum.'

'Arthur thought Cynthia might have done it to get her hands on your mum's inheritance.'

Arthur opened his mouth to point out that had been Phyllis's theory, not his, but a glare from the woman made him close it again.

'But there *is* no inheritance,' Michael said. 'I told you; my dad gambled every penny of it away. Mum had no idea until last week, but Cynthia has known since my dad died that there was nothing to inherit except a pile of debts.'

'Damn it, there goes her motive of greed,' Phyllis muttered.

'Besides, I know for a fact that Cynthia has an alibi for the evening my mum . . .' Michael trailed off, clearly unable to say the word.

'Do you mean that she was with her sister?' Phyllis was squirming again. 'I'm sorry to say this, but Cynthia was lying when she told you that. She wasn't with her sister, she was with—'

'Her lover?'

Arthur looked at Michael in surprise. 'You knew?'

The man let out a weary sigh. 'I had my suspicions, but I didn't know for sure until that day. I had Graham Pierce . . .' He stopped, looking embarrassed.

'Go on,' Phyllis said.

'After Graham traced you, I asked him to follow Cynthia, to see if she was really cheating on me. That night, while I was in the book club, Graham texted me with a photo of Cynthia and this man together. Even though I'd suspected it for a while, it was still a shock to get confirmation.'

'Ah, so *that's* why you ran out of the meeting so suddenly,' Arthur said.

'And those photos give Cynthia a concrete alibi,' Phyllis added, frowning.

'Without a doubt. She was seventy miles away, in the Premier Inn, Torquay.'

'As was Graham Pierce, which ticks him off our suspect list as well,' Phyllis said. 'Which leaves us back at square one, with no idea who killed Eve.'

'And no idea who stole the community centre money either.' It was the first time Nova had spoken this car journey, and her voice was thick with despair. 'Now we know it wasn't Michael, the police are going to think I took it, aren't they? Especially after what happened to Sandy.'

'Or they'll still think it was me,' Michael said. 'You said yourself, it doesn't look good: my mum was killed, and the same night money goes missing and I disappear. In the absence of anyone else, I'm still going to be the prime suspect.'

'No son of mine is going to prison for a crime he didn't commit. We'll prove your innocence, and Nova's too.' Phyllis's words were firm, but even she couldn't hide the concern in her tone.

It was almost eight o'clock by the time they made it to Port Gowan. The lights were on as they pulled up outside Michael's house, and he let out a long, weary sigh.

'Cynthia's going to kill me.'

'I can come in and help you, if you like?' Phyllis offered, but Michael shook his head.

'I disappeared and unwittingly left her with a nightmare to manage on her own. I need to face the music.' He turned to Phyllis. 'I'll telephone you tomorrow, okay?'

Even in the dark of the car, Arthur could see the smile that spread across Phyllis's face.

They drove back to St Tredock and dropped Phyllis and Craddock off at her house.

'What's your address?' Nova asked Arthur, as they watched Phyllis and the dog head inside.

'Oh, just drop me at the community centre, I can walk from there.'

'Don't be silly, I can drive you home. You must be in a hurry to get back to Esi.'

'And you must be in a hurry to get back to Craig. Honestly, after sitting in the car for so long I could do with a walk.'

Nova didn't say anything, but drove them to the community centre, where she pulled into the car park and turned the engine off. For a moment they both sat in silence, and Arthur studied the girl's drawn face. What would Esi say if she were here right now? She always had the right words, the gentle way of putting someone at ease so they'd confess whatever was on their mind. Arthur had lost count of the number of times he'd come home from work to find some stranger sitting at their kitchen table, sharing their deepest worries with his wife, while she nodded encouragement and filled up their mug with hot, sweet tea.

Arthur turned to Nova. 'I don't suppose you have time for a quick cuppa, do you? I'm gasping for one.'

Nova looked at him in surprise. 'Don't you need to get home?'

'Esi will be all right for another half an hour.' He cleared his throat. 'I called her friend earlier, before I set off with Ash and Dan, and asked if she'd stay with Esi. The two of them will be happily gossiping with a fish and chip supper, so they won't miss me for a bit longer.'

Nova looked at the darkened community centre, chewing her lower lip. 'I'm pretty sure I've been banned from going inside, but given how much trouble I'm in already, I guess a bit of illegal trespassing can't make things much worse.'

She gave a dry laugh and Arthur chuckled.

'Excellent. Let's hope they have some bickies too.'

Nova unlocked the door and led them down the dark corridor to the office. Once inside, she put the kettle on while Arthur sat down. They didn't speak until Nova had placed a mug in front of him and pulled up her own chair next to his.

'Would you like to talk about what's going on?' Arthur said, as Nova blew on her tea.

'What do you mean?'

'I know it's none of my business, but I get the sense that things are a bit tricky with you and your lad.'

Nova took a sip of tea, and Arthur waited for her to tell him to mind his own business.

'I wasn't entirely honest with you earlier,' she said, putting her mug down. 'Craig wasn't understanding about me missing the rehearsal. In fact, he completely freaked out and told me that if I want to get married tomorrow then I need to promise I'll quit my job.'

'What? But that's blackmail.'

'I don't think he meant it as blackmail. He just . . . oh God, it's so complicated, Arthur. He's worried about me, and maybe he's right. I mean, I did miss my own wedding rehearsal today so I could drive eighty miles and take part in some madcap rescue mission. That's not the behaviour of a normal, rational person, is it?'

'Maybe not, no. But Nova, you're not a "normal" person, and I mean that in the best possible way. None of the great characters in books are "normal"; they're complicated and flawed and utterly unique. Just like you.'

'My dad used to say something similar,' Nova said with a small, sad smile.

Arthur paused. There was something he wanted to ask her, but he wasn't sure how she'd react.

'Do you think that maybe you went searching for Michael today because you didn't want to go to the rehearsal?'

'You mean like self-sabotage?'

'I'm not saying it's true. It's just a thought.'

Nova didn't reply straightaway. 'I don't know. I have been feeling nervous about it all, but that's normal, isn't it?'

'Of course it is. I was absolutely terrified the night before my wedding, didn't sleep a wink. I was convinced Esi was finally going to realise I was just a Cornish oik and she could do much better than me.'

'That's what I keep trying to tell Craig, that it's natural to have a few nerves before your wedding. But what if you're both right and it's more than that?'

'I don't know, lass. I guess you need to ask yourself what you really, truly want? And if you're willing to sacrifice a job you love for the man you love.'

Arthur took a sip of his tea and waited for Nova to speak.

'I do love Craig, and he's been so supportive over the past year. He held me together through my dad's sickness and death, and again when I had to leave my old job because of a serious incident. Each time I fell apart, Craig picked me up and put me back together again. I honestly don't know if I'd even be here without him.'

'I'm so sorry to hear about your pa. How long ago did he die?'

'Ten months.'

Arthur swallowed. 'That's no time at all, Nova. I'd say it's not a surprise you're feeling a little wobbly: you must have all sorts of emotions about tomorrow and your dad not being there.'

'And now my mum's not going to be there either. Her flight's been cancelled and she's stuck in Colombia.'

'Oh no, I'm so sorry.'

'It's such a mess.' Nova leaned back in her chair and ran her hands through her hair. 'If I really did want to get married, would I be feeling so . . .' She faltered, clearly searching for the right word. 'So *ugh* about it all right now.'

Arthur couldn't help smiling. 'We all feel *ugh* sometimes.'

'Yeah, but I bet you didn't feel *ugh* the night before your wedding?'

'No, you're right there. I might have been nervous, but I knew before I even set foot in that church that my wedding was going to be the happiest, most important day of my life.'

'I don't know what's wrong with me, Arthur. I know I love Craig, and even though I've never been that bothered about the whole marriage thing, I know how important it is to him. So why can't I feel more excited about this?'

'Maybe you need your *Much-Ado-About-Nothing*-Bridgerton-Star-Wars moment?'

Nova looked at him as if he were speaking Dutch. 'My what?'

'Ash and I were talking about how in all those stories, a character is having doubts and then something happens to make them realise that they do actually want to spend the rest of their life with the other person. In *Much Ado About Nothing*, Claudio is feeling pretty *ugh* about his fiancée – in fact, he calls the whole wedding off – until he thinks she's dead, at which point he realises his mistake. In *The Viscount Who Loved Me*, it takes Kate being crushed by a carriage for Anthony to realise he wants to be with her, and in Star Wars . . . Well, it was all a bit confusing but there was something about an emperor and lightsabers.'

'So, you're saying I need Craig to nearly die for me to get over my *ugh*?'

Arthur chuckled. 'Maybe not that extreme. But if I told you now that if you don't marry Craig tomorrow you might lose him for good, how does that make you feel?'

Nova thought for a moment. 'Terrified. Sad. But also . . . Oh, I don't know! Seriously, why does this all have to be so complicated? I bet it wasn't like this with you and Esi.'

'No, it wasn't complicated. There were things that made it difficult: we faced a lot of prejudice and neither of our families were delighted with the match. But for me, marrying Esi was the simplest decision I ever made.'

Nova smiled, the first time he'd seen her do that all day. 'Tell me about you and Esi, Arthur. Tell me your love story.'

He paused to take a sip of his tea, and also because of the emotions that were suddenly swirling inside him. He put his mug down on the desk carefully, aware his hands had started to shake.

'I've read hundreds of romance books, and in each one there's almost always some grand gesture of love: someone saves someone else's life, or they risk their own reputation or make a big public declaration to prove their love. But for me and Esi, it was never about the grand gestures. Instead, it was the hundreds of little ones, every single day. The bowl of porridge she used to make for me every morning before work, even though it meant her getting out of bed at four a.m. when she could have stayed asleep. The love notes I used to leave hidden round the house for her to find during the day, or the fact we've never once spent the night apart since our wedding day. I know they're not worthy of a romance novel, but for me, those tiny gestures are what love is really about.'

'Oh Arthur, that's more romantic than anything I've ever read in a book,' Nova said.

'I don't know about that. But I do know that every good thing in me was put there by Esi. Without her . . .' He faltered for a moment, suddenly lost for words. 'Without her, I'm nothing.'

'You two are very lucky to have found each other, and to still have each other after all this time.'

'We—'

Arthur started to speak but then stopped. He suddenly felt exhausted, his whole body heavy, as if he were carrying a great weight on his back. Although in truth, he'd felt like this for months now, even if he tried to ignore it. He looked across at Nova, who was watching him with her open, trusting face. What would Esi say if she were here now? The same thing she always said, of course. The truth.

'Nova, I've not been entirely honest with you.'

'About what?'

Arthur felt as if he were standing on the edge of a precipice, looking down into a vast, bottomless hole.

'Arthur?' Nova was still watching him, concern on her face. 'Are you okay?'

'No,' he said, and it was the first time he'd admitted this out loud. 'Esi died four months ago, and I'm not okay at all.'

Chapter Thirty-Four

Nova

Nova watched as Arthur bowed his head and let out a long, low wail.

Without stopping to think, she leaned forwards and wrapped her arms around his shoulders. This seemed to trigger something in Arthur, and he began sobbing, his whole body shaking. Nova didn't say anything and just held him as he cried.

'I'm sorry,' he gulped after several minutes. 'I haven't cried since the day it happened so . . .' He trailed off, hiccupping.

'Please, don't apologise. Believe me, I know how you feel right now.'

'I'm sorry about lying to all of you; I just wasn't ready to admit she was gone. I still talk to her at home and imagine her replies in my head.'

'That's completely understandable, Arthur. You and Esi have been together for so long.'

'I kept promising myself I'd tell people soon, but the longer it went on, the harder it's become.'

'Does anyone know the truth?'

'A few, but no one at the community centre, and I liked it that way. I could come down here and carry on going to my Carers Support Group and the book club, and everyone assumed Esi was still alive. While I was here, I wasn't a widower grieving the loss of his wife but just plain old Arthur. That makes me sound like a fraud, doesn't it?'

'Of course not. It makes you sound like a man who lost the love of his life and has been in shock.'

'It's why I read the romance books too,' Arthur said, wiping his eyes with the back of his sweater sleeve. 'When I started reading them to Esi, I thought they were so daft. But over the years, I've come to love them as much as she did. And now I read them as a way to stay connected with her. When I'm with the Bridgertons or any of her other favourite books, it's like she's still here with me.'

'Oh Arthur, I understand. I still wear my red coat because it makes me feel close to my dad.'

He smiled, his eyes bloodshot from crying. 'I know I need to tell everyone the truth. It's not like the lie's going to bring Esi back, however much I want it to. I have to start being honest with people.' He exhaled slowly, leaning back in his chair. 'I'm sorry. We were here to talk about your wedding, and I've just sobbed all over you.'

He pointed at the damp patch on her shoulder and Nova smiled.

'That's okay. But let me find you a tissue.'

She stood up and began to look round the office. There was always a box on Sandy's desk, but given all the recent upheaval, it looked like she'd used them all up.

'Hang on, Lauren usually has a pack.'

Nova opened her colleague's drawer but there were none there. Then she spotted Lauren's coat hanging on the hook.

'Excuse me,' she said, reaching past Arthur and putting her hand in Lauren's pocket. Sure enough, she felt the familiar plastic of a tissue pack and pulled it out. As she did, a piece of paper fluttered to the floor. Nova handed Arthur a tissue and then reached down to pick up the paper. She was about to put it back in Lauren's pocket when she spotted what was written on it and stopped.

'Everything all right?' Arthur asked.

'Yes, fine. It's just . . . Why does Lauren have my computer password written down in her pocket?'

'I don't know. Did you give it to her?'

Nova shook her head, trying to work out why this was bothering her so much.

'I'm sure there's a simple explanation,' Arthur said.

'Maybe.' But as Nova said this, she reached forwards and put her hand into Lauren's other pocket. She felt something cold and metal, and her heart sank before she'd even pulled it out and confirmed her suspicion.

'The sports cupboard keys,' she said, staring at them in disbelief. 'The keys I supposedly lost.'

'Lauren must have found them again,' Arthur said.

But Nova wasn't so sure, her mind whirring. The lost keys. The messed-up community centre bookings and forgotten messages. All this time, Nova had thought the mistakes were her fault; that she was being forgetful and disorganised. But what if that wasn't true?

'I think Lauren has been trying to sabotage me,' she said, wincing at how strange the words sounded coming out of her mouth.

'Why would she do that? She's your friend, isn't she?'

'She is; or at least, I thought she was. But what is it Phyllis always says? If all the facts fit your theory, then it must be the right one. And look at the facts: the keys I supposedly lost are in Lauren's pocket, along with my log-in details that would allow her to go onto my computer and change diary bookings under my name.'

'But still, what's her motive?' Arthur said, sounding as bewildered as Nova felt.

'I don't know. Maybe she wants to get me fired? Lauren knows better than anyone how financially precarious this place is. Maybe she thought if I lost my job, hers would be safe?'

'Goodness, that's properly evil, especially from someone who pretends to be your friend.' Arthur stopped, his nose wrinkling. 'You don't think she's behind the stolen money, too, do you? What if she took it from the office, knowing you'd be blamed because it happened during your book club?'

'Oh my God!' Nova said, looking at Arthur with wide eyes as her mind raced ahead. 'But I didn't get sacked, did I? So, what if she then had to try harder. Shit, what if Lauren's the one who attacked Sandy to try and frame me?'

'Bloomin' heck,' Arthur said, exhaling. 'If that's true then we need to report her to the police now. She's clearly unhinged.'

'But we don't have any evidence. Finding the keys in her pocket is hardly proof, plus Lauren can always deny all knowledge and say I planted them there to frame *her*.'

'You're right, we need something more concrete,' Arthur said. 'We need to find a way of getting her to admit what she's done.'

'But why would she do that? If our theory is correct then now that I've been suspended, she's won. She's hardly going to suddenly confess all for no reason.'

'There has to be something we can do,' Arthur said, frowning. 'I can't believe I'm saying this, but I wish Phyllis were here right now. She'd know exactly what to do.'

Nova stopped pacing and looked at Arthur.

'You're absolutely right. I think it's time we call an emergency meeting of the St Tredock Community Book Club.'

Chapter Thirty-Five

Phyllis

At 11:30 the following morning, Phyllis stood in the churchyard of St Piran's Church, staring at the tall, austere building in front of her. As with her previous visit, she could feel her mother's presence everywhere.

You're a sinner, Phyllis Hudson, Eliza Hudson's voice called on the wind.

No amount of prayer will ever make up for what you did, she screamed with the seagulls.

That when lust hath conceived, it bringeth forth sin: and sin, when it finished, bringeth forth death.

'Oh, go away, Mother,' Phyllis muttered, gripping Craddock's lead. 'My lust wasn't a sin. I was a young girl who made a mistake because I knew no better. And you stole my son from me. *That* was the sin.'

My son.

Michael.

At the thought of that name, Phyllis turned to look at the man standing in front of a grave a few metres behind her. Michael had called her this morning after he'd been to the police station to give them his side of events. They hadn't arrested him on the spot, thank goodness, but he had been told to go back on Monday morning for further questioning. Cynthia had been rather less forgiving of his reappearance and had apparently spent much of the night screaming at Michael. As a result, he'd been in no rush to go home, so when Phyllis had mentioned what she was doing today, he'd asked if he could join her. Phyllis's heart had soared so high she thought it might burst out of her chest.

'Are you all right?' she asked now, walking back to join Michael.

'I still can't believe she's really gone.' His eyes were fixed on the grave in front of them, its earth still fresh from Tuesday's funeral. 'I didn't get to say good-bye; to carry her coffin or tell the congregation what a wonderful woman she was.'

Phyllis faltered. There'd been something playing on her mind since yesterday; something she wasn't sure if she should confess. 'I was at your mum's funeral.'

Michael looked at her in surprise. 'You were?'

'At the time, I thought you might have been behind the theft and murder, and I had this theory you might come to the funeral and then . . .' She trailed off, feeling embarrassed at the confession, but Michael smiled at her.

'I'm glad you came. Although you never got to meet Mum, I think the two of you would have got on. She had a great imagination too.'

'There was a good turnout. She was obviously a popular woman.'

'Yes, she had lots of friends. She was one of the kindest people I've ever met.' Michael stopped and looked back at the grave, his brow creased. 'Ever since I found out I was adopted, I've been so angry at her. Mum and I were always close – much closer than me and Dad – but I began to question everything. Because if she could have lied to me about something as massive as the fact I was adopted, had she lied about everything else too? Did she even love me?'

He kicked a loose piece of turf under his feet, sending it skidding across the graveyard.

'I was desperate to tell her what I knew and ask why she'd kept it a secret all these years, but even in the heat of our last fight, I didn't. I think I was scared of what she might admit once the truth was out in the open. So instead I let the rage fester inside me like a cancer, eating me from the inside out.'

'That's understandable, given everything you've been through recently.'

'Maybe. But this past week, while I've been down at Chy Pysk, I've come to realise that the reason Mum didn't tell me the truth was because she was scared too. Scared that I'd love her less if I knew she wasn't my biological mother. Scared that I might be so angry I'd push her away. And so I made a promise to myself that as soon as I got home, I'd tell Mum what I knew, and also that it didn't change anything. She might not have given birth to me, but she raised me and loved me with all her heart, and I was so lucky to have her as my mother.'

As he said these last words, Michael glanced at Phyllis, as if suddenly realising the implication of what he'd just said.

'It's all right,' she said quickly. 'You *were* lucky, and I was lucky too. I've spent the past sixty years hoping that you were raised by a loving family.'

Tears had appeared in Michael's eyes, and he blinked them away as he looked back at his mother's grave. 'Our last words were cruel, angry ones, said in the heat of a fight. I really hope she knew how much I loved her.'

'She did, Michael, for exactly the same reason you knew she loved you. However misguided it might have been, your mum kept the adoption a secret because she loved you and wanted to protect you from hurt. Just like you kept your dad's debts a secret because you wanted to protect *her*. So, while you might have fought, actions speak louder than words, and your actions showed nothing but love.'

Michael gave a small smile and wiped his eyes on his suit sleeve. 'I hope you're right, I really do.'

'Michael Watkins, how dare you show your face here, you scoundrel!'

Phyllis jumped at the sound of another voice behind them. She spun around to see Eve's silver-haired neighbour, a bunch of tulips in his hand, his face twisted in shock and anger at the sight of Michael. Craddock started barking as the man strode purposefully towards them.

'There's no point trying to run away; I might be old, but I can physically restrain you if I have to,' Richard said as he approached them.

Phyllis swallowed a smile; she had to give it to Richard, the man was brave. Reckless, but brave.

'I didn't kill my mother,' Michael said, taking a step backwards. 'I've already been to see the police and they know I'm innocent.'

'What?' Richard ground to a halt. 'But your argument? I heard you and Eve fighting and then you sped off.'

'She was alive when I left.'

'Then where in God's name have you been for the past ten days?'

'I needed a break, a chance to clear my head. I had no idea what had happened to Mum; I only found out yesterday when Phyllis told me.'

At the mention of her name, Richard's eyes spun to look at her.

'Phyllis, I'm sorry, where are my manners?' He bowed his head. 'It's lovely to see you again. You must be happy your missing book club member has returned.'

'You could say that.' Phyllis caught Michael's eye as she said this and saw him suppress a smile.

Richard turned back to Michael. 'If you didn't kill your mother then I owe you my deepest condolences. Eve was a magnificent woman and I'm very sorry for your loss.'

'Thank you. Are those for her?' Michael nodded at the flowers in Richard's hand.

'I know how much Eve loved gardening, so I thought I'd bring her some tulips to brighten up the grave.'

'That's very kind of you, Richard. You were a wonderful neighbour to my mum.'

'She was a good neighbour to me, too, and I'll miss her very much.' Richard paused, his brow furrowing. 'So, if it wasn't you, then who did kill her? The police seemed so certain she'd been pushed down the stairs.'

'I don't know,' Michael said. 'When I talked to the police this morning, they said it's possible she slipped and fell. She had been getting a bit wobbly on her feet recently.'

'I suppose that is possible,' Richard said. 'And if that's the case then I'm sorry I suspected you, Michael. Please don't blame me for jumping to that conclusion so quickly.'

'It's all right. I know it must have looked suspicious, especially when I disappeared.'

'What a terrible business it's all been,' Richard said, shaking his head. 'But it is nice to see you again, Michael. And you, too, Phyllis. You're looking very elegant, if I may be so bold.'

'Oh, this old thing,' Phyllis said, self-consciously touching her old church hat. She'd not worn it for years, but when Nova had asked her to come to the wedding, Phyllis had felt she ought to make an effort.

At the thought of the wedding, she glanced at her watch. It was eleven forty-five; she needed to get inside. 'We should be going, Michael. The service starts in fifteen minutes.'

'Are you here for the wedding?' Richard asked. 'I saw guests arriving when I walked over here.'

'Yes, one of our fellow book club members is getting married.'

'How lovely. Well, I'll be letting you both get along, then. Michael, I suppose I'll see you back at Mountfort Close.'

'Yes, see you later.'

Richard nodded to Michael and then turned to Phyllis. 'It was lovely to see you again. Perhaps we could meet up another time? I know you never got to enjoy the scones last week, so I'd be delighted to take you for afternoon tea one day.'

Phyllis felt her face getting hot. 'That would be nice, thank you.'

Richard smiled at her and then turned to leave, and Phyllis bit her lip. Would it be strange if she asked him to join them? Nova had said herself that most of the village were coming to the church, so one more guest wouldn't make a difference. And it had been a very, very long time since anyone had looked at Phyllis in the way Richard did. She glanced at Michael, who was clearly trying to hide another smile.

'I don't suppose you fancy joining us, do you?' she called after Richard. 'I'm sure the bride and groom won't mind one more member of the congregation.'

Richard turned round, beaming. 'I would love to! Thank you, Phyllis.'

'Well, in that case, we should get inside. I have someone I need to speak to before the service begins.'

Chapter Thirty-Six

Nova

Nova sat in front of the mirror, applying her make-up. She'd barely slept last night, what with her late-night meeting with the book club members, followed by a long, emotional phone call with Craig. He and his parents were staying at his aunt and uncle's for the night, so that Nova and her mum could have the house to themselves this morning. Only her mum was currently five thousand miles away in South America.

Nova smeared concealer under her eyes to try and hide the dark shadows that were threatening to appear.

'Easy there, Nono, or you'll look like a panda.'

Nova glanced at her phone screen, which was leaning up against the mirror so her mum could see what she was doing.

'That better?'

'Yes, but make sure you blend it well. Are you sure you don't want to call Katie or Faye to come and help you? Their hotel isn't far.'

'Nah, it's fine. Honestly, after the twenty-four hours I've had, it's quite nice to have a bit of time on my own.'

'I still can't believe Lauren's behind all your problems at the centre,' Maddy said. 'From everything you've said about her, I really thought she had your back.'

'Yeah, me too.'

'What did Craig say when you told him? He must have been furious with her.'

'I haven't actually told him yet,' Nova said, and she saw her mum arch an eyebrow in surprise. 'He already thinks I've turned into a conspiracy theorist over this stolen money, so I figured it was best to wait until we have some actual evidence before I started making wild accusations about one of his best friends. I'll tell him after the wedding.'

'And you're sure this plan you and your book club friends came up with is going to work?'

Nova thought back to their meeting last night. As Arthur had predicted, Phyllis had been full of ideas about how they could prove what Lauren had been up to, almost all of them inspired by her beloved Miss Marple. For once, Nova hadn't dismissed them but had listened to what Phyllis had to say, and with a few tweaks suggested by her, Arthur and Ash, they now had a plan in place. But was Nova sure it was going to work? Absolutely not.

'Darling, I think I might be about to lose phone signal,' Maddy said. 'I'll try and call you in a bit but—' The screen froze before flickering back into life.

'Mum, don't worry, my car will be here soon,' Nova said. 'I'll speak to you later.'

'I love you, Nono. And remember, you can always—' The screen froze again and then went blank.

Nova applied her mascara and then stood up and crossed to the wardrobe. Her wedding dress was hanging in its cover, and Nova unzipped the bag and pulled out the long white gown. It was a beautiful dress, there was no doubt about it. The silk was soft to touch, and the hundreds of hand-sewn crystals glistened in the late morning sunlight. Pamela had been right: millions of women would dream of getting married in a fairy-tale dress like this. So why could Nova still not see herself walking down the aisle wearing it?

There was the sound of a horn outside the window. Shit, if that was her wedding car then she was running late. Nova crossed to the window to call down to the driver that she'd be ready soon, but as she looked through the glass, she let out a laugh of surprise.

It wasn't a Mercedes waiting for her, like Pamela had arranged. Instead, it was a huge, rusty tractor, black smoke belching from its exhaust and a white ribbon tied to its bonnet. In the cabin sat a ruddy-faced farmer, dressed in a suit and flat cap. He turned off the engine and gave Nova a cheery wave when he saw her, and she opened the window.

'Arthur, what are you doing here? Shouldn't you be in place at the church already?'

'The others have it all under control. Besides, it occurred to me that you might need a lift.'

'Are you seriously suggesting I ride to my wedding in that old thing?'

'Don't you dare insult Bessie! She might look a bit knackered but there's life in the old girl yet.'

Nova smiled. 'That's a very kind offer, Arthur, but Craig's mum arranged a car.'

'You don't want a boring old car, do you? A girl as unique as you deserves something more original than that.'

'You know what, you're absolutely right! Give me a few minutes and I'll be down.'

Nova laughed as she turned away from the window, then stopped when she saw her wedding dress hanging up, waiting for her.

A girl as unique as you deserves something more original than that.

Ten minutes later, she left the house and found Arthur standing by the tractor, waiting for her. He looked distinctly uncomfortable dressed in his suit, but when he saw her, he took off his cap, and she saw his eyes had misted up.

'Bloomin' heck, Nova. You look like Sophia Loren or one of those golden age movie stars.'

Nova smiled. She'd chosen a 1950s red dress which she'd bought with her parents years ago in a flea market in Paris. It was cinched at the waist with a full skirt, and she'd paired it with Mary Jane shoes and dark red lipstick. Craig's mum was going to have a heart attack when she saw it, but Nova didn't care. After all, it was *her* wedding day, not Pamela's.

'You're going to have to give me a leg up into that thing,' she said, pointing up at the tractor cabin.

'Of course. But before we set off, there's something I wanted to ask you.' The man looked even more uncomfortable, and Nova could anticipate the difficult question he was about to ask.

'It's okay, Arthur. I had a long chat with Craig last night and we cleared the air. I'm not going to quit my job, and he's apologised for ever asking me to do that.'

'Oh, I was—'

'I know I told you yesterday I wasn't sure about getting married, but I've thought about it long and hard and it's what I want to do. I love Craig, and even though today might not be my dream, it's his and I want to make him happy.'

'Actually, it was something else I was going to ask.' Arthur was staring at his shoes, wringing his cap between his hands. 'I know you said your mum was going to walk you down the aisle today, but she's not going to make it. So, I wondered if maybe I could have the honour of accompanying you instead? I never had a daughter, you see, and . . .'

He trailed off and Nova felt tears spring to her eyes. She blinked them away before her mascara smudged.

'Oh Arthur,' she said, putting her arms around the old man and pulling him into a hug. 'Thank you.'

Chapter Thirty-Seven

Phyllis

By the time Phyllis made it to the church door, a steady procession of guests were making their way up the path. Most of them were faces she recognised from St Tredock, but there were a few unfamiliar figures dressed in bright clothes that made them stand out from the local crowd. These must be Nova's London friends, although they were vastly outnumbered by Craig's guests. Phyllis scanned the congregation inside but there was no sign of the one guest she was particularly interested in. She did, however, see Ash sitting in one of the pews. He caught Phyllis's eye and gave her a quick nod, and she nodded in return.

'Richard and I will go inside and find some seats,' Michael said from beside her. 'Good luck.'

'Thank you.'

Phyllis turned her attention back to the guests walking up the front path. Where was Lauren? Nova had said she was definitely coming, but maybe the girl had worked out they were onto her and decided to skip the wedding? No, that seemed unlikely. Most criminals believed they were smarter than everyone else and so rarely suspected they'd get caught.

And sure enough, there was Lauren, wearing a skimpy pale pink dress and holding hands with a tall, muscly man as they walked up the path to the church. At the sight of her, Phyllis felt a stab of rage. How dare that rat stroll up here as if she didn't have a care in the world, while all along she'd been trying to frame the bride and get her sacked. The absolute gall of the woman! For the hundredth time since Nova and Arthur had told her what they'd discovered, Phyllis kicked herself for not having suspected Lauren sooner. She'd allowed her judgement to become clouded by her dislike of Cynthia, something Miss Marple would never have done. Still, Phyllis was going to make up for that mistake today.

'Phyllis, hi!' Lauren smiled as she reached the church door. 'I didn't know you were invited.'

'A last-minute addition,' Phyllis said, fixing a fake smile on her own lips. *Two can play that game, missy.* 'Did you hear what happened yesterday?'

'Do you mean the book club road trip? Craig told me that you'd all gone down to Lizard Point.'

'That's right. And we found the missing man, Michael.'

Phyllis watched Lauren's face as she said this, but the girl didn't so much as blink. She was looking over Nova's shoulder, her eyes searching for someone inside the church.

'The murder suspect who stole the money? Wow, well done.'

'Ah, but that's the thing. It turns out that he didn't kill his mother or steal the money.'

'Are you sure? He might have been lying to you. Unless you think it was someone else at the book club who took the money?'

No, you're the one who's lying and took it, you little snake. Phyllis kept the smile glued on her face as Lauren's boyfriend excused himself to head inside. Lauren turned to follow him, but Phyllis reached out to grab her arm.

'Did you hear the other good news?'

'What's that?'

'Sandy's remembered who attacked her.'

This caught the girl's attention, and she swung back to look at Phyllis. 'What? When did that happen?'

'Apparently she woke up this morning and suddenly remembered she'd seen their face. Isn't that incredible!'

'And has she told anyone who it was?'

'I don't know. But I heard she's going to call the police straight after the wedding.'

'Sandy's here?' A pink flush was spreading across Lauren's cheeks, turning them the same colour as her dress.

'Yes, she felt well enough to come. She's inside the church now.'

'Right. Wow . . . that's great.'

Yet Lauren looked anything but delighted as she hurried past Phyllis. She stopped for a moment in the doorway, her eyes scanning the congregation, and then she saw who she was looking for and headed over to join them. Phyllis watched her go and smiled in satisfaction.

'There we go, Craddock,' she whispered. 'Stage one of the book club plan is complete.'

Now, like Miss Marple in *A Murder Is Announced*, Phyllis just had to sit back and let the criminal hang herself.

Chapter Thirty-Eight

Ash

Ash had never been to a church wedding before. Or at least, not since he'd been a page boy at his Auntie Shilpa's wedding, aged three, when apparently he'd been so nervous about walking up the aisle that he'd wet himself. He was feeling pretty nervous today, too, although for entirely different reasons.

One, any minute now he was hopefully going to catch a violent criminal confessing her crime. And two, and even more terrifying, Dan Gates was sitting in the aisle next to him, looking so handsome in his suit and tie that Ash worried he might wet himself again.

'She should be here soon,' Dan whispered, leaning in to Ash so that their shoulders touched. 'You ready?'

'I think so,' Ash whispered back, clutching his phone between his hands.

He was still amazed Dan had offered to come. After Ash had met up with the book club members last night, he'd messaged Dan to let him know what they'd discovered about Lauren. To his surprise, Dan had texted back immediately, and they'd ended up spending an hour messaging each other. And then at the end, when they were saying good-bye, Dan had asked if he could come today as well. Ash knew he was only here because he wanted to help catch Lauren, but still, he couldn't believe he was getting to hang out with Dan for the second day in a row.

'I can't get over the fact Lauren was trying to stitch up her own friend like that,' Dan muttered, shaking his head. 'That's Lando Calrissian levels of treachery.'

Ash laughed at the Star Wars reference. 'Hopefully we can put an end to that today. Thanks for coming to help, by the way. I know spending your Saturday in church isn't the most fun.'

'Are you kidding me? Road trips, terrifying cliff climbs and now entrapping a criminal at a wedding . . . this is awesome! It's better than any first date I could have planned.'

Ash nearly choked at the word *date*. He glanced at Dan, assuming he'd misheard him, and saw that Dan was smiling at him.

'Although next time, maybe we can try for something a little less dangerous; say, pizza and a movie?'

Ash felt his cheeks burn and all he could manage was a mumbled, 'Great.'

Dan laughed and then stopped as he caught sight of something over Ash's shoulder. 'She's here!'

A second later, Ash heard the sound of heels clicking down the aisle and saw a blur of pink as Lauren slid into the pew in front of him. Hardly daring to breathe, Ash pressed record on his phone, and he saw Dan do the same thing.

'Sandy, hi!' Lauren's voice was low, and Ash surreptitiously moved his phone closer to her.

'Hi, Lauren.' Sandy was sitting in front of Dan, and she didn't turn to look at Lauren as she sat down.

'It's so great to see you here and looking so much better. How are you feeling?'

'I'm still getting headaches, but the doctor said that's normal after a concussion.'

'You poor thing. I heard that you've remembered more about the night of your attack?' Lauren's voice was light, but Ash could hear the slight tremble in it.

'Oh, you heard that, did you?' Sandy was still looking forwards, avoiding eye contact with Lauren, who slid closer to her on the pew.

'Phyllis said you remembered seeing who hit you. It was Nova, I assume?'

'Why do you say that?'

'Well, your neighbour said she saw Nova's red coat outside your house. And the police think it was her as well, given she has a motive and . . .'

Sandy had finally turned to look at Lauren, and her stare was so beady that Lauren ground to a halt mid-sentence.

'It wasn't Nova, as well you know.'

'What do you mean?' Lauren was whispering now, and Ash leaned forwards to hear her.

'Don't play dumb with me,' Sandy hissed. 'You know exactly what I mean.'

For a moment, Lauren didn't speak. She was facing the front so Ash couldn't see her face, but he could see the tension in her whole back as she tried to work out what the hell to do. Then her shoulders sunk.

'Sandy, I can explain . . .'

'Don't waste your breath. You can explain it all to the police; they should be on their way to the church as we speak.'

'I'm so sorry, I never meant to hurt you. I didn't even think you'd be at home; I know you usually babysit your grandkids on a Wednesday night. But then you came downstairs and caught me at the door and I panicked. I'm so sorry, it was just a horrible accident.'

Ash's heart was racing. He kept his eyes glued to his phone to make sure it was still recording, while Dan's leg knocked against his in excitement.

'Why were you even at my house in the first place?' Sandy said. 'And why were you wearing a red coat identical to Nova's?'

Lauren let out a long sigh. 'It's complicated to explain, but I was just going to break in your front door and then leave; I honestly never intended to hurt you. Please don't tell the police it was—'

She was interrupted by the blare of the church organ. Immediately, everyone began to stand up.

'Please, Sandy.' Lauren's voice had risen to be heard above the music. 'We've known each other for years. Meet me somewhere private after the ceremony and I'll explain it all to you, then you'll understand.'

Sandy didn't answer, and Ash saw Lauren glance back towards the door.

'There's no point in trying to do a runner,' Sandy said. 'There's a woman outside with a dangerous dog, and believe me, they won't let you get away.'

Beside him, Ash heard Dan give a faint snort at Craddock being described as dangerous. Ash swallowed a smile and pressed the stop button on his phone. That was it, then; they had the piece of evidence they needed. For the briefest of seconds, Sandy glanced back at Ash, and when he gave her a quick nod, she nodded back.

Behind him, the church doors creaked open, and Ash turned

around to see Nova stepping into the church, a familiar white-haired figure at her side. Ash grinned at the incongruous pair as they began to walk down the aisle: Arthur in his ill-fitting suit and flat cap, and Nova in her awesome retro dress. A second later, his grin grew even wider as he felt warm skin brush against his. Dan took his hand and gave it a gentle squeeze, and Ash squeezed back, feeling like he might explode with happiness.

Chapter Thirty-Nine

Nova

Nova gripped Arthur's arm as they walked slowly up the aisle. At the far end, she could see Craig watching her with a look of pure delight on his face. To his left, Pamela was looking considerably less delighted, although whether that was about Nova's dress change or the unsanctioned, slightly dishevelled old man walking her up the aisle, Nova didn't know, and frankly, didn't care. She looked away from her future mother-in-law to the sea of faces on either side of the aisle. Most were unfamiliar, but every now and then she'd catch the eye of one of her old London friends, and Nova smiled. God, she'd missed them all.

Halfway up the aisle, she saw Ash and Dan sitting on the end of a pew. When he saw her looking, Ash raised his hand into a thumbs-up, and Nova felt a flood of relief. So, their plan had worked, just like Phyllis had said it would. Nova hadn't been so confident. Just because Miss Marple always managed to set a trap that would make the criminal confess didn't mean that Lauren would fall into theirs. Thankfully, when Nova had called Sandy first thing this morning and told her their theory, Sandy had been so horrified that she'd agreed to go along with the plan and pretend that she'd remembered seeing her attacker. And by the look of things, it appeared that Lauren had not only believed Sandy but also confessed her involvement, and that Ash and Dan had got that confession recorded. Which meant that Nova was now officially a free woman.

She smiled at Ash and turned back to look at Craig ahead of her. At some point Nova would have to tell him that she'd entrapped his best friend at their wedding, and hopefully he'd understand, especially now that it had cleared Nova's name. But for the moment, all that mattered was what was about to come: the wedding ceremony, their vows, and the moment they became husband and wife. Nova felt her stomach twist. She'd hoped that once she got the thumbs-up from Ash her nerves would subside, but she still felt as if she had a swarm of butterflies circling inside her. Still, it must be normal for a bride to feel like this as she walked up the aisle in front of hundreds of people.

As if sensing her whirl of emotions, Arthur gave Nova's arm a gentle squeeze. As he did, she remembered his words last night. *I knew before I even set foot in that church that my wedding was going to be the happiest, most important day of my life.* But Arthur's love story was like a romance novel: beautiful and all-consuming. Whereas Nova and Craig's love story was like real life: messy and complicated, full of wonderful ups and difficult downs, just like her dad always said life should be. So just because Nova wasn't skipping up the aisle right now, it didn't mean that she and Craig didn't deserve their happily ever after too.

She'd reached the top of the aisle, and Arthur leaned forwards to whisper in her ear.

'You're a very special young lady, Nova, and you deserve every happiness in the world.'

'Thank you,' she whispered back, as Arthur moved to sit in one of the front rows.

'You look incredible.' Craig had come to stand next to Nova, and his voice wobbled with emotion. 'If your dad had been walking you up the aisle right now, I know he'd have been the proudest father in the whole world.'

Nova swallowed down a lump in her throat. This was one of the things she loved about Craig; he'd known and adored her dad, just as her dad had known and adored him in return. And Craig was right; he would have been so proud of her today.

'Dearly beloved,' the vicar began, and Nova heard the congregation settle behind her. 'Welcome to St Piran's on this beautiful October day, to celebrate the wedding of Nova and Craig.'

Her heart was still hammering in her chest so loudly she could barely hear what the vicar was saying. Nova took several deep breaths, willing him to hurry up so they could get to the 'I do' part and she could finally relax.

'We have a wonderful ceremony ahead of us, with two of my favourite hymns plus a beautiful reading by Lauren, a friend of the couple, who has kindly agreed to step in in the absence of the mother-of-the-bride.'

Nova's breath hitched. Lauren, the 'friend' who'd tried to get her sacked and arrested, was doing a reading? She glanced at Craig, but he gave a small shrug in a way that suggested this was news to him too. So, it must be Pamela's doing, then. Nova felt a spike of anger and took another deep breath.

'Before we begin, I must ask if there's anyone present today who knows of any lawful reason why Nova and Craig may not be married.'

There was a pause, and Nova heard a few awkward titters of laughter, as always happened at this moment.

'Wonderful, well in that case—'

'Wait!'

A voice rang out from the back of the church, and Nova and Craig swung round as one to see where it had come from.

A small, squat figure was marching up the aisle from the rear doors, a dog waddling at her feet. The woman was backlit by the outside light so that her blue-rinsed perm looked almost like a halo round her head. Only the words coming out of her mouth were anything but angelic.

'I know a reason why Nova and Craig can't get married. This wedding has to stop.'

Chapter Forty

Phyllis

Phyllis was aware of every eye in the church on her, and not in a good way. The mother of the groom looked as if she was about to jump up and murder her in cold blood, while the groom's face had gone bright red. Nova, for her part, looked as if she was about to be sick; this had *not* been part of their plan. Still, Phyllis wasn't going to let herself be distracted. This was her big Miss Marple moment, and she was going to make the most of every second of it.

She walked up the aisle until she was about ten metres away from the bride and groom.

'Who on earth are you?' Craig said.

'I'm Phyllis Hudson, or "the old busybody from the book club", as I believe you know me.'

'Well, what is it?' the vicar said, in the indignant tone of someone who clearly wasn't used to being upstaged.

Phyllis ignored him and turned to face the congregation. 'Ladies and gentlemen, I'm afraid to tell you that there is a criminal in our midst!'

This elicited the exclamations of surprise she'd been hoping for.

'Sitting here in one of the pews is an individual who has stolen, deceived and even committed acts of violence over the past few weeks. All of it aimed at discrediting and hurting an innocent person who stands in front of you now, about to say her vows.'

'Phyllis, not *now*,' she heard Arthur hiss.

'Lauren Cook,' Phyllis boomed, rounding on the woman to her right. 'Do you deny that you've been targeting Nova, sabotaging her at work and even going as far as to frame her for theft and assault?'

There was another, louder gasp from the congregation. Lauren, who Phyllis had hoped would be quaking in her silly pink stilettos by this point, just frowned.

'I've got no idea what you're talking about, Phyllis. Have you been drinking?'

'Don't deny it! We have your confession on tape, don't we, Ash?'

Phyllis was going out on a bit of a limb here, given she wasn't certain that Sandy had managed to extract a confession from Lauren, or that Ash had recorded it. But when she glanced at the teenager, he nodded, and she inwardly sighed with relief.

'What on earth does any of this have to do with the legality of the marriage?' the vicar said, his tone growing impatient.

'I'm coming to that. The theory my fellow book clubbers came up with is that Lauren is concerned for the safety of her job, and so she's been sabotaging Nova in order to get her sacked. But something has been bothering me about this theory; something that doesn't quite add up.'

Phyllis began to pace up and down the aisle.

'I understand why Lauren might have undermined Nova at work, but why would she steal the roof money, knowing that would put the community centre, and therefore her own job, at risk? And why

would she attack her own boss? These, to me, seemed crimes dispro-
portionate to the motive of simply being fearful for her job security.'

'Right, I've had enough of this,' a voice said, and Phyllis looked
around to see the groom glaring at her. 'This isn't an episode of
bloody *Columbo*. Get out of here before I throw you out.'

'But a few minutes ago, while I was standing at the back of the
church, the penny dropped,' Phyllis continued, unperturbed. 'I was
watching Nova walk down the aisle, and I remembered something
that Arthur Robinson had said to me, about how in romance novels,
people do the strangest things for love. And that's when it hit me.'

Phyllis paused for dramatic effect, then kicked herself because
that was the kind of nonsense Hercule Poirot would do. Still, she was
on a roll now, and she drew breath before she continued.

'Lauren hasn't been going after Nova because she wants her *job*.
She's been going after Nova because she wants her *man*!'

At this, a clamour of shocked voices rang out around the church.

'It's true, isn't it, Lauren?' Phyllis said, shouting to be heard
above the noise. 'You're having an affair with Craig, and you've done
everything in your power to destroy Nova so you could stop this
wedding from happening.'

'Have you been shagging my girlfriend?' The tall man who'd arrived at the church with Lauren stood up and glared at Craig, a vein
visibly throbbing in his forehead.

'Don't listen to a word the old cow is saying,' Craig spat. 'The
woman is clearly deranged.'

'Hey, don't talk to Phyllis like that,' said Arthur, jumping up from
his seat too. 'You can't insult her just because she's uncovered your
secret.'

'Is this true, Craig?' the vicar asked, stepping forwards. '*Have* you been having an affair with another woman?'

'No, of course not!' Craig turned back to Nova. 'You don't believe any of this rubbish, do you? You know I'd never cheat on you.'

Nova didn't reply, her eyes wide with shock. Phyllis looked over at Lauren, who was staring at Craig, her cheeks bright pink.

'I'm not wrong, am I?' she said to the girl. 'You and Craig have been sleeping together and that's why you've been trying to destroy Nova.'

Lauren opened her mouth and Phyllis held her breath.

'Craig and I haven't been having an affair,' she said, and Phyllis's shoulders sank with disappointment. Miss Marple always managed to elicit a full public confession with remarkably little fuss.

'You see!' Craig said. 'Now can someone please get this old woman out of the church so we can get on with the wedding?'

'No!'

There was another audible gasp as Lauren stood up in her pew. The church fell silent as everyone waited to see what would happen next.

'Do *you* have an objection as well?' The vicar raised his hands in defeat.

'Craig, you can't marry Nova,' Lauren said, her eyes on the groom. 'She's not good enough for you.'

'Stop it this instance!' This was the mother of the groom. 'Be quiet and stop embarrassing yourself, Lauren.'

'You think the same, Pamela, I know you must,' Lauren said, and there was a pleading note in her voice. 'Nova doesn't love Craig, she told me herself she'd been having doubts about marrying him. But Craig wouldn't listen to me when I tried to warn him, so I had to do *something*.'

'So have you really been behind all of Nova's problems?' Craig said.

Phyllis saw Lauren visibly swallow. 'I thought that if she got sacked then the wedding might be called off, and you'd be spared from the massive mistake you're about to make.'

'But your early efforts to get Nova sacked for incompetence didn't work, did they?' Phyllis said. 'Which is why you got desperate and started to take things further, like framing her for stealing the money.'

'I was sure she'd get fired over that, given she was alone in the building and had to go to the office to get her book I'd hidden,' Lauren said, shaking her head. 'But then Nova forgot to lock the office and that bloody man, Michael, ran away, and everyone thought it was him who'd stolen the money instead of her.'

'So then you tried to frame Nova for a violent attack by wearing a coat just like hers when you hit Sandy.'

Lauren glanced back at her boss. 'I never intended to hurt Sandy, I swear. I just wanted to make sure someone saw me trying to break into her house wearing a red coat. But then she opened the door and surprised me, and I panicked and pushed her. I'm so sorry, Sandy.'

'Bloody hell, Lauren!' said her boyfriend, who was looking slightly green. 'What the hell is wrong with you?'

But Lauren ignored him, looking back at Craig instead. 'I love you, I always have. And I couldn't bear to see you make the biggest mistake of your life by marrying Nova.'

'And so you tried to get her fired and arrested?' Craig said. 'That's psychotic!'

'Oh my God, are you the one who cancelled the wedding photographer?' Pamela screeched.

'I bet she poisoned Craddock as well,' Ash called out from the pews.

At this, Lauren frowned. 'No, that wasn't me. I've done a lot of shitty things lately, but I'd never hurt an animal.'

'In fairness, she might be telling the truth there,' Phyllis said. 'I think Craddock possibly ate a chocolate biscuit and poisoned himself.'

There were a few sniggers at this. Nova, who up until now had been watching proceedings unfold with a look of shocked horror on her face, suddenly spoke up.

'I thought you were my friend, Lauren. I trusted you.'

Lauren sniffed. 'I'm sorry, but you're not suited to being Craig's wife, and deep down you know that too. And as his friend – and someone who's been in love with him since I was eleven – I couldn't stand by and watch you ruin his life.'

'You're the one ruining my life!' Craig said, and in a sudden movement he launched himself towards Lauren.

'Craig, stop!' Nova screamed.

There was a flurry of activity around Phyllis. Both Ash and Dan leaped from their seats and jumped forwards to protect Lauren, and at the same moment, her boyfriend also rushed towards Craig and grabbed his arms. Craddock, who had been in the process of stealing food out of someone's handbag, also jumped into action and began barking loudly. For a moment, Craig and the other man struggled in the middle of the aisle, but Lauren's boyfriend was much bigger and pulled Craig away from her.

'Right, this is getting out of hand,' the vicar said, his face scarlet and visibly sweaty. 'Can someone please get this woman out of my church?'

'The police should be waiting outside,' Phyllis said with satisfaction, as a couple of guests stood up and walked towards Lauren.

The girl looked like she was about to put up a fight, but then she turned to the groom. 'I love you, Craig. Please don't do something you'll end up regretting for the rest of your life.'

She lowered her head and allowed herself to be led away. Her boyfriend, or probably now ex-boyfriend, stormed after her.

'Nova, I'm so sorry about what Lauren's done,' Craig said.

Phyllis turned her attention back to the front and saw him reach out and take Nova's hand.

'I swear I had no idea she was in love with me, or how much she hated you. You do believe me, don't you?'

Nova didn't immediately answer, staring at her hand in Craig's, and Phyllis found herself willing the girl to tell him to bugger off and run out of the church too.

'I do believe you,' she said eventually, and Phyllis's heart sank. After all that, Nova wasn't really going to marry this chump, was she?

'Thank you,' Craig said, smiling. He looked up at the altar. 'I'm sorry about the disruption, vicar. Any chance we could carry on with the wedding now?'

The vicar, who looked utterly perplexed by the whole situation, shrugged. 'I suppose so. Nova, are you happy to proceed?'

Chapter Forty-One

Nova

Nova's heart was thumping in her chest. Craig was smiling at her, waiting for her to answer the vicar's question, as the events of the past ten minutes flashed through her mind: Lauren's confession, Craig yelling at Phyllis and launching himself at Lauren, the book club members jumping to her defence. She took a deep breath, aware everyone was hanging on her next words.

'I'm sorry, Craig.'

'What?' The smile disappeared from his face. 'I told you; I had no idea what Lauren was doing.'

'This isn't about Lauren.'

'Then what is it about?'

'It's about us. Lauren was right on one thing: I won't make you happy. You want a wife who'll settle here in St Tredock, give you babies and take part in the pub quiz with your parents every Wednesday. And I don't think that's me.'

He narrowed his eyes and took a step closer, lowering his voice so only Nova could hear. 'And you're only just realising this now? As we literally stand here in front of our friends and family on our wedding day.'

'But that's just it. It's *your* friends and family, *your* wedding day, not mine.'

'Of course it's yours, you're the bride! And you promised me that you weren't getting cold feet.'

'I'm sorry,' Nova said, and she really meant it. She should never have allowed things to get this far. 'I love you, Craig, and you've been the most amazing support to me over the past few years. And because of that, I really wanted to make you happy. But I've been so focused on giving you what you want – moving to Cornwall, planning your family's version of a dream wedding – that I stopped thinking about what *I* actually want.'

'Which is?'

Nova paused. 'To be honest, I'm not really sure. My life has been on hold since Dad got sick, so maybe I'd like to travel and see some more of the world. But, whatever I end up doing, I want to be the main character in my own story again, not a side character in yours.'

'This is crazy, Nova. I never asked you to prioritise what I want. I only made all the decisions because you stopped making any.'

'I know I did. After Dad died and everything that happened with Declan, my confidence was destroyed, and I became way too reliant on you. But my dad always said that they don't write novels about people who sit around waiting for life to happen to them, and he was right. It's time I took charge of my own life again.'

'Can't we do that together, as a married couple? I know I've been a bit overprotective lately, but I can change. And if you really don't want to live in Cornwall then we can move somewhere else. We can compromise, Nova; that's what couples do.'

Nova took Craig's hand, aware this might be the last time she held it and felt its comforting warmth. 'I don't think we can. I might not know what I want from my life yet, but I know it's not all of this; and *this* is what you want.'

She indicated around her at the congregation, who were all

muttering awkwardly among themselves, clearly wondering what on earth was going on.

Craig opened his mouth and for a moment Nova thought he was going to try and convince her to change her mind. Then he let out a long sigh. 'Okay. If this is what you really feel, then you should probably go.'

'Hang on a second!' Pamela's voice rang out, and Nova looked over to see her not-mother-in-law striding towards them. 'You can't just stand my Craig up in front of everyone, young lady.'

'Mum, not now,' Craig said.

'Yes, now. Do you have any idea how much money your father and I have spent on today? And now Nova thinks she can just ditch you at the altar and swan off like none of it matters. We *paid* for a wedding to happen, and it should damn well—'

'I said not now!' Craig snapped, and Nova saw Pamela startle at her son's sharp tone. 'I should have stood up to you a long time ago, Mum. If I had then maybe none of this would be happening now.'

Pamela's mouth flapped open and closed like a fish, but she was clearly too stunned to speak.

Craig turned back to Nova. 'You should go. I can handle this.'

She looked at him, the man who'd held her together through the past few years. The man who she'd thought she was going to spend the rest of her life with. 'Really?'

'Yes. Don't worry about me, I'll be okay.'

Nova raised up onto her toes and placed a light kiss on his cheek. 'Thank you, Craig.'

And then she let go of his hand and walked down the aisle and out of the church, alone.

Chapter Forty-Two

Nova

As soon as she heard the heavy doors slam behind her, Nova felt the tears start to run down her cheeks. But along with them she felt something else: a lightness in her chest that she'd not felt for months. The wind blew, bringing with it the smell of sea air, and Nova pushed her hair out of her face and began to walk up the path, towards the road. Where she was going now or how she was going to get there, she had no idea. But for the first time since her dad died, that thought didn't terrify her.

'Hey, Nova! Wait up!'

She looked back round to see the church door opening and her book club members hurrying out, along with an unfamiliar silver-haired man. Nova stopped and waited for them to reach her.

'Are you all right?' Arthur asked, his face strained with concern.

'I am, thank you. And thank you all for what you did in there today.'

'It looks like the police have arrested the criminal,' the silver-haired man said, nodding out of the church gate towards the road, where two police officers were talking to Lauren.

'I'm sorry, who are you?' Nova asked him.

'Oh, my apologies; I'm Richard Digby-Rice, Eve Watkins's next-door neighbour. I hope you don't mind me gate-crashing your wedding, but Phyllis invited me.'

As he said this, Nova glanced at Phyllis, whose face had gone uncharacteristically flushed.

'Phyllis, you were amazing in there,' Ash said. 'I can't believe you worked out that Lauren was in love with Craig.'

'I saw it in her eyes when she arrived at the church,' Phyllis said. 'She was standing talking to me, but the only person she was looking at was Craig.'

'It turns out being a busybody is useful after all,' Arthur said, winking at her.

'Well, I suppose I can't take *all* the credit. You were the one who gave me the idea that love could be the motive.'

'Didn't I say that romance novels would have the answer?' Arthur chuckled. 'In the end, everything always comes down to love.'

'But still, we have to give Miss Marple here credit for solving the mystery,' Ash said.

The older lady gave an embarrassed cough and turned to Nova. 'I'm sorry for disrupting your wedding like that, only I thought you should know what was going on.'

'It's okay, Phyllis. That whole thing was horrible, but I do feel . . . I don't know: relief, maybe? And thanks to you, I'm no longer a police suspect.'

'Well, I'm very glad I could help clear your name,' Phyllis said, and then she frowned as she looked at Michael. 'I'm just sorry we're no closer to clearing yours.'

'I do wonder if Michael's right and Eve tragically tripped and fell of her own accord,' Richard said. 'With no other suspects, surely the police will decide it was an accident?'

'So perhaps her death was never a murder mystery after all,' Phyllis said. 'Nor a romance.'

'Now will you and Arthur admit that not everything can be answered by Miss Marple or a romance novel?' Ash said, smiling at the pair. 'Not everything comes down to greed and love.'

The others all laughed at this, and despite her life having spectacularly imploded moments earlier, Nova found herself laughing too. And then she saw Phyllis stop and frown.

'Greed *and* love,' the woman muttered to herself.

'Is everything okay?' Nova asked her.

Phyllis ignored her and turned to Michael. 'Who knew about your father's financial affairs, apart from you and Cynthia?'

'Phyllis, is now really the time for this?' Arthur said, glancing back towards the church doors, through which the wedding guests were starting to exit.

'We can leave in a moment, but I want to hear what Michael has to say first.'

Michael was looking confused, but he shrugged. 'Eh, well apart from the bank, credit card companies and our family solicitor, I don't think anyone knew. We were careful to keep Dad's gambling debts a secret so Mum wouldn't find out.'

Richard opened his mouth to say something, but Ash got there first.

'Cynthia might have told her lover! Is that what you're thinking, Phyllis? That Cynthia's lover might have killed Eve?'

'That's an interesting theory,' Phyllis said, nodding approvingly at the teenager. 'But I don't think it was him; he doesn't have a strong enough motive. Yet there is someone else with a strong motive; someone who had no idea about the debts and still thought Eve was a wealthy woman sitting on a decent inheritance.'

'Hang on, I'm the sole beneficiary of Mum's will,' Michael said. 'So I'm the only person who'd have a motive to kill her for the inheritance, and as previously discussed, I definitely didn't do it.'

'Hypothetically speaking, there are other ways someone could have got their hands on your mum's money. Someone could have convinced her to sell her house, for example, and give them the money?'

'Why on earth would Mum have done that?'

Phyllis smiled at Michael sadly. 'As Arthur so frequently reminds us, people will do all sorts of crazy things for love.'

'Hang on, are you saying my mum was in *love*?' Michael's voice had risen with incredulity. 'I'm sorry but that's ridiculous. She adored my dad and was devastated when he died.'

'I know this must be hard to hear, Michael. But if it's any consolation, I know what it's like to be heartbroken and lonely, and then for someone to come along who makes you feel special. Someone who smiles at you with kind eyes and makes you feel like a teenager again.'

Phyllis looked at Richard as she said this, and Nova glanced at the man, too, expecting to see him blush at Phyllis's compliment. But her words seemed to have had the opposite effect, as his face had gone deathly pale. Why was he looking so—

'Oh my God, it was you!'

Richard's eyes flicked between them all, but before he could do anything, Ash and Dan both jumped forwards and grabbed him by the arms.

'Get off me!' Richard shouted, finding his voice. 'This is outrageous!'

'I can't believe it took me so long to see it,' Phyllis said. 'I was blinded by my own silly vanity, too flattered by your attention to remember Miss Marple's number one rule: always believe the worst in people. You did the same thing to Eve Watkins, didn't you? Twinkled your blue eyes and flashed her that charming smile so she wouldn't question your motives. All because she was, like me, a lonely older woman who you thought you could manipulate to get your hands on her money.'

'I've never heard such nonsense!' Richard said, struggling to get out of the boys' grip.

'You must have spent months wooing Eve: being a good friend, a comforting ear and a shoulder to cry on. It all looked so innocent from the outside: as Michael himself said, you were a wonderful neighbour. But all the time, you were trying to make a grief-stricken woman fall in love with you.'

'Oh, you scoundrel,' Arthur said with a growl.

'On the way to Eve's wake, you told me that Michael and Cynthia had been putting pressure on Eve to sell her house, but it was you who was putting pressure on her, wasn't it? You were trying to convince Eve to sell the house and give you the money.'

'Oh my God, that's why the solicitor told my mum about Dad's debts!' Michael said with a gasp of realisation. 'Mum must have told him she was thinking of putting the house on the market, and the solicitor wrote back saying that the house was no longer hers to sell.'

'Richard must have overheard you and your mum arguing about the solicitor's letter and discovered that instead of sitting on a small fortune, Eve was penniless,' Phyllis said. 'And this made you furious, didn't it, Richard? All that time and effort you'd put into making her fall for you had all been for nothing. And in a fit of rage, you went round and murdered her.'

'I didn't mean to kill her!' Richard shouted, and his shoulders sagged. 'After I heard Michael leave, I went round to ask her about the letter, but Eve was so upset she ended up screaming at me too. She started hitting me and I defended myself, but I never meant for her to fall.'

There was a moment of stunned silence as they all took in what he'd just said.

'Then why didn't you go to the police and tell them what had happened?' Arthur asked.

'Because I knew how it would look. After my first wife died in a freak accident—'

'My God, it's not the first time you've done this,' Michael said. 'You absolute bastard!'

He lunged clumsily at Richard, his fist connecting with the man's shoulder. Richard yelped and jerked backwards, and in the moment of chaos, he managed to slip free from Ash and Dan and started to run towards the road. A second later, Dan set off after him at a sprint. He caught up with Richard at the gates, just as the police car containing Lauren was about to drive off.

'Perfect, the police can take the two criminals at once,' Phyllis said, and when Nova looked back, she saw a satisfied smile on the woman's face.

'Are you okay?' Nova asked Michael, who was leaning on a gravestone looking like he might be about to pass out.

'I can't believe Richard killed her. I encouraged Mum to spend time with him; I thought their friendship would be good for her. And all along he was a trickster trying to scam her.'

'It's one of the oldest tricks in the book, I'm afraid,' Arthur said. 'In one of Esi's romance n—'

'Not now, Arthur,' Nova interrupted.

'Ah yes, you're right, sorry,' he said with an embarrassed smile.

Behind them, Nova heard voices, and she turned round to see the congregation had all spilled out of the church, and in their midst, Craig's family were glaring across at her.

'I should probably get out of here,' she said.

'Where will you go?' Arthur asked.

'I don't know. Not to Craig's parents' house, that's for sure.'

'You're welcome to come and stay with me for a while, if you like?'

Nova smiled at him. 'Thanks, but I really, really want to see Mum, so maybe I'll head to the airport?'

'That sounds like a grand plan. I'm not sure Bessie will get us all the way to Heathrow, but I can give you a lift to the station if you like?'

'Arthur, in any of your romance novels, has a bride ever run away from her own wedding in a tractor?' Ash asked.

'Not that I can remember. But it feels very fitting, don't you think? A unique getaway vehicle for a unique young woman.'

Nova laughed. 'It sounds perfect. Now let's get out of here!'

Epilogue

Phyllis

Phyllis stared at the clock on the wall. It was now five past eight, so the others should be here by now. As the self-appointed chair of the book club, she'd taken it upon herself to send out not one but two reminders about every meeting, stressing the importance of punctuality, but no one ever bothered to reply.

'Where on earth are they, Craddock?'

The dog didn't respond, too busy chewing on a mankie old sock he'd found on the walk over.

Phyllis reached into her bag and pulled out this month's pick, *The Left Hand of Darkness* by Ursula Le Guin, a science fiction novel Ash had chosen. Phyllis hadn't been sure at first, but the more she'd read, the more she'd found herself cheering Genly Ai and Ekumen on; not that she'd admit this to the others, of course. Arthur would no doubt have enjoyed the story – the old fool liked anything with a hint of romance – and Dan loved anything Ash loved. As for what Michael would have thought of it, Phyllis wasn't so sure. Her son – that word still brought a smile to her face – was like an Agatha

Christie novel: seemingly simple on the surface but full of twists and hidden depths. Phyllis was enjoying working out the mystery more than she'd enjoyed anything in her entire life.

'It looks like they've all forgotten,' she said with a sigh, as the clock hand hit ten past. 'Come on, let's go and tell Sandy she can lock up.'

Phyllis put the book back in her bag and was about to stand up when—

'Surprise!'

She jumped and looked round to see a crowd of beaming faces coming through the doorway, along with several bottles of wine, some presents, and a birthday cake shaped like a book.

'Happy birthday, Phyllis!' Arthur bellowed.

'You should see the expression on your face, you look like you've seen a ghost,' laughed Dan.

'We made you a cake, but I apologise if it tastes rubbish; neither Dan or I are natural bakers,' Ash said, putting the cake on the table and sitting down opposite Phyllis.

She stared at them all, gobsmacked. 'How did you know it was my birthday? I didn't tell a—'

She stopped, her eyes flicking to Michael, who was still standing in the doorway, holding an envelope.

'I saw the date in that old photo album you showed me,' he said. 'I hope you don't mind the surprise?'

Phyllis opened her mouth to reply, but no words came out. No one had ever thrown her a birthday party before, not even her mother.

'Why don't you open your present?' Michael said, coming to sit next to her and handing Phyllis the envelope.

Her hands were shaking as she tore it open. She pulled out the card inside and read the message, then looked at Michael in confusion.

'I know you said you'd never been on holiday, so I'm taking you to London for the weekend,' he explained. 'We're staying at Brown's Hotel, which was apparently Agatha Christie's inspiration for Bertram's, and I've got us tickets to see her play, *The Mousetrap*.'

'Don't worry about Craddock; I've agreed to look after him for the weekend,' Arthur called over. 'I've recently joined the St Tredock Ramblers so he can accompany us on our walk.'

There was a lump in Phyllis's throat so large she thought she might choke. She stared at Michael mutely, hoping he understood how much this meant to her.

'Happy birthday, Mum,' he said, giving her a shy smile.

Tears jumped to her eyes, and all Phyllis could do was smile back.

'Right, shall we get this meeting started?' Arthur said, and for once, Phyllis didn't jump in to remind him she was in charge. 'I bloomin' loved this book. I know it wasn't strictly a romance novel, but I thought Genly Ai and Ekumen's relationship was wonderful. As Esi would have said if she'd been here, they're a classic opposites-attract trope.'

'You and your tropes,' Ash said, rolling his eyes affectionately. 'What did you think, Phyllis?'

Phyllis was still fighting back tears, and all she could do was shake her head.

'Let me guess, it wasn't an Agatha Christie novel, so she hated it?' said a new voice from the doorway.

They all spun round to see Nova's suntanned face poking round the door, and the room erupted into cheers. She stepped inside and Phyllis did a double take. The nervous, jumpy girl of last year had gone, replaced by a confident young woman wearing a vintage polka-dot sundress, sandals and a huge grin.

'Happy birthday, Phyllis,' she said, crossing the room and sitting down next to Arthur.

'I'm so glad you could make it, lass!' Arthur said. 'When did you get back?'

'I landed on Saturday and then moved into my new houseshare in Camden on Monday,' Nova said. 'I start my youth worker job next week, but I wanted to come and see you all before then.'

'Did you see the community centre has its new roof?' Ash said. 'We held a charity read-a-thon that helped raise the last of the money.'

'Sandy told me. Excellent work, St Tredock Community Book Club!'

'Actually, that's not what we're called anymore,' Dan said.

'Oh?'

Arthur grinned. 'We decided that was a bit of a mouthful. Besides, we thought we needed a name that reflected the group's ethos a bit better.'

'I see. So what are you called now?'

Everyone turned to look at Phyllis, and she finally regained her voice. 'It's good to see you again, Nova. Now, if we're all ready, I call tonight's meeting of the Busybody Book Club to order.'

Acknowledgements

And now to the bit of the book where I struggle to find enough super-latives for all the amazing people who've helped bring *The Busybody Book Club* into the world!

I have to start by thanking my incredible agent, Hayley Steed. This book has been a roller-coaster ride, so thank you for your continued belief in me, your guidance, support and eternal good humour. *The Busybody Book Club* is dedicated to you, but really all my books should be . . .

I'm so excited to be working with the brilliant, dynamic people at Dialogue in the UK. Thank you to Christina Demosthenous for your enthusiasm, creativity and kindness; I can't tell you how happy I am to be working with you on this book. Thanks as well to Eleanor Gaffney, Emily Moran, Mia Oakley, Annabel Robinson, Saida Azizova and Chevvone Elbourne for everything you're doing to bring *The Busybody Book Club* to UK readers. And thank you to Lucia Gaggiotti for the beautiful cover illustration.

Thank you to the phenomenal Berkley team in the US. This is our fourth book together, and I feel so lucky to get to work with such a talented and passionate gang of book lovers. Particular thanks to my fantastic editor, Kerry Donovan; my publicists, Tara O'Connor and Kaila Mundell-Hill; and my marketing manager, Jessica Plummer, as well as Genni Eccles for all you do to help us. Lila Selle is once again the genius behind the gorgeous US cover, which made me purr with happiness the first time I saw it, and thanks to my copy editor Lisanne Kaufman and proofreader Pam Feinstein for catching my many errors! Also a big shout-out to the fabulous PRH creative marketing department for everything you do to help get my books out into the world: you really are the dream team.

Thanks to the wonderful people at Janklow & Nesbit Associates, especially Mina Yakinya, who's an absolute gem. I'm so grateful to their world-class rights team for helping my books reach readers around the world: Mairi Friesen-Escandell, Nathaniel Alcaraz-Stapleton, Maimy Suleiman, Janet Covindassamy, Ellis Hazelgrove and Ren Balcombe. Thanks as well to Kirsty Gordon for making sure I get paid!

A massive thanks to Sarah Hoyle for your excellent advice (and hilarious stories) about life running a community centre. I know that if you'd been in charge of the St Tredock Community Centre, none of this nonsense would have happened.

As always, I'm hugely grateful to my two writing groups for all the help, humour and (virtual) hugs you've given me as I wrote this book. I'm so lucky to be able to call the gorgeous 'Berkletes' my friends: I appreciate you all so much and am still holding out for our IRL writing retreat one day! And thanks to my beloved buddies from the 2017 Faber Academy writing class: you've been there since the very beginning, and I don't know what I'd do without you all. Particular thanks this time round to Lissa Price, who read an early draft of this book and gave me some much-needed feedback and encouragement.

Finally, my immense gratitude to my gorgeous friends and family. Special thanks to Bethany for keeping me sane (if not always sober); to my wonderful parents, Roy and Ali; to Callum, Jess and the fabulous Kocen crew; and, of course, to Andy, Olive and Sid. I love you all.

KEEP READING FOR A PREVIEW OF

Nosy Neighbours

Chapter One

Dorothy

Years later, when the residents of Shelley House looked back on the extraordinary events of that long, turbulent summer, they would disagree on how it all began. Tomasz in flat five said it started the day the letters arrived: six innocuous-looking brown envelopes that fell through the communal letterbox one Wednesday morning in May. Omar in flat three claimed the problems came a few weeks later when an ambulance pulled up in front of the building, its siren wailing, and the body was loaded into the back. And Gloria from flat six said her astrologer had told her way back in January there would be drama and destruction in her near future (and, more importantly, that she'd be engaged by Christmas).

But for Dorothy Darling, flat two, there was never any question of when the trouble began. She could pinpoint the exact moment when everything changed: the single flap of a butterfly's wing that would eventually lead to the tornado that engulfed them all.

It was the day the girl with pink hair arrived at Shelley House.

That morning had started out like any other. Dorothy was woken at six thirty by thumping from the flat overhead. She lay in bed for several minutes, her eyes squeezed shut as she chased the last shadows of her dream. When she could put it off no longer, she rose, her knees clicking obstinately as she moved through to the bathroom to perform her morning ablutions. In the kitchen, Dorothy lit the stove with a match and did her morning stretches while she waited for an egg to boil and her pot of English breakfast tea to steep. Once they were ready, she carried a tray through to the drawing room, where she consumed breakfast sitting at a card table in the bay window. So far, so normal.

As she ate, Dorothy observed her neighbours depart the building. There was the tall, ferocious man from flat five, accompanied by his equally ferocious, pavement-fouling dog. Next came the pretty-if-only-she'd-stop-scowling teenager from flat three, staring at her phone and pointedly ignoring her father, who followed her carrying a battered briefcase under one arm and an overflowing box of recycling under the other. As he emptied the contents into the communal bins, a tin can missed the deposit and rolled onto the pavement. The man hurried off after his daughter, oblivious. Dorothy reached for the diary and pencil she kept near at all times.

7:48 a.m. O.S. (3) Erroneous rubbish disposal.

Once the morning rush hour had passed, Dorothy washed up her crockery, dressed, brushed her long silver hair, and put on her string of pearls. She was back at the window by eight fifty, just in time to see the redheaded woman from flat six departing hand-in-hand with her current paramour, a tall, bovine man in a cheap leather jacket. After that there was a lull and Dorothy changed the beds and dusted the picture frames and objects on the mantelpiece, accompanied by Wagner's *Götterdämmerung* to block out the din from the flat above.

And then, a little after ten, she was brewing her second pot of tea when she heard a tremendous bang from outside. Dorothy abandoned the kettle and rushed to the front window, where she watched an old, ramshackle blue car pull up in front of the building, its rear wheel mounting the curb. A great cloud of black smoke burped from the exhaust pipe as the engine puttered out, and a moment later the door opened and the driver emerged. It was a young person who looked to be somewhere in their twenties, although at first glance, Dorothy was unsure if it was a man or a woman. They had short, unkempt hair dyed a lurid neon pink and were dressed in a pair of dungarees of the sort one might expect a labourer on a building site to wear. The youth did not seem to have any kind of coat or knitwear, despite it being unseasonably cool for early May, and Dorothy could see tattoos snaking up their arms like graffiti. The person reached into the back seat of the car and heaved out a large, well-worn backpack, then kicked the door shut, causing the vehicle to shake precariously. It was only when they turned to face Shelley House that Dorothy realised she was looking at a young woman.

The girl's face gave nothing away as she surveyed the building, but Dorothy could imagine her taking it in with a mixture of apprehension and awe. After all, one did not come across dwellings like Shelley House every day. Built during the reign of Queen Victoria and named after the English Romantic poet, its broad façade was a mixture of precise red brickwork and embossed white masonry, topped by an ornate balustrade. Wide stone steps led up to the imposing front door, over which the words SHELLEY HOUSE, 1891 were engraved in Gothic script. Impressive bay windows framed the door on the first two floors, while the highest floor – once the servants' quarters before the building was converted into flats – had smaller, rectangular dormer windows. Dorothy could still remember the first time she had seen the building herself; how she had stopped in the middle of the pavement and stared, mouth agape, marveling at its grandeur and history. It was the most beautiful house she had ever seen, and Dorothy had pledged there and then that it would become her home. Thirty-four years later, it still was.

The pink-haired girl continued regarding the building, and as her eyes swept along the ground floor they seemed to pause for a moment on Dorothy's window. Dorothy instinctively drew back, even though she knew nobody could see her through the net curtain. Still, she found her heart beating a little faster as she watched the young woman climb the steps and disappear from view at the front door. Who was she coming to visit in the middle of the working day? Perhaps the uncouth new tenant in flat four? Dorothy waited to hear the sound of a distant bell ringing and was therefore utterly confounded when she heard the unfamiliar chime of her own. Good gracious, it was for her! Should she answer it? It had been a long time since Dorothy had had a caller, and the girl hardly looked trustworthy. Perhaps she was one of those scoundrels who preyed on vulnerable elderly people, tricking her way into their homes, robbing them, and then leaving them for dead? Of course, Dorothy was neither vulnerable nor stupid enough to fall for such a trick, but this young rapscallion was not to know that. Should she fetch a knife from the kitchen drawer, just in case?

The bell sounded again, jolting Dorothy. She reached for her pencil – the nib was sharp enough to be used as a weapon, if circumstances required – and moved to her front door. Some years earlier, a previous landlord had installed an overly elaborate entry system whereby when someone rang her bell, a video appeared on a little screen by her door, showing Dorothy who was there and even allowing her to speak to them before she 'buzzed' them in. Dorothy had been horrified by it, even when the engineer insisted that the video was one-way and the person outside could not see her. Now she lowered her face so that her nose was almost touching the screen. It showed a grainy black-and-white image of the woman, who was chewing a fingernail as she waited for an answer. What could she possibly want?

The bell sounded a third time, a longer, more persistent ring. Dorothy cleared her throat before she pressed the button labelled INTERCOM.

'Who are you and what do you want from me?' She had to shout to be heard above the third act of *Götterdämmerung*, which was still playing in the background.

'I've come about the room.'

Dorothy frowned. 'You must be mistaken. There is no room here, I assure you.'

She heard an audible sigh through the intercom. 'Has it gone already? You could have let me know; I've driven all the way here especially.'

Dorothy bristled at the girl's impertinent tone. 'Then you can go back whence you came. And take that menace of a car with you.'

Even on the tiny monitor, Dorothy could see a flash of anger in the girl's face.

'It is parked illegally,' Dorothy clarified.

The visitor did not even look back at the vehicle. 'No, it's not.'

'Yes, it is. Your rear wheel is mounted on the curb, in contravention of Rule 244 of the Highway Code. So unless you move it, I may be forced to telephone the council.'

The girl let out a sound somewhere between a laugh and a snort. 'Wow, you sound like a right barrel of laughs. Maybe I dodged a bullet after all.'

Dorothy had no idea what bullet the girl was referring to, but before she could say something suitably caustic she saw the youth turn and start down the steps, without so much as a thank-you or good-bye.

Dorothy stepped back from the door in triumph. She had no doubt that the girl had intended to ring for flat one, whose ghastly tenant made a habit of illegally subletting his second room. Dorothy had reported him to the building's landlord on three separate occasions, but so far there appeared to have been no obvious sanctions. Still, she took some satisfaction in having thwarted this particular attempt. Standards in Shelley House might have been slipping for years, but she could quite do without that disrespectful young hoodlum living across the hallway.

Dorothy glanced towards her diary on the table. She should write this interaction up now, while it was still fresh in her mind.

> 10:17 a.m. Impertinent pink-haired caller mistakenly enquiring about room. Educated her on Highway Code and sent her away.

But that could wait. More pressing at this moment was the abandoned pot of tea in need of resuscitation. Dorothy returned to the kitchen, accompanied by the soaring notes of Wagner's Brunhilda riding to her death in the flames.

Chapter Two

Kat

Kat opened the boot of the car and chucked her bag in, slamming the lid shut. What a waste of time that had been. She'd even texted last night to make sure the room was still available and had been reassured it was. Now she'd lost a whole morning driving here when she could have been searching for a room and job elsewhere. Kat had been wary about coming back to Chalcot in the first place; perhaps this was a sign she shouldn't be here after all these years? She yanked the driver's door open with force, grimacing as it gave a wail of protest.

'Sorry, Marge,' she muttered, patting the frame. The last thing she needed was the car giving up on her today as well.

Kat climbed into the driver's seat as gently as possible, but as she was about to close the door, she heard someone shout her name. She glanced back at the building to see a white-haired man standing in the open doorway, waving in her direction.

'Hello? Are you Kat?'

She nodded but stayed where she was.

'Don't tell me you've made up your mind already?' The man gave her a crooked smile.

Was this some kind of a joke? Kat began to close the door again.

'I know it doesn't look like much from out here, but the room is lovely,' he called. 'You should come and take a look before you write it off completely.'

He was still smiling at her hopefully. Kat opened the door and spoke slowly and loudly in case he had trouble understanding.

'Your wife told me the room has gone already.'

The man frowned. 'My wife?'

'Yes. She said there was no room.'

He paused for a moment and Kat felt a tug of sympathy. The poor thing really was confused if he couldn't even remember his own wife. Then he grinned, his eyes crinkling.

'Oh dear, I think you may have rung the wrong buzzer! Don't worry, you're not the first.'

Now it was Kat's turn to frown. 'So is the room available?'

'It most certainly is. Come on in and I'll show it to you.'

He stood back from the front door, holding it open for her, but Kat remained in the car. Did she really want to stay here? She could still remember the building vividly from her childhood. Whenever she'd been sent to live with her grandfather, Kat used to walk past Shelley House to get from his farm on the outskirts of the village to Chalcot Primary School. Back then, the other kids used to say that the creepy, crumbling old house was home to a wicked witch who locked children in the attic, and so Kat used to speed up whenever she passed in case the witch tried to kidnap her too.

She scanned her eyes over it now. Kat was no longer scared of child-eating witches, but there was still something eerie about Shelley House. The brickwork was faded and crumbling, the window frames warped and peeling, like something from a horror movie. Bits of the stone balustrade were missing from the roof, and the whole structure seemed to tilt ominously to one side. If this was what it looked like on the outside, God knows what state it must be inside. No wonder the rent on the room was so cheap; Kat couldn't imagine anyone willingly choosing to live here.

The man was still standing in the doorway, watching her. Above his head she could see the building name engraved into the stone. Since she'd last been here someone had vandalized it so that rather than reading SHELLEY HOUSE it now said HELL HOUSE. Kat couldn't help smiling at this, and the man grinned back at her.

'Come on, then! I've just put the kettle on.'

What the heck? She'd come all this way; she might as well take a look at the place that had scared her so much as a kid. She climbed out of Marge, taking care to close the door softly.

When she reached the top of the steps, the man held out his hand.

'Joseph Chambers. Pleased to meet you.'

'Kat Bennett,' she said, keeping her own hands in her pockets.

She followed him inside, the door slamming heavily behind them. There was no natural light in here, and it took a moment for Kat's eyes to adjust to the gloom. When they did, she saw that she was in an unremarkable entrance hall. Black-and-white checkered floor tiles hinted at the building's grander past, but now the space seemed to largely be a dumping ground for unwanted possessions. There were piles of unopened post on a shelf, and from somewhere farther up the building Kat heard the sound of drum and bass music, but there were no other signs of life. Two unmarked doors led off either side of the hall and Kat looked between them.

'I'm in number one, over here,' Joseph said, pointing towards the left-hand door. 'Flat two belongs to Dorothy Darling. I believe you may have had the pleasure of chatting to her already.'

Kat had nothing polite to say about the old woman who'd shouted at her on the intercom, so she kept her mouth shut. Joseph chuckled.

'As I suspected. Don't worry, Dorothy's an eccentric but her bark is worse than her bite. Speaking of which . . .' He moved towards the left-hand door. As he reached it there was an explosion of yaps on the far side. 'You're not allergic to dogs, are you?'

'No.'

'Good.' He pushed the door open and immediately a small brown-and-white Jack Russell came charging out of the flat, circling Joseph before skidding to a halt at Kat's feet. Its barks reached a new crescendo as it jumped up against her leg.

'Meet Reggie,' Joseph shouted above the noise. 'He'll calm down in a moment. He just gets excited when he meets new people.'

Kat bent down and offered Reggie her hand. He sniffed it eagerly, his nose wet against her skin. Kat ran a hand over his head and as she did she had a flashback of another dog, his fur short and wiry like this one's, and the comforting smell of cigar smoke that always accompanied him. Reggie stopped barking as Kat scratched between his ears.

'He likes you!' Joseph clapped his hands together with glee. 'Well, that's an excellent omen. He wasn't at all keen on my last lodger. Used to pee behind his wardrobe but I don't think we'll have that problem with you. Come on, Reggie, let's give Kat the grand tour.'

At the sound of his name the dog trotted back into the flat. Kat swallowed as she moved towards the door, preparing herself for what was to come, but as she stepped inside her breath caught. The room she found herself in was huge, its ceiling vaulting high above their heads and a polished wood floor underfoot. The walls were in need of a repaint and there was a slightly musty smell, but light poured in through the large bay window and the biggest fireplace Kat had ever seen took up much of the far wall. Never in a million years had she imagined the inside would be so striking. Kat felt like she'd walked onto the set of a period costume drama, only the furniture was from IKEA and there was a flat-screen TV in the corner.

'Quite something, isn't it?' Joseph said.

'It's incredible.'

'It used to be the home of a rich Victorian industrialist. In fact, the whole road was once made up of mansions like this, all named after famous English poets: Byron, Wordsworth, Keats, et cetera, hence the name Poet's Road. Half of the mansions got bombed during the Second World War and the rest got pulled down after and replaced with smaller, more practical houses. Somehow Shelley House survived, although it was converted into flats back in the sixties.'

Kat didn't say anything as she took it all in. Her grandfather had lived in this village his whole life, which meant he must have known Poet's Road back when it was still all mansions like this. In fact, perhaps he'd even visited Shelley House? The thought made Kat's chest ache.

'If you think it's impressive now, you should have seen the place when I first moved in thirty-three years ago,' Joseph continued. 'It was one of the grandest buildings in the area back then and immaculately maintained. But I'm afraid various landlords have rather neglected it over the years, hence the state it's in now.' He indicated a patch of damp on the wall next to them, the paint flaking off it. 'Anyway, that's enough of the history lesson. Let me show you around.'

Joseph set off towards the two doors at the far side of the room, Reggie scampering and sliding across the floor behind him.

'The kitchen is in here,' Joseph said, pushing open the farthest door.

Kat wondered if it was going to be like something off *Downton*

Abbey too, but when she peered in she saw that it was small and disappointingly ordinary.

'I think this would have once been a scullery,' Joseph said. 'Not palatial but it does the trick. You can make yourself at home in here, there's all the usual pots and pans. And there's an evening meal included as part of your rent.'

'Oh, I don't need cooking for,' Kat said quickly. That hadn't been mentioned in the advert and she had no desire to have an awkward meal with her landlord every day. She had learned at an early age it was best never to get too close to the people you lived with. Kat would never forget the seemingly sweet old lady they'd rented a room from when she was six or seven, who used to give her biscuits when she got back from school and chat with her about her day. Then one afternoon, Kat had come home to find social services waiting for her, asking all sorts of difficult questions. She and her mum had fled that night, her mum cursing Kat for 'blabbing her mouth off' to their landlord. She had never made the same mistake again.

'I'll leave the food in the fridge so you can reheat it whenever suits you,' Joseph said, as if reading her mind. 'To be honest, you'd be doing me a favour. I've not got used to cooking for one yet, you see. It's been three years now but still . . .'

He trailed off and for a horrible moment Kat thought he was about to cry, but he blinked and looked up at her, smiling again. 'It's part of the reason I have lodgers. Well, that and to help me cover the rent now I'm retired. Shall we carry on the tour?'

He showed her through the second door, which led into a small hallway. The bathroom was modest and decorated in avocado green, its wallpaper peeling off in places, but it looked clean enough. The door next to it was closed – Joseph's bedroom, she assumed – but the last one was open.

'It's not very big, but I think it's cosy,' Joseph said, pausing on the threshold. 'It used to be our daughter's bedroom.'

The room was indeed small, but Kat liked it immediately. There was a single bed and a wardrobe, and an old-fashioned rocking chair next to a small bookcase stuffed with well-worn paperbacks. Kat glanced over the shelves: *Pride and Prejudice* . . . *Bleak House* . . . *Moby Dick* . . . all old books that she'd never read and never would. She turned back to the door and was relieved to see a lock on the inside. Joseph seemed harmless enough but you could never be too careful. Above the bed was a window and Kat walked over to see the view. She was expecting a garden or at least some greenery, but found she was looking out onto a concrete car park behind a block of modern flats.

'We used to have a communal garden, but that got sold off by an old landlord years ago,' Joseph said.

Kat turned back to survey the room. It really was small, but that wasn't a problem. All her worldly possessions fit into the old ruck-sack in her car boot, so she hardly needed a walk-in wardrobe. And Joseph seemed nice enough—a bit chatty, maybe, but he'd soon re-alise she wasn't the talkative type and leave her alone. The bigger question was whether she wanted to come back to Chalcot in the first place. After all, there was a very good reason Kat had stayed away for fifteen years, and nothing about that had changed. So what if she'd found herself thinking of the village and her grandfather more and more over the past few months, the memories itching like a mos-quito bite that wouldn't heal. It didn't mean she had to risk coming back here, so surely the sensible thing would be to drive far away and never return.

'So, what do you think?' Joseph was watching her. 'Would you like the room?'

Kat took a deep breath. Now that she was here, she might as well stay for a few weeks. But thanks to Marge outside, she could always make a quick getaway if she needed to.

'Okay, thank you.' She paused as a thought occurred to her. 'Don't you want to know anything about me or get a reference?'

'Why would I want a reference?'

'Well, I dunno, I could be a psychopathic ax murderer for all you know.'

Joseph let out a loud guffaw. 'Oh, you don't strike me as the ax-murdering type. No, if anything I'd say you were more of the poisoning sort.'

Kat couldn't help laughing at this; the guy was bonkers. But if he didn't want a reference, that suited her fine. The less he – or anyone else around here – knew about her, the better.

'Come on, then,' Joseph said, moving towards the door. 'You get your stuff in and I'll make us a coffee.'

Photo by David Levenson

Freya Sampson is the *USA Today* bestselling author of *The Last Library*, *The Girl on the 88 Bus* and *Nosy Neighbours*. She studied history at Cambridge University and worked in television as an executive producer, making documentaries about everything from the British royal family to neighbours from hell. She lives in London with her husband, children and cats. *The Busybody Book Club* is her fourth novel.

VISIT FREYA SAMPSON ONLINE

Freya-Sampson.com
 FreyaSampsonAuthor
 FreyaSampsonAuthor

Bringing a book from manuscript to what you are reading is a team effort.

Renegade Books would like to thank everyone who helped to publish *The Busybody Book Club* in the UK.

Editorial
Christina Demosthenous
Eleanor Gaffney

Contracts
Stephanie Evans
Sasha Duszynska Lewis
Isabel Camara

Sales
Megan Schaffer
Kyla Dean
Dominic Smith
Sinead White
Georgina Cutler-Ross
Kerri Hood
Jess Harvey
Natasha Weninger Kong

Design
Chevonne Elbourne
Charlotte Stroomer
Sara Mahon
Luke Applin

Production
Amanda Jones

Publicity
Annabel Robinson

Marketing
Emily Moran
Mia Oakley

Operations
Rosie Stevens

Finance
Chris Vale
Jonathan Gant

Audio
Rabeeah Moeen

Anglicisation
Rachel Malig